Mycroft Holmes and the Adventure of the Desert Wind

By

Janina Woods

Paperback ISBN 978-1-78705-212-3
ePub ISBN 978-1-78705-213-0
PDF ISBN 978-1-78705-214-7

Published in the UK by MX Publishing
335 Princess Park Manor, Royal Drive,
London, N11 3GX
www.mxpublishing.co.uk

Cover design by Brian Belanger
Cover painting by Lou B / diogenes art

This book is dedicated to everyone, who supported this crazy idea over the years, and especially to Jeni and Lou.

Contents

CHAPTER 1

It seems I am being summoned

London, January 1896

With a most ungraceful sidestep I avoided the fist, which had been thrown in the general direction of my unprotected head. I could feel the air rushing past my face, which told me that I had saved myself from bodily harm, just barely. To get away from the imminent danger, I had to twist my upper body harshly, which made me lose my balance -- and with both arms tied behind my back, it was a chore regaining it in a timely manner.

"Will you please, for the love of all that is holy, just let me hit you?" one of the shadows around me shouted with clear annoyance in his voice.

I didn't grace it with a response. Ducking low, I evaded another blow from the person behind me, found a stable hold on my right foot and used the left one to kick my assailant's leg. He stumbled and fell into the person behind him. I cursed. How many people had entered the room? In the twilight, I could not make out more than five. The figures around me reminded me of the spectres which had haunted my dreams for days. I shrugged off the uneasy feeling and braced myself for the next impact.

"Get him!" the downed man shouted and suddenly all of the ghost-like appearances jumped me at once.

They didn't use any weapons, so I had nothing to turn against them. A few kicks and twists later, one of the men had my torso in his grip on the floor and another secured my legs. I struggled for a while, but it was no use. My stamina had run out, clothes clung to my body permeated with sweat, and I breathed heavily against the cold, dusty stone paving. Still, I had never been a man to admit defeat. In a feat of strength I twisted and rolled over, and in turn made my attackers lose their grip.

Now I had them. If I could just…

"Mr. Holmes? Sir? A letter for you." The familiar voice of the footman sounded out of place in the darkness. "It is *most* urgent, I might add."

"Alright, game's over," the man on my back said and released his hold.

I rolled over and sat up, drawing great gulps of air into my lungs as I regained my equilibrium. With a few practiced motions I got rid of the rope around my wrists and rubbed the skin to restore a proper blood flow.

"Time?" I asked without looking up.

"Thirty-seven minutes and twenty-three seconds until Crawley interrupted us," someone answered from the other side of the room. A light flickered into existence and illuminated the small cellar room in a sickly yellow. Ah, so they had brought seven agents this time. I had half a mind to remind them of the rules to this game. But the announced time already showed that I had yet again set another record, despite the unfair odds, so I kept my mouth shut. No need to be petty. Their silence told me that they knew.

The footman, Crawley, stepped between us and handed me a folded piece of paper without further comment. I opened it to peruse its contents. What could be so urgent on a dreadful winter night such as this?

"It seems I am being summoned," I said after I had folded the message and jumped to my feet. The motion made me feel the places I had bruised as the result of a particularly badly executed fall, but I didn't let it influence the grace of my movement. "If you'll excuse me, gentlemen."

My fellow agents nodded, some eyeing the paper with curiosity, but no one inquired. It was not unusual for any of us to be summoned at any odd moment in time, so they could detect nothing out of the ordinary in my behaviour. I dropped the rope on an old, wooden table nearby and grabbed my suit jacket from a chair.

Just as I left the room, I could already hear whispers exchanged among them. I consciously didn't pay them any mind. Most of the agents in the service were younger than I and couldn't accept me retaining my high status within their ranks. I had barely entered the 42nd year of my life, which made me the oldest agent to turn down a more relaxing desk job or relocation to a warmer post in a colony further south after more than a lifetime of work.

The fact that I continued not only to outsmart my colleagues, but actually displayed a better physical record than most, was a source of constant talk and jealousy. Adding to that my experience in the field, I made sure that I was still chosen for most of the high-profile work, leaving them to clean up the mess common people made. In short: I was everything they wanted to be, but could never seem to reach - and god, I enjoyed it.

London was sleeping under a thick blanket of snow. Not even the thieves and scoundrels made an attempt of braving the bitter cold. Even evil needs a winter holiday, it seems. Not that I, Mycroft Holmes, would ever step so low as to pursue a pickpocket in the streets. No, I was used to an entirely different class of criminal. But even if the city took a break, the Secret Service would never be still. Its agents worked throughout the British Empire and beyond, ensuring the safety of its citizens.

As I traded the comfortable warmth of the Diogenes Club for a hard seat in a hansom cab, which might as well have been a block of ice, I briefly considered abandoning the effort. Being summoned to handle Sherlock's problems wasn't my favourite way to pass what little free time I had. While I loved my little brother, I did so in the same way one would love a pet cat: Dearly, but with a healthy dose of wariness.

When Sherlock decides to leave the country on one of his errands, he has the gracious mind to inform me of his destination. He doesn't do so out of a generous heart or consideration for his elder brother's feelings, but out of the desire to avoid any complications for himself. After a rather unpleasant stay on an island in a remote fjord in Norway during the winter, from which he only escaped by sending smoke signals to passing fishermen, he had found that informing me was the lesser of two evils.

My thoughts drifted to the note my brother had left behind a week ago, delivered to me by one of his street urchin helpers -- who had almost not been able to gain access to the club after getting in a row with the footman at the door. It had mentioned only the city of Milan and the number nine, indicating both Sherlock's destination and projected days of absence. He was rarely wrong on this account, so I hadn't paid his escapade any mind so far. But now I frantically clawed at any information my brain would provide about the current political and social affairs in northern Italy, as well as any gossip that had made the way over, to give me an idea of the problems he might have encountered.

A knock on the roof of the hansom told me we had arrived. Agitated flurries of snowflakes rushed into the cab as the driver opened the door and I thanked him with a nod as I jumped out into the barely disturbed snow on the pavement. I made my way through the piled-up, crumbly white ice and walked up to the door of 221b Baker Street.

It took no time at all for Mrs. Hudson to answer the ring of the bell, which wasn't surprising, as Watson would have alerted her to my visit. She ushered me into the building and placed a hand on my arm in a familiar gesture, as she welcomed me into the enveloping warmth of the hallway. I returned her greeting with a smile I hoped to be equally kind and declined her offer of tea brought to the sitting room. There were other things on my mind, and I didn't want to spoil the enjoyment of a hot cup of tea on a cold winter night by association with a distressing incident.

"Mycroft! I thank you for responding so quickly," Watson appeared on top of the stairs. He was wearing a simple, for once not ill-fitting, brown suit, looking as worldly and small as ever with his dirty blonde hair and matching mustache. I don't know why he always reminded me of an old dog. Oblivious to my thoughts, the doctor motioned for me to follow him into the sanctum of the building. "While I am aware that it's a nightmare to travel in this weather, the issue at hand simply cannot wait."

"I fully understand," I responded, and my reply was genuine. Problems concerning Sherlock always took the highest priority for us, after all.

"What issue, Dr. Watson?" Mrs. Hudson asked with curiosity, remaining dutifully at the bottom of the stairs while I joined Sherlock's associate at the top and avoided every creaking board as was my custom. "Mr. Holmes hasn't gotten himself into any trouble again, has he?"

"That remains to be seen, Mrs. Hudson," I answered for the doctor.

"Mark my words. That man will put all of us into an early grave," the housekeeper sighed and threw her hands up in a gesture of defeat.

I followed Watson into the sitting room and closed the door behind me. After I rid myself of coat and hat, I took in the familiar scene of 221b with fondness. While I didn't get along brilliantly with my younger brother, I have always admired the way he lead his life. And this room, with all its artifacts and souvenirs, spoke loudly of the way he enjoyed it.

The space was illuminated only by the flickering flames of the fireplace, so when Watson turned on the gas lamp on my brother's desk, I briefly had to squint my eyes due to its much brighter, white light. The doctor then pointed out the reason I had been summoned: A piece of paper, already extracted from the envelope it had arrived in. It was positioned on Watson's old writing desk, on top of what could have only been some of the case notes the doctor always faithfully recorded.

Only a few people would ever know the liberties he took when penning his stories to be published in the Strand Magazine. Take myself for example: No one would recognise me in the streets just following the details of Watson's description. They were indeed the most effective way to camouflage myself while my brother grew as a public figure. In reality I am proud to say that I was everything but corpulent and always took pride in my stately figure, fitting just so in an elegantly tailored, bespoke suit. Frankly, my occupation wouldn't have allowed me to be anything but a paragon of gentlemanly elegance, and I enjoyed every minute of it. But while my physical features and mental faculties were very similar to Sherlock's, the rest of our lives couldn't have been more different.

"Thank you for calling me so quickly," I said as I approached the writing desk.

"Of course," Watson answered. "I didn't catch you at a bad moment?"

"In fact you did."

I pointedly ignored his raised eyebrow at my last comment and proceeded to pick up the rather small, dirty envelope, noting that Watson had opened carefully despite his agitated state of mind. His years in the company of my brother had not been in vain, after all. I let my gaze wander over the slightly brownish, coarse paper surface, illuminated by the light of the gas lamp. A number of faces looked up at me from colourful postage stamps, which took up a quarter of the envelope's front.

Italy. Milan. There wasn't any doubt now.

"The content?"

Watson produced a small piece of paper, evidently ripped from a larger sheet. He held it up to the light for me to see. Only a few words and some stains adorned its surface. It read in a hurried handwriting:

'Find help. I am truly sorry.'

The writing on the torn-off page was unmistakably that of Sherlock. I would have recognised my younger brother's hand anywhere.

"The note was written in a hurry, compressed into a ball and given to someone with dirty hands. Someone then straightened it out again, placed it in the envelope and addressed it in his own, crude hand. The first part simply reads "John Watson, London," but has been amended two... no three times until it arrived here. Observe that

"England" and "Baker Street" have been written by the same person with two different pens. Someone then added your title of "Dr" in front of your name."

"So that means…"

"It means that my brother is most definitely in some sort of… danger. Tell me, where does Sherlock stash his letters, if he doesn't get rid of them immediately? We should find a clue about the nature of his case in Milan there."

"He usually keeps his correspondence ordered by year on a shelf behind his bedroom door."

"You haven't looked at it yet?"

"No, I admit it slipped my mind…" Watson had the decency to sound embarrassed.

"But he *did* receive a letter? There was no visitor to inform him of the case matter?" I was already on my way to my brother's sleeping chamber, Watson at my heels like a trained dog.

"Yes. Well, not that I can recall. I'm not always present when a client deems it suitable to visit," the doctor mumbled while stepping up to help me find the letter in question. "Ah, here it is."

He grabbed a moderately sized ledger, bound in cheap, black leather from the shelf. It looked worn out from repeated use, even though the year had barely started and it shouldn't have seen many hands yet. But where there should've been only the soft whisper of leather being dragged over used wood, as Watson pulled the ledger from the shelf, I heard a rasping noise, like two hard, uneven surfaces screeching against each other.

In our confusion we shared a brief questioning gaze, but were quickly distracted by the sound of heavy sand grains that tumbled onto the floorboards, originating from the bundle of collected paper in the doctor's grasp. I grabbed the curious thing from his hand and opened it immediately to witness the last remnants of dry sand still on the surface of the few letters it contained. I recognised them as the correspondence my brother and I had shared in the aftermath of the delicate issue of the Bruce-Partington Plans.

"What in the name... ?" Watson uttered disbelievingly. "Why would Holmes place sand into his documents?"

"Has anyone visited while he was away?"

"I've received Stamford for tea once, three days ago, but otherwise it's just been me and Mrs. Hudson in Baker Street."

I hummed noncommittally and carefully put the ledger down on the adjacent work desk, which was as cluttered as my brother's mind. Even in the feeble light of a single lamp, there was no mistaking the substance, which was now scattered across the floor for anything but coarse grained, reddish sand. With my right index finger, I cautiously picked up some of the remnants in the ledger, to roll them between my fingertips, test the smell and taste. But as soon as they came in contact with my skin, I recoiled and snapped my hand back in alarm.

"Mycroft?" Watson moved in to see what had surprised me so. "What happened?"

"Interesting..." I mumbled. "The sand... it felt electrifying. My skin grew hot the instant I touched it," I explained, a bit of wonder colouring my tone, as I rubbed my fingers, still feeling the remaining heat. But that's impossible? No, there must be a chemical…

The reaction hadn't injured my fingers, just caught me completely off guard, similar to the shock you feel when you expect the liquid in your glass to be water and after a big gulp it turns out to be vodka instead. I decided to test the substance again, this time mentally prepared. Slowly, under Watson's curious scrutiny, I applied another of my digits to the paper and touched the grains to exposed skin.

Nothing happened.

I placed my whole hand on the paper. Still nothing. A closer inspection of the ledger revealed only two letters to be present, both of which I penned myself. And the sand on the floor was just that: a pile of slightly brownish coloured, thoroughly ground down rocks.

What just… Was my tired mind playing tricks on me?

"There's nothing wrong with the sand, except for the fact that it's fallen out the ledger, where it clearly has no right to be," Watson concluded, and deposited a handful of the treacherous material on top of the desk. "Could you have been… mistaken?"

His question was posed cautiously. A wise move when he thought it prudent to address me with an accusation like this. But I wasn't in the mood to discuss the issue.

"Yes, I must've been mistaken," I answered, voice clear even though my thoughts were still muddled. "There is no time for this. If there's no written record to be found, I will have to visit the root of the problem."

My irritation with this whole incident grew by the second, so I didn't hesitate to leave the room and the accursed pile of particles behind me and return to the chair to which I had relinquished my coat and hat earlier. I had felt determined to chase after Sherlock since I received Watson's message at the Diogenes and was annoyed at the strange occurrence, which single-handedly managed to completely derail my train of thoughts. My feet led me to the stairs automatically, while I wrapped a woollen scarf around my neck several times, so I was ready to depart once more into the frosty winter air.

"Mycroft!" Watson exclaimed and drew my attention back to the present. Only then did I realise that I had completely forgotten the doctor in my pursuit. "Would you *please* explain what's going on?"

"You know Sherlock wouldn't ask for help if not pressed for it by extraordinary circumstances. The fact that he didn't even have time to post the letter himself speaks for itself." I had already departed the room and made for the entrance door of the building, so Watson had no option but to follow me.

"That's not what I was talking about! The sand ..."

"Is of no consequence," I said with emphasis. Whatever had happened was strange, but didn't change a thing about the obvious course of action. "The post office stamp is already six days old. There's no time to lose -- I need to depart for Milan immediately."

"Milan?"

"Yes, Dr. Watson. I am going to Italy," I said and opened the door to the building with force, so it swung wide open, much to the dismay of Mrs. Hudson, who had exited her room to investigate the commotion. Freezing air rushed in, bringing with it snowflakes, which melted on contact with the warm hallway floor.

"Farewell."

Watson quickly stepped in front of me, and blocked my path with crossed arms, legs spread wide. "I will not sit idly by while you rush off to the Continent. In fact, I insist on accompanying you."

For a moment I blinked confusedly in the face of the doctor's persistence. Even though my brother held him in high regard and had subsequently taken to bringing him along on any case he could possibly manage, I had my reservations. It was easier to move alone. Improvisation had always been my most prized skill -- impossible to employ when you have a short, slow and untrained man glued to you side.

But even though I could have easily brought forth any number of convenient arguments, I couldn't use them. If something should happen to Sherlock while I had forced Watson to stay behind, I would have a hard time reconciling with him. The secret-keeper could quickly become a great liability. I sighed internally and cursed myself for allowing the circumstances evolve like that, just out of lazy convenience. No... there was no choice in the matter.

How could I have even thought of leaving the *faithful* Watson behind?

"I will be back in half an hour and expect you to be travel ready by then."

Watson nodded and gave way for me to exit the building. I could see some fear and uncertainty in his face, but also resolve and gratitude, and that was enough ... for now. I prayed that I wasn't going to regret the decision.

My hansom cab was still outside, the driver wrapped in a thick blanket, the horse breathing steady clouds of steam into the winter air. I didn't turn around as I climbed into the cab and gave the order to take me back to the Diogenes. There was no time to pick up anything from my private residence, and I had some things to arrange which would require the facilities of the club.

The Diogenes Club was my home away from home, housing not only the Secret Service city headquarters, but also an office space I almost never left while I conducted my business for Queen and country. And, yes, I did indeed possess a much used armchair. That much of Watson's account was true, even if his stories of Greek interpreters have been the product of his boundless imagination.

I entered my office, relished in the way the world fell away as soon as I closed the door behind me and breathed in the smell of old wood and paper. It was quiet here, as always -- an island of silence in the middle of the bustling city. I lit a single lamp at my desk, which threw an ornate shadow on the ceiling and put the room in a warm twilight. The selection of spirits in their crystal decanters sparkled invitingly from a sideboard, but as much as I felt the need for a stiff drink, there were more pressing matters. At my desk, I was privy to the luxury of a telephone, which enabled me to call in a few favours to make the start of our travel as painless as possible. In this situation there was no need to play humble, and I had every intention of using my high status within the Secret Service to my advantage, even if not on official business.

A note, with a rudimentary explanation for my absence, was quickly drafted and placed into an envelope to be delivered to my superiors in the morning. I wouldn't wait for permission and was fairly certain that my lapse would be frowned upon, but Sherlock had been a valuable asset to the agency on several occasions. And if I had overstated his importance sometimes, it only served to enable my self-proclaimed consulting detective brother to carry out his job as he saw fit.

In the end, the siren call of the spirit was too strong and I gave in, quickly downing a glass of whisky to keep me warm, before I left my office. A bag of travel essentials was always prepared for me, so I wouldn't have any problems starting the journey immediately. I left the note for my superiors with the footman at the door and once again made use of a cab.

Dr. Watson was already waiting for me when I called upon him again at 221b and exited the building together with Mrs. Hudson. They exchanged a few words, during which both tried to assure the other not to worry, but it was a futile effort. When they were finished, I approached the housekeeper and handed her a small envelope.

"I am sure Dr. Watson has already suggested that you take leave for a while. In fact, prepare the house for a longer absence, take the dog and stay with your family until you are sent for again." I tried to put on my best encouraging smile. "Christmas might be over, but there is never a bad time to visit your loved ones. Consider this a late gift from myself to you."

Much to Mrs. Hudson's credit, she didn't open the envelope, but put it into the side pocket of her skirt, in which I knew she also kept the keys to Baker Street. She looked at Watson in a way a mother looks at her son, before she faced me with a much sterner expression.

"I don't know what's going on, but please, Mr. Holmes. Bring those two home safe. I am too old to look for another employer," she joked, but there was an almost undetectable waver in her voice.

I made myself smile again, this time reassuringly, then tipped my hat and motioned for Watson to join me in the cab before the housekeeper could utter more sentimental words. The situation had a feeling of finality to it, which wasn't unusual to me, but served to make the doctor feel anxious, which spoke clearly from his every movement. He watched Mrs. Hudson see us off until she disappeared behind a thick wall of snowflakes. The hansom plowed on through the piled-up white. Progress was slow, even though we were travelling on the main road. The familiar sounds of horseshoes on cobblestone were muffled by the icy blanket, and the whole atmosphere felt as if the world were wrapped in cotton wool.

For a long time, neither Watson nor I seemed willing to disturb the silence. What little warmth I had retained slowly slipped

16

away as a creeping cold began to set into my limbs. I watched the doctor wrap the thick coat tighter around his shoulders and rearrange the scarf to cover more of his face, as the carriage wasn't entirely draught proof. For myself, I didn't feel the need to take any action to counter the cold. On the contrary, the freezing temperatures helped me to focus my thoughts. And there was so much to contemplate. Oblivious to my inner turmoil, Watson cleared his throat noisily. I inclined my head slightly to indicate that he had my attention.

"From your hasty reaction I assume you know a great deal more about the situation than I do." As soon as the words had left the doctor's mouth, I saw him flinch in the corner of my eye, probably because he realised that he could have insulted me with his wording. "I mean, there must be a reason…"

"Dr. Watson, I simply have the desire to return my brother to London. Preferably alive. I assure you that I had no prior knowledge of the situation and was confronted with the information in the same way as you were."

There was no need to inform him of the note Sherlock had left me, as it made no difference at this point. I turned towards the man, who would now have to be described as my traveling companion, and picked up on a few conflicting emotions displayed openly on his face. While I had never given the man any reason to doubt my actions, it didn't offend me to see a healthy amount of distrust in his. I can't stand people who trust blindly.

"I couldn't refrain from an examination of the strange sand briefly before I had to depart," Watson said, proud but still in a

17

slightly apologetic tone. "There wasn't time to do a proper analysis, but in the end I could detect nothing out of the ordinary. Simple, coarse sand grains, slightly reddish from exposure to iron. No foreign matter."

I nodded, not letting my surprise show. Sometimes I forgot that the addendum to my brother was capable of individual action.

"Then I can't explain the reaction I felt by anything other than my imagination," I concluded, even though it pained me to say it.

"You said it felt... electric?"

"Like a small lightning bolt entering my fingers," I confirmed. "Exceedingly hot to the touch. Maybe a thing on the desk had a charge I wasn't aware of. I wouldn't put it past my brother to have any kind of odd implement lying out in the open."

The doctor nodded in a way that told me more than any words could have.

"As I said earlier: It's of no consequence. Odd as it may be, a bit of sand is no reason to question the road lying in front of us."

"You are right, of course. So... do you have a plan?"

I produced a small pack of paper from a hidden pocket on my coat and handed it to the doctor. While he untied the string around it, I started to explain.

"As I am leading this excursion, we will work by the book, which means taking every possible precaution. This contains everything you need for your temporary identity on our journey," The occasional light falling into the hansom from the street was not enough to illuminate the papers sufficiently, so I elaborated on their

18

contents. "Your alias will be *Richard Brewer* and mine *Ian Ashdown*. We are to be tailors on our way to Rome to find new trading partners. I have used these aliases many times and they have always served me well."

Watson shook his head, but quickly added words to indicate that it was not out of disapproval but rather disbelief. "I have no qualms with the identity, but is this really necessary? It seems like an excessive measure."

"Dr. Watson," I pinned him down with one of my most icy stares to emphasise the point I was about to make. "If you want to travel with me, you *will* follow my rules. There is no other option. You either agree or leave this cab right now."

Watson was stunned into silence by my strong words and stared at me for a few long moments. I could clearly see the disapproval of my behaviour in his eyes.

"There is only one problem…"

"And what might that be, *doctor*?"

"I know nothing about tailoring."

CHAPTER 2

I have taken the hippocratic oath

When we arrived at Victoria station, it was void of the usual hustle and bustle of the city. The last trains of the day had not yet departed, but passengers were few and far between. While this made it easy for us to move quickly, I felt dreadfully exposed out in the open. There shouldn't have been any threat for us at Victoria, but I had been caught off guard once already that day, which was one of the reasons why we didn't depart from Charing Cross.

Watson joined me after I stepped out of the cab and looked as nervous as I was secretly feeling. I appraised his appearance more out of routine than curiosity. The short man looked very much like the middle-class city dweller he was, in a dark coat, bowler hat and worn-out shoes peeking out from underneath dark-brown tweed trousers. He gave no indication as to his profession in his outward appearance and at least he blended in, so it would have to do.

I turned on my heel and walked through the entrance of Victoria station, once again leaving the doctor no choice but to follow me. He hurried along, but didn't complain, as he was probably used to this kind of treatment from my brother. I led the way to a small carriage attached to a single engine, which had been arranged for us per my earlier request sent out from the Diogenes. This was my last chance to leave the doctor behind, but I pushed the thought out of my head as soon as it appeared, as it was clearly beneath me to be as fickle-minded.

The train carriage was uniformly black and as non-descriptive as the cab we had arrived in, with curtains blocking the view to the inside and no signs or writing anywhere on its exterior to give a clue as to its origin or destination. We were greeted by a very small man in an even smaller coat, who was standing on the platform. He hid his face behind a voluminous scarf and what remained of his head under a large top hat. On first glance you might've not even recognised him as a person, but rather a pile of discarded cloth, on which someone had the silly idea to place a hat. I sighed an exasperated sigh. Of course it must've been *him* to deliver the goods -- who else would be present for work on such a dreadful night?

"Good evening Ignatius," I said in a low but mock-cheerful voice. Watson was not to listen in on our conversation, so I had to bow down considerably to meet my colleague's ear.

"Holmes," he answered curtly and held up a small bag. "The requested items."

"Most kind."

I grabbed the container, but Ignatius wouldn't release his hold on it. Instead he raised his head and stared at me with narrowed eyes, which peeked out barely from underneath his large hat. We held eye contact for only a few seconds, but it was enough time for me to soak up all the annoyance he projected about being called out here in the middle of a freezing winter night. My pride prevented me from a simple pull at the bag, but I couldn't let go either.

"Next time you go frolicking off to the Continent, you fetch your own damn things, Holmes."

"My sincerest apologies," I mouthed, not even attempting to make it sound truthful. "I am *most* grateful for your assistance and I am sure my brother will extend the same gratitude to you once I have plucked him off the streets of Milan and dragged him back to London."

"Ah, so it's about Sherlock," Ignatius said. Immediately his features softened and he let go of the bag.

I refrained from rolling my eyes at what I had come to call *Behavioural Pattern A*: Disdain for my own person, consideration and fondness for my little brother. That people should choose him over me was a riddle I seemed to be destined to chase after my whole life.

"Much appreciated," I added and didn't let my own irritation get the best of me. "Now, if you'll excuse us. We have a boat to catch."

"Right. But are you sure about that?" the small man inclined his head towards Watson, who stood at a wise distance and made no attempt to join the conversation.

"*That* is my brother's associate and *not* taking him will get me into more trouble than leaving him behind."

"I didn't think anyone would be able to get the *great* Mycroft Holmes into trouble. How far you have fallen," Ignatius smirked, satisfied by the unfortunate situation I had found myself in. He beckoned Watson over, then indicated we should board the train.

"Not one more word, Ignatius Craig," I warned him and he showed me a broad grin as a response. "Or I will tell everyone just *what* you did on Christmas in 1893."

That one usually got me punched, but this time Ignatius merely squinted his eyes at me. I boarded the carriage via some narrow steps and watched Watson follow me as he exchanged only a polite nod with my colleague.

"Godspeed, Holmes," Ignatius said before he closed the door behind us.

"Thank you," I answered, this time with sincere gratitude.

No matter how much we tended to tease each other, in the end we were fellow agents.

What greeted us on the inside was easiest to be described as a comfortably sized room, furnished with everything one could desire for a relaxing evening, complete with a low dining table and a well-stocked bar. With the only light in the carriage emanating from a small lamp over a writing desk opposite a divan, you could almost mistake the space for a tiny, but expensively furnished living room -- constantly in an earthquake. It was obvious that the carriage hadn't been heated recently, but it wasn't freezing either. The small dose of whisky from my office had long since deserted me, so I took a seat in the armchair between the bar and the desk -- just in case.

The carriage was already on its way to exit the station and rattled over countless railway switches in the progress. From my seated position, I could see Watson struggling to keep his balance until he ultimately lost it and stumbled rather ungracefully onto the divan in front of me. I could not refrain from showing an amused smile as I watched him fight and lose against the forces of the train.

"So," the doctor said as soon as he had sorted his limbs. "This is a private carriage, isn't it? *Your own* private train?"

"Dr. Watson, you overestimate me," I answered with a smirk on my lips, both out of amusement and to cover my pleasure about the fact that he considered me as someone who could afford such a thing. "No, this is one of the royal carriages -- used when wanting to travel in comfort, but hidden from the prying eyes of the public."

Watson actually sputtered. "A *royal* carriage? But how…?"

"Let's just say that a lot of people owe me a lot of favours. I rarely call them in, which makes it easy to get what I need in a real emergency, which our current situation more than qualifies for."

The thick, blue, velvety curtains, which were draped over all windows and the items decorated with golden ornaments on an even darker shade of blue, should have been obvious clues. I watched the way Watson studied the details intently, waiting for the moment when the realisation would hit him. And that moment was recognizable ever so easily.

"This is *Queen Victoria's* carriage!" he exclaimed and jumped up from the divan as if stung by a whole swarms of bees. "Mycroft…?"

I still wasn't used to him calling me by my given name, and really saw the use only when my brother and I were in the same room, as to not confuse us. But there was no need for needless hostility. Besides, watching the doctor grow red in the face and jump around like he was standing on coals with naked feet, was amusement enough to pacify any desire to quarrel.

"Calm yourself! We needed a means to reach Dover within the hour and the carriage was present in the station. It's as simple as that," I explained and started to pull a number of small packages from the bag, which I had received from Ignatius at the station, and place them onto the writing desk next to me.

"Oh, *do* sit down. You are making me positively nervous."

I watched Watson fight with himself for a few seconds, but a sudden jolt of the carriage, as it drove over yet another switch, took care of that problem and made him tumble back down most ungracefully. It was so sudden, I was unable to suppress a chuckle, but had my face back under control when Watson frowned upon me.

"Let me get this straight. The Queen *herself* owes you a favour?"

"Several in fact," I said with a decidedly neutral expression. "One less now, I suppose. But who keeps count?"

Watson shook his head. His face was like an open book for me to read -- emotions washing over it undisguised. Astonishment, annoyance, contemplation, doubt.

"You have a habit of overthinking."

"And you have a habit of reading my thoughts."

"Merely observing. Your face is very... liberal."

The doctor had the audacity to smile at my comment. "There are times when I can't tell you and your brother apart."

Only years of rigorous training helped me avoid a slip in my expression. Comparing me to Sherlock had always been an insult of the highest order. Few people knew about our filial bond, and those

25

who did valued their lives too much to dare make any comment. Watson knew this, of course. I narrowed my eyes briefly, more out of acknowledgement than disapproval, and filed the comment away for later. Watson had his own little room in my head, and the things which had accumulated there over the years would have been his downfall long ago, were my hands not tied.

To change the subject, I pointed to the small packages on the desk, which the doctor had been eyeing with unabashed curiosity. There were two piles, in fact, and I pushed the smaller one towards Watson unceremoniously.

"The matter at hand is an urgent and potentially dangerous one. We have to assume some sort of resistance at our destination. It can never hurt to be prepared, even if we might not need any of these," I handed Watson one of the boxes, as he seemed to be hesitant to touch them. "I requested a number of items to be put at our disposal for the trip. I would have called for additional backup, but..."

My voice trailed off. There was no need for the doctor to know about my very unsanctioned departure, and I had let on too much already. He frowned, but didn't pry, and we turned our attention back to the task at hand.

Each of the mystery bundles was a small, wooden box, wrapped in coarse, brown packing paper and fastened with a black string. I opened them all, one by one, just as Watson was doing the same.

Ah, those people... I shook my head. They always want to remind me that their tools were *expensive and precious.* '*Dear*

Mycroft. This item is one of only two in existence. I would like to see it returned to England in one piece.' As if I would ever…

I read the note, which I found in the biggest box, in the mocking tone Ignatius always adopted, hearing it clearly in my head. There really was no point to it, as I had always brought back at least half of the items they supplied me with. And if one or two exceptionally good ones sometimes ended up in my own pocket… well, that was no one's business but mine. The Service had sufficient means to produce more tools than I could ever ruin.

"This is a concealed carrying belt for your gun, which I am quite certain you brought with you, carelessly concealed in one of your coat's pockets," I said and pushed said belt towards the doctor. One would think he'd take better care of his firearm after serving in the military. "Now this is a regular pocket watch on the front, but if you press the switch on top three times very fast and pull the chain out, you can see it's attached to a very robust piano wire, useful for all kinds of situations. Here we have a pen, which is filled with ink, but when this part is turned, it can be used as a means to inject a potent poison …"

"Mycroft!" Watson stated with emphasis, body straightening in an instant. "I will *not* kill a person! I have taken the Hippocratic oath!"

Again I suppressed the obvious urges as the muscles in my body tensed. The deadly pen was still in my hand, and I twirled it several times between my fingers in an effort to release some of the nervous energy that had taken hold of me. I could still dump Watson in Dover...

"Yes, you are a doctor. But you are an *army* doctor and you carry a gun on your person almost religiously. How many of your patients have you shot before patching them up?"

"The difference between a gun and this pen is that the former provides me with the chance to do *exactly* that," Watson said between clenched teeth, as he picked up on my mood and visibly braced himself. "I shoot to incapacitate. *Not* to kill."

"With all due respect, *Dr.* Watson," I replied and put as much venom in pronouncing the man's title as I could muster. "My tools, my mission, my rules. You agreed to take my lead, and I will *not* take you along if all you prove to be is a liability."

Watson slammed the pocket watch, which he had still held in his hand, back on top of the writing desk and rose to his feet. He looked more than ready to launch into a heated argument, maybe even a physical one.

Then, all of a sudden, the carriage shook violently. A gale so fierce, it made the windows rattle and the whole structure tilt precariously, hit the train with full force. Watson tumbled onto the floor and, out of instinct, I threw myself on top of his form as I saw the items on the desk follow suit. Several heavy things hit my back, but their impact was cushioned by the thick layers of clothing I was still wearing. The wheels of the carriage screeched and it shook again, making the alcohol bottles perform a cacophony of clinking sounds.

Expensive drinking glasses fell to the floor and were only saved by the plush carpet laid out beneath.

A shock of pain from my right index finger made me shout something unintelligible as not only the skin on my fingertip, but my whole hand felt as if it were made of liquid fire. I couldn't conceal it and released a groan of anguish at the unfamiliar and horrifying sensation as I threw myself back, thereby releasing the doctor.

Then the wind calmed down, the short train picked up speed, and the weird feeling in my hand disappeared as quickly as it had arrived -- leaving only an irritated tingle. I stared at my skin, but there was no visible sign of any damage or even burns to be seen.

"Are you alright?" Watson uttered with concern as he righted himself up.

"I didn't hurt myself when the carriage shook," I answered, truthfully in part. "Merely bumped my knee at an unfortunate angle as I fell."

The doctor nodded. "Thank you for... shielding me."

"My rules," was the simple reply.

I could pinpoint the moment that our earlier argument popped back into the doctor's head, but the commotion had taken all the wind out of his sail. Neither of us seemed comfortable in acknowledging the second strange happening of the night. I knew I wouldn't admit to the pain I had felt, thereby making it a real thing that hadn't happened just in my head. Though the other option wasn't much better.

"Alright, Mycroft. This time it's your rules. If Holmes is in danger, I'm the last person who wants to create any problems during his rescue."

So there was something good to be had today, after all.

CHAPTER 3

Like handing a mouse to a hungry cat

The abominable weather seemed intent to stand in our path at every junction. Upon our arrival in Dover, we learned that the wintry gales of a blizzard made a crossing of the channel temporarily impossible, and we had to resign ourselves to wait until they subsided. Our hasty departure had been in vain and all hours saved were now wasted.

Brilliant.

I stood at the seafront and watched the ships being battered by waves that should have had no business being so large and vicious in the safety of the harbour. All my curses did nothing to calm the gales and my voice was drowned out by the roar of the storm. There I was, foolishly thinking that I could bend Nature to my will, when it was all futile. I hated being put in my place like this, no matter by whom. We couldn't afford to be delayed.

Sherlock had never, in his life, sent a request for help like this. My brother was and had always been an ingenious, secretive and above all self-sufficient person. If I could trust anyone to battle his way through life alone and come out on top every time, it was him. But I also knew that he would rather shoot himself than ask me for support, no matter how freely I would give it. Though, sometimes I wondered if I should offer to do the shooting.

Then Watson approached me, arms raised to shield himself from the worst of the storm, which really was a futile endeavour.

"There is a man, who wants to see you," the doctor shouted over the wind.

"A man?" No one was supposed to know we were there.

"He seemed insistent. Sent me out to fetch you, even," Watson stated, clearly bristled about the fact that he had been ordered about like that. "He is waiting in the lobby of our hotel."

A peculiar feeling overcame me. "Does he perchance happen to have red hair, a wild beard and wear small glasses on a large nose?"

Watson frowned, but nodded all the same. "You know the gentleman?"

"Yes, unfortunately. I had temporarily forgotten about him." No, that's not right -- I made myself forget him. How did he know...? We hadn't even been there for more than an hour... Ah, of course, we gave the hotel our real names. What a stupid, stupid mistake. There was no excuse to let my guard down just because we were still on British soil.

"Should I be worried?"

"No, not exactly worried."

Watson seemed confused and I couldn't blame him. I prayed that the night wouldn't take a turn for the worse -- though with the way that I was feeling, my patience was already running thin.

The walk from the harbour to the hotel was a short one, but to brave the wind was a challenge all in itself. The heavy snowfall clouded my view and the freezing water on the ground made every step a potential pitfall. Still, we made it to the welcoming warmth of the hotel lobby in one piece, where a pageboy offered to dry and then bring our coats to the room we had bought for the night.

I surveyed the space as we approached the bar in the room next to the lobby, which was furnished in warm tones, with heavy curtains to keep out the cold and many different palm trees to give the place a bit of colour. It held a large number of low tables and chairs -- almost all occupied by guests, who were held back by the weather as we were, enjoying a drink or maybe two. The fine aroma of cigars permeated the air as the smoke drifted lazily through the light. Watson was a bit unnerved in these surroundings, but I would accept nothing but the finest lodgings to raise my spirits at least a little.

"So, are we in trouble?" the doctor asked in a small voice, already spying the person, who had sent him on the errand to fetch me. "Because of the carriage, maybe?"

I laughed softly at his train of thoughts. "Not because of that. Follow me, please. And… try to keep quiet."

The familiar man sat at a table next to the bar. He didn't look out of place in this establishment, even in his simple, brown suit. A lanky figure, nursing a glass of amber spirit nervously, with a shock of bright red hair, which stood up as if fleeing from his scalp in horror. In hindsight, maybe a smaller hotel… maybe something unregistered might have done as well. But, no. There was no use in prolonging the inevitable.

"Leonard!" I uttered the name as warmly as I could muster, as we approached his table. "A absolute pleasure to meet you here!"

"Mycroft!" he shouted -- excited, shocked and gleeful at the same time. "So good to see you! You're looking well!"

"You must be joking," I countered. My face must have looked even more tired as I was feeling.

Leonard Hawkins laughed in his own, unique way, sounding like a dry-heaving chicken. He gestured to the empty chairs at his table and just as we took a seat, a waiter placed two drinks in front of us, evidently of the same spirit that Hawkins was enjoying a bit too freely. He looked nervous, and I couldn't blame him.

"I am delighted to see you, friend. It has been too long."

"Seven months and twenty-three days," I stated flatly.

Watson looked back and forth between me and the tall stranger and implored me with his eyes to explain what was going on. I shrugged and took a big gulp of the liquid in my glass, which turned out to be a damn fine cognac, which immediately started to thaw me. At least Hawkins had taste in alcohol.

"Dr. Watson, this is Leonard Hawkins -- we share the same employer. He overlooks all business going on in Dover," I explained while the man puffed himself up. He had all the reasons to do so -- to observe the traffic going through Dover and to take care of any problem arising, was a challenge that could only be organised and carried out by the best. It wasn't because of his job or abilities that I had grown to dislike the man, but for a completely different reason.

"Charmed, Dr. Watson. No need to introduce yourself, I most certainly know of you. Associate to the great detective Sherlock

Holmes. And now on the road with the magnificent Mycroft Holmes? My, my…" Hawkins smiled.

Watson nodded curtly. "All circumstantial, I assure you… A pleasure to make your acquaintance, Mr. Hawkins."

"Leonard, please. For friends of Mycroft's, always Leonard."

"I do *not* recall informing you of my location," I said amicably enough while Watson acquainted himself with the cognac. "How did you …"

"It's my job to know where everyone in this town is," he answered and smiled broadly.

"Yes, well, if you put it like that."

Watson seemed content to stay out of the conversation, and I couldn't blame him. Hawkins had always been a strange bundle of nerves, always just a bit… too much. I had learned to avoid him, but that wasn't always possible. Despite this, he didn't recognize any negative feelings I harboured for him. Or maybe he simply ignored them. The redhead waved for the waiter to top off our glasses, even though I refused out of politeness.

"Mycroft, my friend," the agent said happily, but with a barely perceptible tense edge to his tone. "You know that you are my friend, right?"

"*Right.*"

"You must know that I am overjoyed to meet you here, no matter the circumstances, and that I would never want for any harm to …"

"Get to the point," I cut him off. He was clearly torn between his loyalty to the Service and the one to a fellow agent. I already knew why he had sought me out.

"There was a message, you see," Hawkins stated, nervously, opening the unavoidable part of the conversation on an uneasy note. Everything could hinge on my ability to handle Hawkins right now. Maybe even my brother's life.

I leaned back into the uncomfortable chair, held the crystal glass up to my eyes and swirled the amber liquid around in a way the light sparkled on its surface, doing my best to look thoroughly unimpressed.

"Headquarters told you to intercept me. Tell me off. Worst case even detain me?" I stated the obvious.

"Your trip is unauthorized, and so are your supplies. You could slip through the cracks because we weren't quick enough to catch up with you in London, and you even managed to fool Craig... but here I am now. Before we have to employ more drastic measures, I was sent here to talk to you."

"Damn that blizzard!" Watson exclaimed and slammed the glass down onto the table just a little too hard. Fortunately it was already empty. I would've hated for this fine spirit to go to waste.

"Now, now," I smiled. "Don't be so agitated, dear doctor. Yes, the blizzard prevents us from proceeding, but it also gave me the opportunity to see an old friend again. Isn't that right, Leonard?"

I hated to resort to this, but the last thing we needed was a holdup right at the beginning of our journey. I smiled at the precious effort of headquarters. They didn't have any choice but to contact him, as he was the only man who could potentially stop me in time. But to place Hawkins in my path was more like handing a mouse to a hungry cat, as he had long been my self-proclaimed number one admirer.

"I *am* happy to see you, no matter the circumstances, Mycroft. But this is irregular and I can't just let it slide."

Watson narrowed his eyes, but refrained from attempting any intervention on his part, which I was very glad for.

"I will tell you the reason for this unusual trip, and only because I know I can trust you," I said, my voice sweet, but not overly. It wouldn't be good to overdo it.

"You can always trust me, Mycroft," he replied readily. "But I don't see how this would change anything."

"Well, you see, the real reason for our hasty departure -- and for Dr. Watson's presence -- is that my brother could be in mortal danger. We need to find him posthaste, as his life depends on it. You understand, surely, that I cannot wait for permission in such a dire case, if it's about my beloved brother!"

Watson's eyebrows seemed to disapprove of my acting, but I knew just how far I could push it with Leonard Hawkins, who was all too ready to see in me the noble saviour -- the same kind of hero figure I had cut when we had first met on a mission in Edinburgh all those years ago. And I could already see that my gamble was about to pay off.

"I see… the message didn't say any of this," Hawkins acquiesced quietly. "But are you really telling me the truth?"

"Have I ever lied to you?" I asked, hurt in my voice. And it was true. No matter how much I despised my colleague sometimes, he was still a fellow agent, whom I'd always assume to have the noblest of intentions and didn't deserve being lied to. Hawkins smiled cautiously. There was a long moment of silence, that stretched between us like warm taffy and I could actually hear Watson hold his breath.

"I suppose I will have to tell headquarters that I missed you."

Oh, he would get hell for this. Not as much as myself, when I eventually made it back to the island, but it wouldn't be pleasant at all. Now, the battle was over, but it wasn't in my nature to back down and accept the easy win. No, the little voice in my head challenged me to see how far I could take this. A lesser man would be led to ruin by this voice, but I made it work for me instead.

"I will be in your debt, Leonard," I said with emphasis to seal the deal. "If I can ever do something for you when I return, please don't hesitate to reach out."

"The knowledge of having been of use to you shall suffice, Mycroft," Hawkins nodded amicably, but it was clear that this would come to haunt me at some point.

The atmosphere was not as antagonistic as in the beginning of our meeting, but the air wasn't cleared either. There was still an annoying, noticeable tension that wouldn't be dispelled as easily, simply because Hawkins and I had a history. The only thing that kept us from falling out again was the shared goal of aiding Sherlock. It was still a miracle to me how a person like my brother, who was the very impersonation of self-centred behaviour and tactlessness, managed to rally us like this.

"Leonard I understand that is an irregular situation for you, but -- no, let me finish, please. All ships we wanted to hire refused to carry us over the channel tonight, and--"

"Mycroft, we can't! That would be suicide!" Watson shouted, loudly enough to make other the patrons of the hotel look our way.

I cleared my throat and shot the doctor a warning look. "With any *normal* ship, yes. I do happen to know, though, that the Service is in possession of a more sturdy specimen that could just make the crossing."

Hawkins shook his head. "Even if such a ship existed, this blizzard would be the best way to ensure it didn't."

"Leonard!" I said, almost pleadingly, putting all my emotion into this one word.

The agent looked at me, then the good doctor... and shook his head. I was just about to open the argument again when he burst out laughing. "You never change, do you, Mycroft? Is your brother worth that much to you?"

I swallowed dryly, not only because the last cognac had disappeared long ago, then exchanged a glance with Watson, who was also looking at me expectantly. There was no use in lying.

"No matter his shortcomings, he is the only family I have left. And I intend to keep it that way," I uttered gravely.

There was no time to lose, so we departed into the direction of the Service base of operations in Dover immediately, after picking up our luggage. It was conveniently situated in the middle of the harbour and in this way had access to most of the trading docks. It also oversaw the masses of people traveling between the island and the Continent. Concealed in an inconspicuous property, you wouldn't attach any significance to it, which was very much the point.

Luckily for us, the boat we were headed toward was being kept in a separate building, a sort of private dock, in which the aptly named *Interceptor* was waiting day and night -- always ready to move out at a moment's notice. The Service used it mainly to do exactly what she was named for: Chase and capture rogue elements on the channel around Dover. With three newly developed and so-called "internal combustion engines," the *Interceptor* was not only faster than any other boat around, but also kept up high speed more reliably. This was exactly why she could make the trip across the channel -- even in the blizzard.

It was not without guilt that I felt a small amount of glee at the thought of being able to finally make use of the boat. I had only heard about its magnificence from my colleagues and never had the chance to enjoy her special features so far. But for all the positive thoughts I allowed myself to have, nature was determined to find a contrary answer. The wind had picked up and seemed even fiercer than before our brief stay in the hotel lobby. We kept away from the water's edge, as the gale whipped the waves into menacing shapes, crashing onto land and freezing over anything the water touched.

"Mycroft?" Watson grabbed my shoulder and leaned in to shout in my ear as it was impossible to hold a normal conversation over the storm. "Do you see that?"

My eyes followed his outstretched arm, pointing with one finger into the distance at the end of the pier we had just walked past. I squinted to make out whatever he had spotted, but in the darkness, with water vapour and a flurry of snowflakes filling the air around us, I confessed to not seeing anything.

"Something lit up. Like a fire, but only for a moment," he explained. "Maybe I imagined it."

I was about to agree with the doctor when a red-hot glowing light flickered into existence for just a second, spread out like a piece of cloth fluttering in the breeze. Watson gripped my arm and instinctively pulled me a step back.

"What...?"

By now, Hawkins had realised we were no longer directly behind him and turned around to join us with a question on his face. Watson wasn't about to move, so I took action by shaking my head and pulled him along, pointedly ignoring whatever had presented itself to us in such a dramatic manner. I heard the doctor protest, but that was no reason to stop. The freezing cold of the blizzard was already so deep inside my bones, I feared it would never leave me again should I stay in it any longer.

Hawkins was temporarily bewildered, but followed me as I pulled Watson along. Any comment he gave was lost to the wind, and I heard nothing but the roar of turbulent air and the crash of the waves

41

on hard stone. Then it happened again -- and from the reaction of my companions I could conclude it wasn't just my own mind, that seemed to be playing tricks. Between us, and the building we were attempting to reach, the light appeared again, flickering like a flame, floating disembodied in the air.

"Are you seeing this?" Hawkins shouted and walked towards the phenomenon, unaware of its implications. As it flared up, a sharp pain shot all the way from my fingers to my shoulder, and it took all I had in me not to convulse on the spot. Instead I grabbed the now useless limb with my healthy hand and clutched it to my body. Unable to utter a sound as I gritted my teeth, there was no way for me to hold back the red-haired agent, who walked on, transfixed by the light.

Then, suddenly, Watson sprinted ahead. He must've seen my reaction and concluded that only he could stop Hawkins in his tracks. I saw him reach the man and pull him back by a sharp yank of his coat.

It wasn't a moment too soon.

The red fire disappeared, but almost like emerging from it, a figure, enveloped in a wide sheet of fabric, jumped at the pair in front of me. The cloth moved violently in the gale and obscured the actual silhouette, but I could see glinting steel raised high with overwhelming clarity. The pain in my hand was forgotten as I propelled myself forward, crossing the distance against the winds in seconds. I threw myself at the apparition -- but where I expected to hit a solid body, there was only flimsy fabric in my path, through which I passed without resistance and subsequently got acquainted with the hard pavement in a rather sudden fashion.

My vision went black for a second as the shock of the impact rippled through my entire body, but once again I was saved by the substantial amount of padded clothing on my frame, which cushioned the blow. For a while I could only hear, but not see the commotion around me, while I fought against gravity and the churning air masses. Firstly, and most importantly, there was the tell-tale sound of metal as it hit stone, shortly after my fall. At least my actions seemed to have dislodged what I thought to be the weapon of our attacker. Then, barely audible grunts of exertion drifted over, and I fiercely hoped that the occasional sounds of pain didn't stem from my colleagues.

"Mycroft?" Hawkins shouted, just as I had managed to push myself upwards.

"I'm alright!" I replied as loudly as I could.

I turned towards the action behind me, which I had seemed to have missed most of. Still shrouded by what I now properly recognised as a cloak of black and white patterned cloth, there was a man on the ground beneath Watson, who put all his weight into keeping him exactly there. I could only see the back of our assailant's head, which was cleanly shaven and the bruised skin of his hand, which Hawkins kept pressed to the floor with his boot.

My first reaction was to pick up the knife, which lay discarded at my feet, to prevent the man from taking control of it again. It was a short dagger with a thick blade, which ended in a round, lavishly decorated handle. Even in the darkness of the night it glinted golden, invitingly and ominously.

"He seems to be unconscious," Hawkins shouted. "We should take him with us to the dock."

I nodded my agreement. It would be much easier to detain and control the attacker out of this dreadful weather. My heart was still beating fast and the sudden spike of adrenaline left me a little dizzy, but I kneeled down next to the exotic figure and helped Watson turn him over. The cloth around his body was blown up by the storm and revealed that the man was not only tanned, but entirely naked underneath it. But his body was limp in our grasp and it was safe to say that the punch he had received on his nose, had not only broken it but also rendered him unconscious. His face was bloodied and bruised, but what struck me most, was that he was completely hairless. Not even a faint arch of an eyebrow or the stubble of a beard could be seen.

I left Watson to sort out the man's limbs and wrap the cloth around his body so we could carry him, and I could examine the dagger. It was a simple thing, but it felt heavy and strangely consequential in my hand. Not only because both the metal and my skin grew ever warmer the longer they touched. I was drawn in by the feeling, as the weight felt more comfortable in my grasp and the connection seemed to make my hand tingle -- for once pleasantly -- and removed all the pain I had felt before.

A scream ripped me from the almost meditative state I had slipped into within such a short amount of time. I whirled around to

44

see Watson and Hawkins on the floor -- and the unknown man, hurtling himself toward me. His arms stuck out from the cloth like thin branches with gnarled fingers. Everything seemed to slow down as he managed to grab the dagger with one hand and tear it from my grasp. It didn't seem to bother him that he clutched the blade tightly in his hand and thus spilled his blood on the frozen ground.

A curse, loud and fierce, in a language I had never heard before, emerged from his lips, deeper and more forceful than I'd ever thought this emaciated body capable of producing. Once again I felt pain well up in my hand. There was no way to deny the unholy connection anymore.

Despite everything, I braced myself for an attack -- which never came.

I saw the cloth fly away from us like a ghost dancing in the storm. With surprising speed the man ran towards the churning ocean and jumped into the freezing waves without any hesitation. As he disappeared, the burning sensation on my skin left me... but that wasn't the only thing which had deserted us. The wind died down in an instant, as if someone had flipped a switch. Where there had been roaring, icy gales, there was now only light snowfall in a gentle breeze, and a silence, which was almost deafening in its suddenness. The sea moved back into its usual bed and the only evidence of the earlier storm were the puddles of seawater strewn about the pavement.

Watson was sitting on the floor, eyes wide and stared at the place where the man... no, the spectre had jumped into the depths. Hawkins had tumbled to the ground in the commotion and lay on his back, snowflakes falling ever so gently on his face. Just like me, they were both stunned into silence by the events, which had taken place in such a short amount of time, but had shaken us all to the core.

"Is there something you want to tell me?" Hawkins was the first to regain his composure and righted himself up to a sitting position.

I shook off the remaining fuzziness in my head and walked over to him, then offered the man a hand, which he took gratefully. He groaned slightly as I pulled him upright, but there was nothing in his movements which would have suggested a serious injury.

"Frankly, I don't know," I admitted. "Sherlock has been abducted and we're on our way to reverse the situation. Someone knew exactly where we would be, which leads me to believe that the communication we received has been... monitored. That's all I know."

"Who was that man?" Watson asked, and it struck me that I could hear him talk clearly, despite the distance between us, which grew as the doctor approached the edge of the walkway to look for our assailant in the waves.

The storm was well and truly gone.

"I have never seen the like," I answered.

"Are you sure you want to tackle this alone?" Hawkins sounded concerned.

"Have you forgotten why you were sent to intercept me? I'm well aware that I am leaving for the Continent without sanctioned support," I cocked an eyebrow. "It has to be this way if I'm to act fast. This... happening is no reason to abandon my brother."

No, if anything, it only spurred me on.

"Well, you'll have me," Watson said as he joined us and placed a hand on my shoulder, smiling collegially. "As for the... person who attacked us, I can't see him anywhere."

"There's no way he survived the plunge into the freezing water."

A twinge in my hand made me look around in a brief moment of agitation, but then I turned my eyes back to the skin of my palm. Where I had held the dagger, the grooves of the metal had burned into my skin, leaving red, angry marks. They didn't hurt -- miraculously -- but tingled as if an army of ants were crawling across my skin.

"Are those... signs? Writing?" Watson grabbed my limb and pulled it closer. "It's too dark to see, but..."

"Quick, let's enter the dock," Hawkins said nervously. "I'd prefer to get away from the sea, and we have a light inside."

There was no other sensible course of action, so I followed the two men along the waterline. Without the wind to work against us, we reached the wooden building within minutes. My fellow agent grabbed a lantern from a hook next to the door with a well-practiced gesture and set the wick on fire. The smell of burning oil was a welcome and homely one.

"Now, let me see that hand," Watson gestured for me to step closer and hold out my palm, which I did without complaints.

But as I put my skin into the light, there wasn't a single mark to be seen. My hand was as unblemished as it had been before the attack, showing only some old scars, which had long since healed. I flexed my fingers, but couldn't feel any discomfort. In that moment I shared an uneasy glance with Watson, which didn't escape Hawkins' scrutiny.

"Now you *have* to tell me what the devil's going on here!"

"A series of pranks and coincidences," I answered gravely. "Little actions to throw us off our rescue mission."

"You call a lunatic attacking you with a knife *a prank?*" Hawkins exclaimed. "I'm sorry, Mycroft, but I don't buy it."

"You don't *have* to buy it. Just get us across the channel."

"Mycroft …," Watson started, trying to sound amicably.

"No! There is now *nothing* on my hand, and the man is gone. We need to go."

"You can't deny …"

"I'm not denying anything, doctor. Every happening makes me grow more fearful for my brother's life. But it doesn't change the need for us to proceed as quickly as possible. Please."

"Just tell me I'm not delivering you to your death."

"I've survived worse."

Hawkins laughed. "That you have, my friend. That you have."

CHAPTER 4

You're not comparing me to a dog, are you?

After the storm had died down, the *Interceptor* made the crossing of the channel within only half an hour. Hawkins returned to the island on the same night, but not without thoroughly lecturing me on... well, apparently anything that came to his mind. I let him talk his heart out, as he was indeed doing us the biggest of favours. That, and because of the fact that he tended to babble when nervous, and nothing about the situation we were in was in any way reliably reassuring.

Watson warmed up to the man, and they shared stories about the work we had carried out together with Sherlock, to pass the time. Stories that he hadn't been able to tell anyone before because of their sensitive nature. But I kept quiet through it all and cautiously monitored the sky. No one had said anything about the way the storm had just... vanished, as soon as the man disappeared between the waves, but I knew the other two must have realised it too. Maybe it was one of these things that was simply impossible, and didn't actually happen until someone acknowledged it and another confirmed the facts. I wouldn't be either of those people.

A train journey through Europe was our next step. We crossed most of France and some of Switzerland before we entered Italy. When you think of the southern country, most of us have this picture of a perfect summer day in a quaint, little cafe in mind, maybe even at the seaside. While I had visited Italy many times during my life, the excursions had always been work-related. That didn't mean I couldn't combine hunting down the odd enemy of the British Empire with a few pleasurable days in the countryside. It's my firm belief that anyone should be granted a bit of respite after wrangling with an actual lion.

Just when I felt like I'd be on a train for the rest of my life, we reached the south side of the Alps. It turned out that the snowfall didn't only plague northern Europe, but also put a blanket of white ice on Italian soil. As the monotonous landscape passed by the window, I willed the train to go faster, as Sherlock's chances sank with every passing hour. Still, some part of me expected to find my brother in said quaint cafe, where he would sip a local spirit and greet us with a sheepish grin as soon as we'd arrived -- and for once I wouldn't even hold it against him.

For a while, at least.

We arrived in Milan in the early morning hours, tired and beaten, after an uneasy sleep in a rattling carriage. While I was ready to soldier on, Watson looked like he had reached the limit of his stamina, and our search hadn't even begun yet. The relaxed years in London, away from military training, had taken its toll on the good doctor. Still, one would think he'd be in better shape from running after my brother all the time.

A hotel to stay at was quickly found, as January was anything but a prime time to take a holiday in northern Italy. The atmosphere in Milan was muted, in that peculiar way only a harsh winter can achieve. We opted to take a room in a respectable establishment run by a bumbling, elderly Italian man, who despite his age reminded me of a nervous sparrow. The hotel was situated right next to the Milan Duomo -- an impressive cathedral built of white stone and decorated lavishly with countless ornaments -- in the middle of the town. Watson briefly protested the money waste, but I would hear none of it. After several nights on the train, my body felt stiff and hurt in places it had no right to. I have never seen any use in denying yourself the luxury you clearly deserve.

But there was no talk of sleep after we deposited our luggage in the cozy room. We had finally reached our destination and I longed to devote all of my time and energy to the search for my brother in this unfamiliar city. To my surprise Watson chose to forgo a rest and joined me in the investigation of the most obvious clue: The stamp of the post office, where the letter had been sent off two weeks ago.

Several inches of powdery white snow covered all surfaces in the city. While it was indeed eerily quiet and almost deserted, I just couldn't put my finger on why it felt so off. The early rays of the winter sun barely filtered through the clouds and most of the city was still shrouded in a dim twilight. A harsh wind pushed small snowflakes onto my skin and I felt every impact like the prick of a needle.

Watson had covered most of his face with a thick scarf, his shoulders drawn up and a permanent frown affixed to his forehead. He struggled to keep up with my walking pace, falling behind a number of times. I was eager to reach our destination, because of the wind, which assaulted my face mercilessly and transformed my skin into a layer of ice.

"We are here," I announced and stopped Watson by holding my cane into his path like a barrier. "After you, doctor."

The post office was on the ground floor of a tall building. It was recognisable as such only by a small sign next to the door. We entered quickly, as it was a relief to get out of the unwelcoming weather, but then the sudden warmth of the room enveloped me and almost took my breath away. The snow started to melt and water dripped down my face in a rather uncomfortable fashion. I took off my hat and with a practiced gesture I smoothed down my hair to get rid of any drops that remained.

There was only one man in the room, on a chair behind a worn, wooden counter opposite to the door. He wore an oversized cardigan made of brown wool and a flat, grey cap on his head of short, dark hair. His features were plain, but he had an attentive look about him, which gave me hope to receive at least some helpful answers. The space looked bland and unimaginatively furnished with worn out appliances in front of a dated, yellowish wallpaper -- there really wasn't anything of note to it. The air smelled predominantly of dust and old paper.

"*Good morning*," the man straightened as I addressed him in Italian. "*I wonder if I may ask you a question.*"

"*Depends on the question*," he answered with a smile.

I mimicked his expression and pulled the envelope, which contained the fateful letter from my coat pocket, then placed it on the worn counter next to a small bell. *"Do you remember this letter? It was sent to a good friend of ours who has recently passed away due to illness. We need to find the person who sent it, so we can take care of our friend's affairs in Milan."*

The post officer pointed to the address on the envelope.

"I wrote this. 'John Watson, London'. So it actually arrived? That's a small miracle. This John was a friend of yours?"

I nodded with a sad expression on my face and pointedly ignored the confused look of Watson upon hearing his own name uttered by the stranger.

"Who then brought this envelope here, if he couldn't write the name himself?" I asked the man, who now eyed the pair of us with unabashed curiosity.

"It was a child. I think it might have been one of the homeless children, who normally loiter on the cathedral square... because he couldn't even write. He had money to pay for the postage, though, which was even more curious," the post officer recounted.

"I take it you asked him where he got the letter from?"

"Naturally. But he refused to answer any questions, just said the name to write on the envelope, paid for it to be delivered and ran off. There wasn't much I could do but post the letter so it might reach its intended destination."

"Did the child have any distinguishing features?"

The man shrugged. "*A small boy, not taller than the counter. He wore baggy clothes and a thick, long scarf. His speaking skills were very poor, but then again, do any of those kids talk properly?*"

"*I see...*"

"*Sorry I couldn't be of more assistance,*" the post officer said, and much to his credit sounded sincere in his apology.

I smiled at the man and shook my head. "*On the contrary. Thank you very much.*"

As we said our goodbyes, I left some coins on the counter and then we were out on the street again. The wind hit me with considerable force. During the brief time inside the building I had almost forgotten about the awful weather, but it was an instant reminder of the uneasiness I had carried since Dover. Dragging my coat closer around my shoulders, I also rearranged the thick scarf and donned my hat again. When Watson looked at me expectantly, I remembered that he wasn't familiar with the Italian language.

"A homeless child," he mused after I recounted the conversation. "That does sound familiar."

"Sherlock associates with the type frequently. It wouldn't surprise me if he has employed the same approach here. The man mentioned the cathedral square, so I suggest we start our search there."

"I suppose ..."

Watson wasn't able to finish the sentence as an exceedingly forceful gale made him tumble and fight to regain his balance. I grabbed his arm to steady him, but the wind died down just as quickly.

"What was that?" he shouted and let his eyes dart around the narrow street nervously. There was no one to be seen -- and why should there have been?

"I don't like this," the doctor mumbled.

I could only agree, thinking back to the freak blizzard in Dover. Suddenly, being outside seemed that much more dangerous. Quickly, I walked ahead and left the doctor no choice but to follow me. It was the most effective way to handle him, as he seemed terrified of being left on his own. He scrambled to keep up my brisk pace and stuck to my side as though our coats had been sewn together. Deep down, I felt just as uneasy, but there was no sense in letting it show. Nothing could be accomplished if not even one of us kept a cool head.

Unconsciously I flexed my right hand inside the coat's pocket, making the leather of my gloves squeak, but I detected nothing out of the ordinary. I hated how I had come to rely on this very... unscientific method of detection.

We walked in silence towards the cathedral. The space around us was covered in white, powdery snow, disturbed only by a few long lines of footprints, which were slowly being filled up by fresh snowflakes. The low buildings around us looked ordinary, simple, boring, with their closed windows and plain colours. The occasional leafless tree made the city seem even more bleak.

"Maybe Sherlock is already back on his way to London and we missed him entirely. Would that not be *amusing*?"

"That does sound like something he would do," the good doctor sighed. "But, still, I'd like to confirm that fact with him in person."

I hummed in agreement. We had almost reached the cathedral square, and I already had an idea of where to look for the homeless children. But I wasn't all that confident in taking Watson along for the more gritty parts of the investigation.

"It *is* curious that he would leave the country for what seems to be a rather simple mystery," the doctor mused then. "There must have been something else to that letter, something which had sparked his interest so. He was still contemplating and recording the affairs of the Bruce-Partington plans, after all. It is peculiar that he should abandon an effort like that."

"It is most curious," I agreed. The case had been of particular interest to both of us, and for once we had worked closely to resolve it.

We turned around a corner, and I could already see the cathedral square at the end of the street, as a now familiar feeling took hold of my right hand. I stopped immediately and scanned the street for any odd appearances. Watson only took one look at how tensely I held my arm close to my body, hand clutched tightly into a fist, before he turned around and pressed his back to mine to cover the part of the street I couldn't see. I recognised with satisfaction that there were some fighting instincts left in him after all. Some of that military training remained deeply ingrained.

"There's no one here except us," he said, voice already coloured with anxiety.

"There has to be," I pushed out between clenched teeth. "My …"

What I had wanted to say was interrupted by the surprisingly high-pitched bursting noise of a ceramic roof tile, which hit the floor just a few feet in front of me. There was another, even closer, then one more on Watson's side. I didn't waste a moment to look up, just grabbed the doctor's arm and ran. Then the sky itself seemed to come down upon us. I could feel the wind, tearing at my clothes and making all the windows in the street rattle so noisily, some part of my mind wondered how they didn't break. The doctor stumbled along behind me, barely keeping upright, both hands above his head for protection.

The roof tiles rained on us from all sides in the narrow street, the cacophony of their shattering noises not lessened by the ice on the ground. Not just one building was affected, because no matter how far we ran, always more heavy tiles came crashing down.

It was only a question of time until one of them hit us. We could have taken shelter in one of the doorways, but I dreaded staying within the cursed street. I needed to get away from all of this, to get far enough for my limb to stop hurting, which only made me feel like being under a curse myself.

I remember the colour of one roof tile in particular. It was of a red-brownish hue, which had been exposed to the sun for at least ten years. There was moss growing on its surface, coarse and almost as brown as the tile, and a slight bit of mold, staining the underside of the tile an ugly black colour. It fell almost gracefully, turned about in the air, and crashed right in front of my left foot. I stumbled, the speed of my run too much for my body to handle, and flew towards the ground.

But I wouldn't let that be it. With both arms outstretched, I used the momentum that had built up and touched the pavement with my hands first, cushioning the blow. My right hand still hurt and almost slipped on the icy ground, but performed its job. I executed a roll, pushed myself off the earth, immediately jumped up to a standing position and resumed my run as if nothing had happened. I heard Watson gasp behind me, but that only served as confirmation that he was indeed still with me. It was a wonder that we exited the street without major injuries, but I didn't stop my run just then. The wind was still strong and we were exposed on the plaza.

"Quick, into the cathedral," I shouted to the doctor, who picked up speed as I mentioned the building and fell in step next to me.

The wind was still at our back as we reached the doorstep, in pursuit like a vengeful ghost. Luckily the front door of the cathedral was unlocked, and even though it was heavy, I could open it easily and we slipped into the large building without trouble. Silence enveloped us as we closed the opening behind us, in a stark contrast to the chaos we had left behind outside. It was that special, reverent silence found only in churches, the one that never failed to make you feel thoughtful and just a bit awestruck. But for now, I was just glad to get out of the cursed weather. I stopped briefly in my steps, made the sign of the cross and took in the view.

An opulently decorated interior welcomed us with rows upon rows of neatly arranged pews, made of dark wood. An intricately tiled floor was scrubbed to within an inch of its life and reflected the columns, which held up the high ceiling. The paintings, hung from chains between the columns depicted various pious scenes from the Bible and especially caught my eye. A sweet smell lingered in the space, a mixture of incense and flowers, barely noticeable. In the distance, behind the altar, I could see someone moving. I took off my hat and walked by the pews to the front of the church, Watson at my side. We pretended to be interested in one of the paintings and stopped to examine it more closely.

"What was *that*?" Watson whispered under his breath, as every loud sound echoed in the space.

"An attempt on our life. Again."

"How could they know we would be in that street to set a trap so effectively?"

"It didn't seem all that planned. More like taking advantage of an opportunity."

"Just like on our journey to Switzerland," Watson shook his head. "The wind… it's an unholy thing."

I didn't answer. Everything could have a rational explanation. Everything except the pain in my hand. I was still ready to believe it all was just coincidences and actual bad weather, but the unwavering ache in my fingers every time *something* happened was always there, mocking me and my beliefs.

"*Sorry to interrupt you, gentlemen. I bid you welcome to our cathedral,*" a soothing voice said next to me in Italian. "*And to Milan.*"

I turned to see the person, who had been behind the altar, stand next to me. He had walked over so silently, I hadn't even heard his footsteps, which was a feat in its own right. To my surprise, the man wasn't clad in any religious vestments I would recognize as connected to the church, but simply in some cloth trousers, a waistcoat over a grey shirt and polished leather shoes, all covering a slender body. The lack of any warmer clothing led me to believe he had some business in the building and was clearly a local. The man showed us a brilliant smile and I just had to observe him closer. Black hair, shoulder length, bound in a ponytail at the back of his head, a small pair of glasses balancing on his nose. He stood closer than a stranger would under normal circumstances and eyed me with the same curiosity I exuded. I admit it was flattering to be the object of such open fascination, but I took a step back, cautious of Watson's reaction.

Internally, though, I raised an eyebrow at the man's keen observation, as I couldn't be sure of his allegiance just yet.

"*Thank you. It's kind of you to welcome us. We've indeed only arrived today,*" I answered amicably. Watson simply nodded his greeting.

"*I haven't seen your face around here before, and there is no way I would ever forget one as handsome as yours. What brings you to our city, if I may ask?*" The man made his advances without batting an eye.

Oh, how I would have loved to respond with an equally charming expression... but even though the doctor wouldn't understand a word, I didn't dare. Instead I closed my eyes for a few seconds, as if trying to compose myself. "*A good friend of mine has recently passed away and left a will, naming a resident of your city as one of his heirs. Now we volunteered to search the man out, but learned that he was thrown out of his apartment and no one has any address on record...*"

As I mentioned my fictitious friend's death, the man crossed himself in acknowledgement and offered his sincere condolences. He placed a hand on top of mine and lingered just a little while longer than entirely proper. I didn't respond, but hadn't drawn back either, which earned a little smile. You could almost think that *I* was the one being roped in for information gathering purposes -- not the other way around.

"*If you are searching for a person without home, I can give you directions you to a shelter, which is supported by the churches in Milan. The man you are searching for might be there, or someone who knows him, maybe.*"

"*I would be most grateful for your assistance in the matter.*"

61

"Excuse me, but I haven't introduced myself yet. The name is Gregorio Taquini," he extended his hand, which I took in mine without hesitation. *"A pleasure to make your acquaintance."*

"Ian Ashdown," I answered without skipping a beat. *"Likewise. And this is my friend Richard Brewer. He doesn't speak Italian; unfortunately, so I'd ask you to excuse his silence."*

"That's perfectly alright," the church worker replied. *"Now, if you want to reach the shelter ..."*

The heavy front doors flew open with a bang, then crashed against the stone walls. A bitterly cold wind rushed into the cathedral with a force that hit me like a wall. The stained-glass windows rattled as they were subjected to such violent air movements from both sides. The suspended paintings now moved about, making their chains creak and twist as wooden frames knocked against stone pillars. Small ornaments and decorative items were blown off various surfaces, crashing to the floor with loud metallic noises. Instinctively I grabbed a hold of both men next to me and threw us all towards the ground, so we could hide behind a solid wooden pew.

Then one supporting chain of the painting above our heads ripped apart with a loud, metallic clang and the frame fell downwards, dangling on just a single piece of metal connected to the ceiling. After a moment of shock, only a slight shower of dust fell down on our heads, as the painting swayed above us and crashed into the pew behind us before coming to a halt at one of the pillars. The spectacle ended as soon as it had begun. The wind waned and reverent silence returned to the holy halls.

The first thing I was aware of after the peace in the building returned, was the motionless body of Watson just to my right. He was still breathing, but unfortunately unconscious. The work of art above our head was still moving precariously, so I grabbed the doctor's body under his shoulders and with Taquini's help, I pulled him out of the row between the pews. We carefully laid him down on the cold floor of the central aisle. The door was still open, but the weather seemed to behave normally again. Still, the incident had done its best to rob me of my temporary feeling of safety in the cathedral.

"*He must've hit his head while falling,*" Taquini said. "*There's a bit of blood on the back.*"

I groaned in frustration and moved a hand through my hair to smooth both it and my emotions over. Then I pressed my fingers to Watson's pulse point on his neck. It was steady and at a reasonable speed.

"*Are you alright?*" I asked the church worker.

"*Yes, I only hit my elbow, nothing to worry about. Thank you for your quick reaction.*"

"*You're welcome.*"

There was a beat of silence between us.

"*I've never seen anything like that before,*" Taquini said and slumped back to sit on the floor next to the doctor. "*The winters in Milan are normally not so... violent.*"

I eyed him cautiously. In my usual work, I tried to never leave a deep impression. Too much depended on me performing my deeds in the shadows. Now this man would certainly remember us, for better or worse. While this wasn't a particular setback right now, it still felt wrong to me. Better to leave quickly. I shook Watson's shoulder to make him wake up, but he wouldn't stir.

"Something hit your cheek."

Only then did I realise a slight stinging pain on my skin and brought my fingers up to feel a bit of blood running down from what felt like a short cut. It wasn't in any way consequential.

"Ah, allow me," the Italian man said then and pulled a white handkerchief from his pocket, then leaned over and carefully removed the drops from my skin, staining the cloth a deep red in the process. *"Can't have that handsome face all bloodied up..."*

I was momentarily frozen in the light of the man's radiant smile, but then Watson stirred from his forced sleep, gasped loudly and grabbed at the air in shock.

"Welcome back."

"Thank... you..." the doctor said slowly, blinked into the light and looked around. As we locked eyes, I briefly shook my head and indicated him to stay silent about the obvious matter. He nodded ever so slightly to acknowledge my request. "What happened?"

"A gale knocked a few things over," I simply said. "Can you stand?"

"My head hurts terribly."

"It seems like you've injured it during the fall. My apologies."

"You acted in good faith," the doctor replied readily under a groan.

I nodded and turned to our new friend. *"Mr. Taquini, I'd like to return my friend to our hotel room and have a look at his wound."*

"Of course," the man agreed. *"Can I assist you in any way?"*

"That won't be necessary. I believe the incident has already created enough work for you."

I surveyed the damage. Not many items were broken, but the whole church was in a bad state of disarray. Add to that three paintings, which had come partially undone from the ceiling. So had the one above our heads been a coincidence? Or was it only made to look like one?

As Watson gave the okay for me to move him, both of us helped him keep his balance until he had reached a standing position, which was still a bit wobbly, but held up. Taquini smiled at me as soon as we were ready for the departure.

"A shame, really. I would've loved to show you the way to the shelter, but it seems like we both have other plans now."

"Unfortunately, yes," I sighed. *"But I should be able to find it on my own"*

"If you don't, I'll be here for the better part of the day."

"I'll make sure to remember that."

There was something about that man I found intriguing -- and whatever that was, it was gracefully helped along by his obvious advances. Still, we politely said our goodbyes without any further comments. This was not the time.

I slung Watson's arm over my shoulder to keep him straight and carry some of his weight. Slowly, we slumped out of the church

65

and closed the entrance doors behind us, which had still been wide open. By then Watson had already found a much more stable footing and detached himself from me.

"So, where are we going now?"

"*We* are going nowhere. You are hurt and will go back to the hotel right now. I will continue without you today."

"But I need to help you. Sherlock would ..."

"What my brother does or doesn't do is none of my concern, doctor."

Watson bristled visibly and -- consciously or not -- took a broader stance. "I am *very much* capable, Mycroft," he huffed, but squinted his eyes in pain. "In fact, I'll be out there right when my brain stops knocking on the inside of my skull."

"Which is precisely why I will undertake this investigation alone. You'll be of no help to me and would only put yourself in further needless danger. What if you have suffered a concussion? Surely as a member of the medical profession, you'd advise anyone in your condition to stay put."

I saw him take a deep breath to hurl yet another argument at me, but something in his eyes had already changed. Especially after I appealed to the rational doctor in him.

"Then what would you have me do?"

"Return to the hotel and rest. If my investigation turns out to be fruitless, we will need to draw up a replacement plan and I need you in better condition for that."

"I don't suppose I could ..."

"No. There is no reason to put us both in harm's way. Still, any information that could connect to the man who attacked us in Dover is just as vital as the interrogation of the child. You remember the look of his clothes and especially the dagger?"

"I couldn't forget them if I tried."

"If you insist on a task, this is your mission, then, and there will be no more discussion. But first you need to return to the hotel and rest that head of yours. Remind me again: Who of us is the doctor?"

Watson huffed again and shook his head, which only elicited a groan of pain and thereby proved my point nicely.

"I guess you're right. But be careful," he said warily. "The things that are happening don't seem… right."

"Not right?"

"Don't play dumb, you *know* what I'm on about! The man in Dover, the storm, the roof tiles… and now this! Something is happening that's beyond our understanding and I don't like it."

I frowned on his words.

"Dr. Watson, you are once again seeing ghosts where there are *none*. Yes, we've been attacked in Dover, which was surprising as well as unusual, but it's nothing that hasn't happened before. Someone simply knew where we would be, which means they were well informed, and as much as that irks me, it isn't reason enough to suspect anything else."

"But the storm! The fire!"

"There simply *are* blizzards in winter, and nature does have a way of behaving unpredictably at the best of times. As for the light we have witnessed: I admit, it seemed a little dramatic, but there are a number of chemicals I could mix without problem, which would produce the same reaction."

Watson seemed as exasperated by my rebuttals, as I was by the fact that he had the audacity to even assume such a... *thing* would be possible. That was exactly what our enemies wanted us to think. To fall into an irrational fear, unable to act. I wouldn't give them the satisfaction.

"And your hand? Mycroft, you have to admit this isn't natural!"

"What about my hand?"

"I've seen you clutch it every time *something* has happened, always contorting your face in pain."

"We have more important work to pursue and no time to think about impossible things," I hissed, acutely aware of my defensive tone. "If we delay our initiative now, we might as well give up on my brother altogether. I will join you at the hotel as soon as I can... and I trust you do your part."

I wasn't proud about how I fled the scene and left Watson behind, but he had his instructions and would perform them. In the end it didn't matter what he thought about me. If there was something I had always hated, it was to justify my actions in front of... well, anyone. Results were what counted, and I got results. Mostly good ones, too, so no one was in the right to complain.

The map of the city in my head provided me with the shortest route to the place the church worker had described, and my feet found the way automatically. The snowfall had waned completely and the wind died down to a gentle breeze. While the sky was overcast, it was still the best weather I had encountered throughout all of our journey. I knew how quickly it could change, though.

There was the matter of the strange sensations in my hand. While I wasn't ready to admit it out loud, there was no way to deny that something *had* happened back in Baker Street and that it was connected to the abduction of my brother. I couldn't ignore it, but to let it dictate my actions was simply a preposterous thought. Still, I flexed my right hand absentmindedly as I walked, repeatedly checking it for any signs of discomfort, but no matter how many times I examined it, there was absolutely nothing wrong. Just as the sand in the ledger had turned out to be just ground down rocks, my skin was unblemished and healthy. A circumstance which irked me terribly.

The streets were empty and I progressed quickly, walking ever faster to put distance between me and Watson with his... irritating questions. Within minutes I was at the building, which was supposedly housing the homeless. It appeared derelict and abandoned from the outside, but looks can be deceiving. It was only sensible to nail shut any windows and fill the cracks to keep the cold -- and any unwanted guests -- outside during the winter. I knew that I wouldn't be welcomed with open arms, but then, was I ever? It had always been my brother's style to mingle with the less fortunate, never mine. But needs must…

At least the front door was recognisable as such. Predictably unlocked, it opened with a minimum of screeching noise and so I slipped into the darkness of the corridor stretching out behind it. The inside was dry, as clean as it could be and surprisingly warm, considering the state of the building, but the air smelled stale and used. No one was present to welcome me, so I had no choice but to venture further on my own. A short walk through a corridor, past closed doors to either side, brought me into a sort of communal area furnished with some tables and a lot of aggregated chairs, all of different makes and in various states of disrepair. Five men were sitting around a table in the far corner, heatedly arguing in the fast and aggressive way only the Italian language can manage. No other people were present, and most importantly: No children.

One of the men became aware of my presence and pointed it out for his colleagues. I was now scrutinised by five gazes across the room, but the dim light and a copious amount of clothing on my person hid important details quite well from their inquisitive eyes. Luckily for me, I didn't suffer the same problem and sized them up while walking through the space without missing a beat. As I dodged the countless chairs, I had ample time to observe the group.

The man closest to me, with dirty blonde hair and a garishly patterned scarf around his neck, which stood in stark contrast to his overwhelmingly dark brown clothing, was obviously the one with the highest standing. I didn't know what role he occupied within their world, but the others glanced at him repeatedly with questioning looks, while he used all of his time to observe just me. He was the only one not shrinking back into his chair as I stopped at a respectful distance and lifted my hat briefly as a greeting.

"*Good evening*," I opened the conversation in what I knew to be a companionable Italian accent. "*I hope I'm not interrupting.*"

"*You're not here to stay the night*," the blonde man stated, and I groaned inwardly. *Of course* it had to be an individual with at least some intelligence. The dumb ones were much easier to manipulate.

"*You are correct. I am merely searching for someone*," I said and smiled briefly when I saw the instinctive reaction of a man, who has had too many brushes with inquisitive police forces already. It was mirrored in three of the other men around the table. "*In a private matter, I might add.*"

A healthy amount of distrust visibly spread across the table. Of course any outsider who just barged in and asked questions would be seen as suspicious. And I was a foreigner on top of it all. But this wasn't the first time I had ever encountered such odds and it wouldn't be the last.

I made sure to keep an open stance and my manners polite enough, as well as my choice of words collegial. No person, no matter his circumstance, appreciates being talked down to or treated in any way less than his conversation partner. It didn't matter that I excelled in these matters and could make a person feel smaller than a fly under my feet -- the current situation called for a more... gentle approach.

71

"I've been sent this way by Mr. Taquini. He was so kind to help me with my search. Could I ask you to extend the same kindness to me?"

The mention of a familiar name took some antagonistic air out the atmosphere. I had assumed that the man was well liked among the people he chose to help and was proven right.

"Alright, then tell us who you're looking for and we'll see if we can help you," the blonde man flashed a smile, showing a surprisingly low number of crooked teeth. *"But if we don't know the person, of course, there's nothing we can do."*

The other men nodded their agreement in unison as if it had been choreographed by an invisible theatre director. Frankly, it was an amusing sight, but that would've been the wrong emotion to show.

"I'm looking for a boy about this height," I indicated it with my left hand, always leaving my right free to act in this unfamiliar environment. *"He helped a friend of mine and I would like to find and thank him for it."*

Unfortunately, the gentlemen in front of me didn't seem to look kindly on strangers, who were interested in children.

"There is no boy of that description here," one of the men with a long, greying beard and unruly black hair said with an aggressive and challenging edge to his voice. *"In fact, there are no children here at all."*

Even Watson would've been able to detect the man's lie. So there *were* children in the building, and by the sound of it at least one boy, who fit the description. But it didn't seem like this was the way I could get to them. It was neither the wisest nor the quickest way to seek a confrontation with the men. Also I wouldn't make myself beg for entrance. No, there had to be a more subtle approach.

"Ah, excuse me, then. Thank you for the information and have a good night."

I nodded, showed them a perfunctory smile and lifted my hat again, then turned around and made my way to the exit in a pace that was neither too leisurely nor too fast. Despite that, I was only allowed to cross half the room before the men had caught up with me and the dirty blonde placed himself right into my path.

I had really wanted to avoid this.

"Now, before we let you leave, why don't you tell us why you're really looking for that boy?"

"I believe I already told you," I answered, still smiling.

"And it has nothing to do with this letter to London, John Watson?"

I whirled around. One of the man had the audacity to pick my pockets while I was distracted. Damnation! He held in his hand the fateful envelope and waved it back and forth. They believed me to be Watson... Someone must've alerted the homeless that a man of that name might come to look for the letter boy. This whole city turned out to be one big, elaborate trap, after all. First for my brother, then for his rescuers. But these men were unlucky.

The gentleman who stood between them was anything but a harmless doctor.

"I would appreciate if you could let me leave."

"Not a chance. There's a price on your head, Watson," the leader laughed, pronouncing the doctor's name Wotto-sen.

"How much is it?"

"None of your concern."

"I believe it is very much my concern, as it is my head you're all wanting to sell."

The dirty blonde threw the first punch. It had been painfully obvious from the way the muscles in his arm tensed. The slight repositioning of his feet told me everything I wanted to know about the direction his fist would approach me in. I ducked, which eliminated the resistance he had calculated to encounter. The man tumbled forward and I could easily push him sideways and to the ground, as there was no way he could regain his balance mid-air. The leader fell against the legs of one of his lackeys, and they both crashed noisily into a table behind them.

The other three stood dumbfounded, hands raised, ready to join the fight, but caught off guard by my sudden defensive moves. Once again I ducked low and pulled the special pocket watch from under my coat. With the hidden mechanism released I threw it, so the attached wire wrapped neatly around a table leg, then I slipped behind the men and pulled. I stretched the wire so strongly, it ripped through their trousers and cut into the flesh of their legs. All of them cursed at the same time, lost their balance one after the other and crashed neatly into the rest of the assorted furniture.

It was all over within seconds, but that was nothing to gloat about. These men were neither trained to fight, nor was there any way they could've expected me to be this skilled. The element of surprise had been on my side. The man closest to me clutched his leg, which was bleeding profusely. I knew that I couldn't have hit any vital blood vessels, but the cut was fine and must've hurt immensely. From personal experience I knew the sensation, which would've be a constant burning, combined with a sharp sting, every time the two sides of the wound rubbed against each other.

I kicked the man's leg. He screamed.

"Now *may I leave?*" I asked again.

"*I will cut you!*" the leader shouted and pulled himself upwards by grabbing at the tabletop. "*Who do you think you are?*"

I smiled and grabbed the letter from the floor, which had fallen during the scuffle. "*Why, John Watson, of course.*"

"*She said Watson was a harmless doctor!*"

She? Interesting.

I quickly grabbed my cane, which I had thrown on a nearby table before the fight and pushed the tip into the man's chest, exactly in the same spot I had hit earlier to make him fall. He grimaced in pain and motioned the man behind him to stand down. There was no need to signal the three man still on the ground, who had crawled out of my way and left a bloody trail on the floorboards.

"*Now you could've just pointed me to the boy, and we wouldn't have had any trouble at all. I don't like being attacked, so before I really beat that bit of knowledge that into you, tell me who put the price on my head.*"

Once again, the leader proved to be slightly more intelligent than his brethren, as he put up his hands in the universal gesture of surrender. His friends mimicked the motion even more quickly than I thought they would.

"Fine. There was a woman... a little more than a week ago, she came to us and put word out that an Englishman was following her. She gave us a name and told us what you might be looking for. Anyone who could capture you would be handsomely rewarded."

"And where should I be delivered to?"

"I don't know."

"Wrong answer."

The man looked properly intimidated as I pressed my cane even further into his chest, holding it like a rapier in front of me.

"Look, I swear I don't know. She said that she would know if one of us captured you and that we'd just have to wait for her to collect you."

From his panicked state I could conclude that there was only a very small chance he was actually lying. And from the way the attacks on us had be orchestrated so far, it wasn't farfetched to assume that this one had also been planned from the shadows. Like the one in Dover.

"Look, I don't want to hurt you any more if you don't give me a reason. Now, you will describe the woman to me. I don't suppose she gave you a name?"

"Just an initial. M."

My eyes widened a fraction before I could regain my composure.

"She wore thick winter clothes... they were... a dark brown. Her hair was long, very long and black as the night. And her eyes sparkled like emeralds, in a green so vivid I have never seen in my life. Her skin was brown, like she had been in the sun for a long time."

A picture of the woman already formed in my head. It wasn't complete, but the man had given me more than enough clues to recognise the individual on the street.

"Thank you. Was that so hard? You may now direct me to the children that are staying in the building."

"What do you want with them?" the bystander asked.

"I told you: Find the boy who helped out my friend and reward him. I'm not the one between us two, who has been lying. Shame on you for accusing me of anything different."

"There's a bunch of kids around here, who have no parents, and stick to each other. They usually group up on the second floor during the winter," the dirty blonde spoke up again. *"Some of them are of the height you indicated."*

While he talked I retrieved the wire and stashed the used pocket watch in my coat's pocket, so I could rewind later and make use of it again.

"Now, you can all wait for me here, or disappear -- I don't really care. But anyone who thinks about attacking me again will face a worse fate than this..."

I pushed the dirty blonde back in earnest, so that he fell onto the table behind him, and as I passed the men on the floor, I knocked on one of their injured legs with my cane. Hurting these misled people gave me no joy, but it was the most efficient way to remind them who they were dealing with. For all their earlier smugness, they now writhed on the floor, all fight taken out of them. It was clear that they could have overpowered me in a coordinated attack, but the odds of that happening *now* were exceedingly low.

An hour later I emerged from the building into the crisp air, which was once again filled with a gentle snowfall. After a thorough search of all the rooms in this repurposed residential house, I had questioned all children, who could've even remotely fit the description the post office worker had given us. But to no avail. None of them had any clue about the letter.

But through lucky circumstance I didn't emerge empty-handed. From the men -- who had disappeared from the room as I had expected -- I had gained vital knowledge about our adversary. A woman with black hair and green eyes... It wasn't often that I was up against a female enemy, but I knew better than to underestimate her. From my colleagues in the Secret Service I knew that women could perform practically any job at least as well as a man, and often they had a tenacious energy about them that made them even better at it.

Now that I knew about her, it would only be a matter of time before she knew about me knowing. If I counted all incidents as actual attacks, she already knew very well what we had been up to, and had chosen not to show herself just yet. Maybe that would change now...

My thoughts drifted back to my traveling companion. There was no reason to assume that Watson hadn't safely arrived at the hotel. My hope was to find him resting in our shared room, exhausted from the day, but unharmed. Still, I couldn't be sure until I saw him. The all-present chill intensified and I somehow found myself in a hurry, despite my own stamina being exhausted after a sleepless night and a physically strenuous day.

We were the only lodgers in our hotel on that January day. I managed to avoid a talk with the kind owners by looking absolutely, dreadfully tired and quickly walked past them to find our room on the third floor. The door was locked and I took the precaution to knock before I unlocked it, therefore alerting Watson to my presence.

"Greetings, doctor," I uttered as I entered the room, well aware he still had his gun ready. "Only me."

Watson sat in an armchair, which was positioned under the window. From his posture, I could easily see that he had been sleeping prior to my arrival. His movements were sluggish, as the haze from his exhausted sleep only dissipated slowly. I saw him slump back into the seat after the initial shock of being wakened prematurely.

"Any luck?" He asked.

"I searched the homeless shelter run by the church, to which Mr. Taquini had pointed us. But there were only a few children, and none of them seemed to lie when I asked them about the letter," I recounted my findings and took a seat on the edge of the bed.

"That's... Well, there are other places we could search?"

"Certainly. But we need to find them first. And there's another matter. I've learned a little about the person, who might be behind this devious plot."

For all the lethargy Watson had displayed before, his eyes sprung open and he leaned forward in his chair, just about ready to jump.

"Is it someone we know?"

"That remains to be seen. All I've learned is that the mastermind is either a woman or represented by one. One of the men in the shelter described her as tanned, with pitch-black hair and emerald green eyes."

"Now that we know what she looks like, we could observe the shelter from the shadows and see if she shows?"

I admit that I was a bit impressed by the doctor's suggestion. "An admirable idea. I start to see why Sherlock keeps you around."

"Keeps me around? You're not comparing me to a dog, are you, Mycroft?"

"Only to its best qualities."

Watson hesitated before he continued, as if he needed to decide if my statement were an insult or a compliment. "So, we go into hiding?"

"Of course not," I rebutted. "Well, it would be a good idea, but the attacks so far have proven that our enemy already knows of our actions, which makes the endeavour pointless. They just choose not to attack directly. So far."

Watson leaned back again and crossed his legs.

"Do you think we should contact the local police?"

I sighed. "*Doctor.*"

"I was just…"

"We are operating without official orders. Also, as soon as we're in alignment with the law, our options will be severely limited." Watson frowned at the implication but didn't comment further. "No, there is a third route of inquiry we haven't taken yet. Before we venture out aimlessly and search out needless danger, I'd like to pursue it first."

"And that would be…?"

From the coat I was still wearing, I pulled the catalyst of our troubles: The dreadful letter. I held it up between us, and couldn't help but notice the confusion on Watson's face.

"The letter itself holds another message. Something must be hidden in it, I'm sure. There's no way that Sherlock would send randomly chosen words in such an important matter."

"I suppose you're right, but there is nothing to the letter except the short note. Do you think there's something in the envelope we might have missed?"

I shook my head. "Sherlock has never touched the envelope. The clue must be in the note itself."

The hotel room was furnished with a writing desk, on which Watson had piled some maps and other informative papers about

Milan and its important places. Most were leaflets for visitors, no doubt obtained from the hotel owners themselves. I had seen several of them lying on the counter downstairs. Still, they were a good start should we need any details about the city.

For now I placed the envelope on a pile of books and removed the letter from it. I turned it around and examined its surface meticulously, held it against the light and tried to fold it in some ways that would produce a hidden meaning from some disjointed lines. But to no avail. There were only the words *'Find help. I am truly sorry.'* They stared at me from the paper accusingly, challenging me with their very presence. Hurried handwriting, a plea for help. A lifeline thrown in the last second, imbued with hope and regret.

"Wait a second…"

"Did you… did you find something?" Watson asked agitatedly.

I had to laugh despite myself. "Have you ever, in your life, heard my younger brother ask me for help, much less apologise for *anything?*"

Watson decidedly shook his head. Sherlock hadn't even come to us for help after the incident at the Reichenbach Falls. Had the obvious been hiding out in the open all this time?

"The phrasing is odd as well. *'Find help'*. Shouldn't that be *'Send help'* or *'Get help'*?" Now that I had thrown the new idea into the room, Watson drew the right conclusions fast. "Then do you think it must be taken literally?"

I immediately grabbed the binder with a selection of maps of Milan from the table and pushed everything else aside, with a few items falling to the ground for what I recognised as an appropriate dramatic effect.

"It must *definitely* be taken literally, doctor. I've been blind, absolutely blind..." I muttered, for once voicing my thoughts out loud, but the reality of my error hit me too hard. "Sherlock trusted my memory and I let him down..."

"Your memory?" The doctor placed a hand on my shoulder, his words steady, but I could feel the agitation through his grip.

"*'Find help. I am truly sorry.'* I have written these words."

"How could you have written the letter, when ..."

"No, I didn't write the letter, doctor!" I shouted, exasperated. "But I *am* the original author of these words. When Sherlock was still a child, we used to play a game of riddles. Over the time we came up with ever more convoluted hints in the hope of baffling the other."

"So that means..."

"Yes, this is one of the riddles I thought up, after we had learned about the Fourteen Holy Helpers of the Catholic Church from our tutor. My brother was supposed to find hints hidden in books about all the helpers and piece them together."

"Then that means we need to find these... helpers in Milan?"

I nodded and grabbed a map of the city, pushed another one towards Watson. "I suggest we hurry. It's only a matter of time before our enemy knows that we are onto her, and I'm very sure that our stay in this hotel has never been a secret. I'd like to be on the right trail and out of here as fast as possible."

Watson spread his map out on the bed to peruse it in detail. I did the same with another on the desk. My mind readily supplied names and details about the Fourteen Holy Helpers, whereas the doctor had to use an encyclopedia, which had been provided by the hotel owner upon his request. My eyes chased frantically across the map while I recited associated poems in my head to help my memory.

'Saint Margaret with the dragon, Saint Barbara with the tower…'

It could've been a street name, or the name of a building. Maybe an important plaza. Sherlock would have trusted me, and only me, to see the hidden meaning in his words and follow the connection, like in our childhood. Therefore I knew that once I'd seen the solution, it would be the only one possible and so glaringly obvious, I'd hate myself for not seeing it sooner.

'St. George, valiant Martyr of Christ, St. Blaise, zealous bishop and benefactor of the poor, St. Erasmus…'

There was nothing on the first map. I had searched it three times, but no feature sprung out at me. I grabbed a stack of leaflets about the features of the city, as no option was to be excluded at this stage. No, these were especially important, as the answer would be unmissable, out in the open.

'When at night I go to sleep, fourteen angels watch do keep…'

There was information about Sforza Castle; the shopping street, Galleria Vittorio Emanuele; the Navigli canals…

"I've found it!" I exclaimed loudly, triumphantly and stepped to the bed, threw a leaflet about the cathedral on top of the map Watson was still searching. "Look at this!"

"This is the cathedral…"

"Yes, but look at the picture at the bottom. It shows an arrangement of statues on the roof, and in the middle is the figure of St. Vitus -- one of the Fourteen Holy Helpers!"

Watson squinted, and in my elation I had to grin at his effort. "I can't even make out the details. Are you sure?"

"More than sure. We need to leave right away."

"But how can a statue be a clue?"

"I don't know yet, but we will find out."

We threw our winter clothing on in a great haste, and all but ran out of the hotel, once again into the freezing air. Thick clouds had darkened the sky, and the wind had picked up just barely, but after everything we had been through I still registered the change with worry. The cathedral loomed in the distance -- an immovable grey and white monument, which we had circled several times already, but had held the solution all along.

CHAPTER 5

You've already lost

There were *a lot* of statues adorning the cathedral. On close inspection, every part of the building was covered in them -- the entrances, the columns, the ledges. Luckily for us, Saint Vitus was one of the better accessible stone carvings, placed right on top of the roof of the large building. The cathedral of Milan is unique, as it allows curious visitors to climb a large number of stairs to reach and wander about its marble covered rooftop.

We made our way up a winding stone staircase in one of the towers in the back of the building. Then a short trip along the side, between decorative columns and carvings, until some narrow stairs helped us reach the very top. All the stonework was covered with a thick layer of barely disturbed snow. I had to carefully place my feet and searched for a proper foothold with every step on the way to the top.

But fate seemed to throw obstacles in our path wherever it possibly could, because as soon as we reached the pillar on which Saint Vitus was supposed to sit, we found it completely empty. I searched the area for a hidden message or any other clue, just in case. With Watson's help I dug through the snow at the base of the pillar, my fingers soon frozen despite the protection afforded by my leather gloves. But we came up with *absolutely nothing.* Confronted with yet another setback, I felt a sudden and powerful rage fuel me. I kicked the deserted stone base with a force, which almost broke my toes.

I cursed myself for the outburst and the statue for being absent, and winced in pain when I heard someone yell loudly on the other side of the roof, running towards us. You didn't need to understand Italian to get the gist of the person's unmistakably angry tirade of colourful expressions directed at me. The man was small, and wiry, dressed in thick work clothes and talked rather agitatedly.

"What do you think you're doing, treating this building so disrespectfully?"

"I'm very sorry," I answered quietly and looked down to the floor.

"We don't keep this place in order for you to vandalize it! Where are your manners, idiot?"

The man certainly didn't pull his punches.

"I... I..." Without warning, I let my shoulders sink and released a loud sobbing noise. I brought my hand up to my face and squeezed the area around my eyes just so, as tears already ran down my cheeks.

Watson stepped up to me and placed a hand on my shoulder. "Are you alright? You kicked that stone pretty hard..."

That was my cue. I turned around, fell into the doctor's arms and cried even harder. Watson seemed genuinely surprised, which worked entirely in my favour, and patted my back in a calming gesture. The worker beside us cleared his throat noisily. His face was a mixture of confusion and commiseration.

"I am sorry for my harsh words, but you must understand..."

"I do, and I am sorry, but my recently departed father..." I crossed myself and looked to the heavens for a moment. "...had always wanted to visit the Duomo and pay his respects to Saint Vitus, who had given him strength throughout his long illness. But he couldn't make the trip before he died."

"And I am so sorry for your loss. If you want to see the statue and pay your respects, you might be able to visit it in the workshop, where it is currently being restored." In just one moment, the man had changed his attitude completely from being angry to supportive. He pointed at a house, barely visible from our vantage point. "It's in the big building directly behind the cathedral."

"You are most kind," I answered with a smile and rubbed the tears from my eyes.

The worker just shook his head and apologised again. We shook hands awkwardly while he looked at me with commiseration and then patted Watson on the shoulder in an empathetic gesture before he left us. As he turned his back, I immediately grabbed the doctor's sleeve and dragged him into the direction of the stairs, which led down from the roof of the cathedral.

As soon as we were out of view, I wiped the last tears from my face with the help of my handkerchief. Seconds later, a pair of slightly red eyes were the only thing betraying the fact that I had actually cried earlier.

"So, what was that about?" Watson asked with curiosity in his voice. "You didn't actually hurt your foot, did you?"

"A simple means of getting information. Most people are uncomfortable when faced with a grown man in tears. They will do anything to get out of the embarrassing situation as quickly as possible," I shrugged, then recounted the contents of our conversation briefly for the doctor.

"You know, I actually believed you back there. Of course I thought you hurt your foot, but the pain was expertly played," Watson laughed. "Just like your brother."

"Quiet, doctor!" I replied in hushed, but urgent tones, and stifled his laugh as I placed my hand over his mouth. "What if the worker is observing us? It would be a rather poor behaviour to laugh while your friend is in grief."

"My apologies..."

"Has my brother taught you nothing?"

"I do tend to get caught up in the moment and let my emotions get the better of me..." Watson's voice had the nostalgic quality of a person talking about a summer long gone by. "But Holmes always says it's one of my better qualities."

"As long as it doesn't interfere with the investigation..." I grumbled and wondered, not for the first, time if Sherlock had grown too soft in recent years.

The cathedral's workshop was just behind the building itself -- the only place still busy while the rest of the city was suspended in hibernation. We approached the entrance with purpose in our stride to get as far as possible into the place before anyone would notice. It's not a secret that it's rather easy to blend into a place if you just pretend like you have every right to be there. People are prone to ignore everything that does not directly concern them. If someone *would* notice us, we could still play the part of a pair of stupid, lost British visitors.

A long, low hallway lead into a large inner courtyard. Despite the cold season, many workers were out in the crisp air, working on various stone elements, which were being prepared to replace broken parts of the cathedral. Several statues were positioned underneath large tents, sheltered from the weather, where they were being cleaned and repaired. Inside the courtyard, it was easy for us to go unnoticed, as everyone was wearing heavy coats, scarves and hats to protect them from the cold, just as we did.

We split up and slowly, as inconspicuously as possible, tiptoed around the place to find the statue we were looking for. Fortunately, the workers didn't pay me any mind, as they were focused on getting their work done as quickly as possible, which enabled me to move between the different tents and look behind the barriers that had been erected to keep the weather out.

While I inspected at the statue of an angel figure, I realised something odd. There was a small girl next to a stonemason, who was meticulously cleaning the surface of a statue. She handed him the required tools, one after the other. Now, as I focused on them, I could see children all around, huddled next to the fires for warmth, or mostly with the workers, engaged in the restoration process.

I pinpointed Watson's location quickly, as I had never left him out of my sight completely, and made my way across the workshop to reach him.

"You have seen them?" I whispered as I had reached his side.

"Yes. Do you think we will find the right boy when we *'Find help.'*?"

"I believe so. We have to," determination overlaid the desperation in my voice. "Saint Vitus is often portrayed as a young man, usually clad in only a sheet of cloth. And I believe I have found him just on the other side of the courtyard, in that brown tent."

The distance was quickly crossed. And then, there he was: The statue of Saint Vitus. We had *'found help'* at last! And at his feet, wrapped up in a thick blanket, was a boy, who couldn't have been older than fifteen. There was no worker around, and he seemed to be sleeping in the middle of the workshop.

"Watch the area," I ordered Watson in hushed tones, then kneeled down next to the boy. I woke him gently, but his first instinct was to run. Of course I had anticipated this. Even if it wasn't the gentlemanly thing to do, I had already placed one hand on his shoulder and another one across his mouth and pushed him down as quickly as he wanted to get up.

"*Sherlock Holmes*," I said quietly and shushed the boy again. As he stopped his struggle, I produced the letter from my coat pocket and held it up, so the boy could see it.

"*I didn't think you'd ever show*," the boy said then, in a broken Italian that was most appalling. "*I've been waiting here, every*

91

day, for weeks. I would've stopped, if that nice man hadn't paid me to do so."

"*That nice man?*" I asked and wondered if he meant Sherlock.

"*Yeah.*"

"*And where is the nice man?*"

The boy shrugged. "*I was told to wait. But I don't know where he is now.*"

"*It's a start. Then tell me what you know,*" I said, as amicably as possible.

"*No.*"

"*What?*"

"*You heard me. Unless you get me something to eat, I won't tell you anything.*"

I groaned but folded immediately. If that's what it was to get the boy to talk, so be it.

"You might want to speed this up," Watson said and turned my head into the direction of a large man, approaching us fast. He didn't seem overly angry, but it was clear that he wasn't happy to be seeing outsiders within the courtyard of the workshop.

The boy reacted quickly and jumped up to meet the man. They exchanged a few heated words, then he motioned for us to follow him. Together we left the premises under the scrutiny of the annoyed supervisor -- the boy still wrapped in his assortment of baggy clothes and rough blankets.

As we emerged from the building, our little friend gestured towards a restaurant behind the cathedral with a cheeky grin. It was in this way I found myself watching our newest acquaintance wolf down a frankly enormous dish of pasta and waited for him to finish his food, just to get the information we so desperately needed. While he had seemed genuinely surprised upon meeting us, it had only taken him a few minutes to realise he could profit from us in exchange for the information we so clearly craved. Street smarts are never to be underestimated.

"*The tall man wanted us to find someone,*" the homeless child recounted while he licked the last remnants of sauce from his fork. "*A woman... how did he say... pitch black hair and striking green eyes.*"

"*A woman?*" I asked, barely able to hide the surprise. "*Did you find her?*"

"*We searched for days, but there was no sign. The man paid us anyway. Then the nice man came to me. The tall man vanished after that. No more money for us,*" the boy sounded sad. If out of concern for Sherlock or for the lost money, I couldn't say, but I suspected it to be the latter. Still... something didn't add up.

"*What did the nice man look like?*" Damn that child for not using any names in his description. Maybe he really didn't know them, but I was still irritated.

"*Normal, I guess. He had an eyepatch, though. He gave me a piece of paper, money and a name. That was the last I saw of him.*"

Eyepatch? What in the world...? I relayed the information to Watson, who had waited with bated breath while the boy talked slowly, at his own leisurely pace.

"A nice man with an eyepatch? I can't think of anyone resembling this description," he said. "Do you think he's the one who …"

"Yes. And now we know why the letter is so short. My brother probably *had* to write it, so it was recognisable as his hand, but that was only intended to lure us here."

"But the riddle… the game you used to play?"

"I don't know. Why would he be allowed to lead us here if the man with the eyepatch could just abduct my brother and escape without any danger of us getting to him?"

The boy looked back and forth between us and waited patiently for more fortune to be bestowed upon him. I took pity on him and handed over a few coins from my pocket, along with the instructions to find us if Sherlock would reappear anywhere in the city.

The boy nodded, then pulled something out of his own pocket and placed it on the table between us. He then snatched the last few pieces of bread from the table and bowed playfully before leaving the restaurant.

"What's that supposed to be?" Watson asked, but the boy made no attempt to stop his leave.

We both stared at a small clay figurine, shaped roughly into the form of a basic human figure with a round head on a cone-shaped body. I picked it up and gingerly turned it around between my fingers, feeling the coarse surface.

"It looks like a play …"

A shot rang out. It pierced the comfortable atmosphere of the brilliant winter day as it echoed through the streets. The doctor jumped up and ran towards the door as if the hounds of hell were at his heels. Curse this man's ingrained desire to help the innocent. In a feat of extraordinary speed, I caught up to Watson and threw myself at him. We tumbled to the ground most ungracefully in a tangle of limbs. It didn't matter because I had achieved my goal: We were still inside the restaurant.

"Are you mad? Stay down!" I hissed and drew Watson under a table, so that we wouldn't be visible from a window. "I should complain to the idiot in charge of your army training, because he left out the chapter about firefights!"

"But the boy!" the fool shouted, the adrenaline from the sudden shock coursing through his veins. I gripped his arms, kept the doctor grounded, as he still looked like he could bolt at any second.

It was clear that other customers and passersby on the street were not as cautious as me, because the noise outside was growing by the second. They couldn't know the implications. Voices grew louder, and from the words I could discern it became clear that the victim had indeed been the boy. But why shoot our informant only *after* he had talked? It made no sense! As soon as the mass of people on the street was large enough to blend into, I gave Watson my blessing to move, but insisted on leaving the door first.

The icy weather seemed to be forgotten, as everyone pushed to get a glimpse of the already cooling body, bleeding out on the pavement. The corpse in front of us was indeed the boy, previously so

95

full of life. Now he lay motionless in the dirty snow of the street. Blood oozed from a large opening in the side of his head that looked very much like the exit wound of a bullet. The bread, which he had grabbed from the table, had fallen from his hands into the puddle of blood, and soaked it up like a sponge.

Watson inspected the body while I directed my attention to our surroundings. None of the onlookers behaved suspiciously, and I didn't expect them to, as the culprit was very likely not among them. The exit wound was on the right side of the boy's head -- a result from an entry on the left. I had only seen a wound like this once before: on a dummy made by my brother. Assuming the boy had wanted to return to the workshop, he would've turned right immediately after leaving the restaurant, which made the only building to have the right vantage point... the cathedral!

I raised my head immediately and scrutinised the top of the building. Night had fallen and it was almost impossible to track anything between the countless columns, decorations and statues. But then I saw it: A brief appearance of light, a glint in the darkness I just knew to be a reflection in a glass lens. There was but one exit from the roof: The very same staircase I had used earlier that day. I wasted no time to explain. My body propelled itself upwards and I pushed my way through the crowd barely a second after I deduced the situation.

There is little that can stop me when I am running with purpose.

The tiled floor underneath my feet flew by and my surroundings faded to a blur. I knew that the entrance to the roof was close. Whoever wanted to leave the cathedral roof would have to go through there, and with the added weight of the rifle, they shouldn't have been able to clear all the steps before I reached the entranceway.

Fueled by adrenaline and armed with desperate determination, I pushed a pair of people out of my way and sprinted up the narrow staircase. My ears strained to make out a sound, and as I was halfway up the tower I heard the unmistakable noise of quick, nervous steps above me. The killer must have heard my approach and turned around. But there was nowhere to go.

The air was burning in my lungs with every breath as I caught up to a tall figure, barely visible around the bend of the tower's central column. With a final effort I doubled my speed and climbed several steps at once, then threw myself at the person, clutched their clothes and restrained their movement by my added weight. The killer released a high-pitched scream as I jumped them, which cut off suddenly, like lifting the needle off a phonograph record, when we hit the floor together.

We struggled for dominance, which was made easier by the fact that I was already on top, when I felt something hit my legs. A figure stumbled and fell over the pair of us. Its speed was sufficient to catapult it out into the open night air and deep into the snow, as we had ended up on the top of the stairs, right at the exit to the roof.

"Release me!" A furious voice screeched from underneath me. "I'll kill you!"

"I will do *nothing* of the sort," I answered coldly, trying to keep my voice as calm as possible and noted with satisfaction that only a hint of the sprint I had just undertaken was noticeable in my tone. "Doctor, so good of you to join us. Please, would you assist me?"

During the short time, I had managed to restrain both hands of the person underneath me at their back and pressed them into the stairs. Their head rested sideways on the top step -- a most uncomfortable position that suited my purpose perfectly. From my viewpoint, I couldn't see their face, only the long, black hair, which had come undone from a bun atop the person's head. Not only from the voice, I could conclude that the culprit was unmistakably a woman.

"My inner left coat pocket, if you would be so kind," I addressed the doctor again, who still drew in heavy breaths, trying to find his equilibrium. He stepped closer and supported himself on the cold cathedral wall, then reached around me to find a pair of iron handcuffs in the aforementioned pocket. A few moments later, I had twisted the killer's hands into the right position and Watson let the metal snap shut around her wrists. Still, as we didn't have any means to restrain her legs, it wasn't wise to release her just yet.

"You will pay for this! I will make you pay, I swear," she hissed, reminding me of a rather angry cat.

The woman lifted her head and glared at me, as much as her position allowed. Her eyes were narrowed and the face was distorted in anger. If she were indeed a cat, her fur would have been standing on edge. She emitted a feral energy, which would make lesser men shrink back in fear, but I didn't move a muscle. It was then I noticed her striking green eyes.

"Her appearance... Is she ..." I shut up Watson with a piercing stare. I put as much non-verbal communication into my gaze as possible, thereby relaying the message that I would like for him to stop talking right now and keep on doing just that indefinitely. His bumbling, careless nature would not help my interrogation at all.

"Can you see the case she dropped? Retrieve it, Doctor," I said calmly. "The murder weapon will be in it and I would very much like to take it with us."

"Leave your filthy hands off it!" the woman hissed.

"It seems like someone wants to do this the hard way," I sighed and pulled my own gun out of a concealed carrying holster around my waist, then pressed it to the back of the shooter's head. "Now, you shot a helpless child in cold blood. While I do need information from you, I do not necessarily need you alive to get the important details. You are clearly very convinced of yourself and the skills you *think* you possess, and have never thought it possible you could be caught by someone as insignificant as the useless, lazy brother of the man you abducted. Let me make this very clear: You make one wrong move and it will most certainly be your last."

The woman had frozen solid underneath me, while I delivered my monologue. I made sure to deliver every detail with enough underlying threat to take the fight out of her before it even began. The words fell readily from my lips as a means to an end. My determination to actually shoot her if she gave me any problems made it even easier.

She had *killed a child*, after all.

"I have the case," Watson said, voice quiet and timid.

"Good," I nodded at him, then turned back to the murderous fiend I had captured. "Now, I will release your legs and you will stand up. Make an attempt to flee and you will quickly notice that it will only last for a two steps at most."

As I removed my weight from the woman, she groaned in pain. Her body had been pressed against the edge of the steps, stone digging painfully into her skin and bones. Without the support of her hands she could barely move, so I dragged her upright with a harsh pull at the handcuffs. After a few awkward twists she stood shakily, battered and disheveled -- still her posture expressed everything but defeat. The woman held herself straight and proud, chest puffed and chin raised. I couldn't see her face, but from the way Watson faltered under her gaze, I imagined it to be a mask of hate.

"Move into the area between the two statues right in front of you, right up against the wall. Good. Now I have a few question for you, which you will answer quickly and truthfully. You answer satisfactory and you might walk out of this alive."

"I don't believe one word out of your dirty mouth."

"That's for you to decide. Now, where is my brother?"

"Gone."

I received a hateful stare as an answer that would've made the gargoyles on cathedral roof proud. Still, I continued the interrogation, but the woman kept quiet, no matter how many questions I threw at her. Fine, we could do this another way.

"You are from London, which is evident from your choice of words and speaking pattern. Well, when I say London, I mean slightly to the north, as it doesn't quite fit with the city centre," I stated and kept a close eye on our captive to observe her reactions, small as they might have been. The abysmal lighting on the cathedral roof made me unable to discern the tiny patterns of her facial expression, but it would have to do. "The hairpin you wear is of a make only a single jeweller in London produces, as it carries his signature style. It would've been possible for you to steal such a thing, but I wager it was given to you as a present and still kept in high regard, as you carry no other adornments on your rather... functional clothing."

Watson stood back as I elaborated on my observations to make the assassin feel as unnerved as possible.

"No answer? Fine. You've been wearing your clothing for about three days. The dark layer on top is made from threads of a plant origin, and the weave pattern would make me place it south of Turkey. The clothing underneath is worn, but well-maintained and of British origin -- mostly sheep's wool. You've spent a lot of time in the sun in recent months, as your skin is visibly darkened, even in the twilight."

The woman made a point of turning her head away from me as soon as I mentioned her skin -- as if that would've made any difference at that point. I cleared my throat before I continued, determined to touch on a detail that would make her crack. There had

101

been so much uncertainty in this mission already, that actually having someone in front of me, whom I could analyse to my heart's content was almost gratifying. It gave me back the sense of control, which had slipped ever further from my grasp during the last days.

"There are many British military operations in the east, which could explain your reason to spend time in the warmer climate, but you wouldn't be here if you were really part of a troop," I continued and exchanged a glance with Watson, whose history gave him the authority to confirm my words. "As you've already told me that my brother isn't here anymore, you're not on this… mission alone."

I could be mistaken, but the possibility of a mastermind, who let herself be caught so easily was negligibly small. So: a group from the Far East, with a grudge towards Sherlock, some substantial resources and a knowledge of his modus operandi. I knew people in each of the listed groups, and had already made a mental comparison to see where they overlapped. But there wasn't one organisation or even person, who shared all aspects. Not a single case of my brother's had taken him this far from London, and I couldn't remember any brush with a group within our hometown that would fit my current line of inquiry.

The assassin showed me a knowing smirk, teeth glinting even in the dark. I knew roughly *where* she was from, but I didn't know *who* she was and more importantly: just who she was working for. She mocked me openly and I wouldn't have it.

"Watson, empty her pockets," I ordered. "And then bring over her weapon."

I desperately needed more information to go on. Maybe there was something in her belongings that could set me on the right path. Without knowing exactly who she was, I would never be able to connect the dots.

As the doctor approached her, the woman actually hissed at him again. My, my. Was this her usual demeanour? My travel companion wasn't fazed by her behaviour and reached into the outermost pocket of her coat-like covering. I couldn't yet see what he'd find, but knew another way to occupy our time.

"What does *this* mean?" I asked and held the clay figurine in front of her eyes.

"That you like to play games, Mycroft Holmes," she smiled, crooked and wrong, uttering my name in a familiar tone as if she had known me for years. "And that you've already lost."

Seemingly to emphasize her statement, a flash of white light exploded and almost blinded me. Watson fell over -- if from the blast or simply from shock I couldn't tell -- squarely on his back. He didn't utter a single sound, which made me highly alert, because I had to assume he was unconscious or worse.

The woman had already jumped to her feet as she took advantage of our confusion. After-images flickered in front of my eyes as I propelled myself forward to apprehend her once again. In my haste, my foot caught Watson's leg. I stumbled and lost precious seconds, during which the assassin made it to the doorway of the stairs.

"Get them!" she shouted and just like that, a number of spectres in wide robes descended upon me. They had exited the stairs after the woman disappeared within the darkness and now swarmed me like a flock of angry birds. Many claw-like hands grabbed at my clothes, pulled me down and the only things I could see were confusing patterns in black and white. Their faces were hidden behind metal masks and their heads adorned with countless red, swaying feathers. For a brief moment I wondered how they could've even made their way through the city like this. I felt dizzy just looking at them and I would've lost my balance, had I not already been pushed down to the ground.

My brain couldn't comprehend this assault on my visual senses and my eyes started to hurt fiercely, but there was no way I could close them now. Tears streamed down my face as I curled up and rolled to the side. I expected at least one of them to brandish a weapon any second. With my motion I pushed two of my assailants off balance and they fell to the floor behind me. Even though I was still positioned horizontally, at least I had left their circle and gained a few vital seconds to contemplate my situation.

Firstly, the woman was gone. From the moment I was hindered by her lackeys, it was clear that there was no way I could get to her again in time. The sudden, but definite, defeat hit me hard. This wasn't something that usually happened to me. I had let my guard down, and now I was suffering for it... No, it would be my brother, who'd be suffering. I could beat these people and get away with Watson, but we had only limited information to get to Sherlock.

My anger and irritation with myself was many times larger than the emotions I felt towards the strange people. But I could still use these aggravated feelings to fuel my counterattack, because no matter how hopeless the situation looked, it would definitely all be over should we die on the roof of the cathedral. I moved backwards in an effort to gain more time and just then my hand touched a familiar object on the ground. At least I had retained a little bit of luck.

With both hands I grabbed my cane and swung it in a wide arc in front of me. The powerful strike was delivered roughly on the height of my attackers' heads, whom I judged to be slightly shorter than Watson. The resistance I encountered proved me right. I hit at least two people hard, strafed another and felled all three bodies in one swift swoop, then jumped to my feet again. Finally the space was cleared and I could see that there were *another* three strange henchmen still with us.

For all their enthusiasm during the first attack, they now seemed almost reluctant to step forward. Maybe I proved to be a more formidable opponent than they had expected. Through my teary, blurred vision I strained to make out their next moves. It was weird that none of them carried any weapons, but I wasn't about to complain. Watson was still on the ground a few feet away, hopefully only unconscious, but at least he wasn't in immediate danger. And I wasn't about to let the attention of our attackers waver.

"Isn't any of you going to attack me?" I asked and held my cane out in front of me, daring the men to step forward. If they came at me one at a time I had a better chance to get rid of them without risking any bodily harm. Well, at least not any additional harm, as my hand and arm were already burning up again and I could barely use them anymore.

But then they all jumped me simultaneously. I was pushed back against the wall, but this time I was prepared for the attack. Leveraging the unyielding stones behind me I kicked out with both legs and hit two of my adversaries squarely between the legs. This single action eradicated all doubts about their gender, because they were on the floor in an instant. I could imagine their pained faces even behind the masks, but this was not the time for empathetic feelings. There was still one man left, and he had decided to go directly for my neck.

Spindly fingers closed around my throat and squeezed with a power that was entirely unpredicted. For just a brief moment, that I would deny outright if anyone asked, I panicked as my air supply was restricted. The mask came close to my face, polished metal glinting menacingly even in the dark. I reached up, grabbed the head full of feathers and ripped the ugly thing from his face. A foul stench assaulted me as he shouted something vile in a language that sounded vaguely familiar but was at that moment incomprehensible. His skin was dark and wrinkled, his hair all but gone. The man's eyes were blown wide, pupils darker than the night. And in the next moment they were gone.

A dull thud was audible as Watson connected his heavy pistol with the lunatic's head, following my earlier example. The grip around my throat loosened as the man slipped away and collapsed into a pile of limbs at my feet. I kicked him once for good measure. Before the other imbeciles could attempt another attack I performed upon them the same treatment, so they were all definitely, and literally knocked out.

"Are you hurt?" I asked the doctor, voice still hoarse from the abuse to my throat.

"I think I hit my head again, but the pain doesn't seem to linger."

"Good."

I smoothed down my hair and righted my clothing, then pulled my own pistol from a pocket of the suit jacket and trained it on the head of the closest attacker. I fired without skipping a heartbeat. There were six of them and we only needed one to answer our questions. Before Watson could tell me otherwise, I had already gotten rid of the remaining, superfluous baggage. With my cane I poked the man I had chosen to be our informant -- the one that had had the audacity to put his hands around my neck. He didn't move, which wasn't surprising, so I placed my boot on his shoulder to keep it that way.

But something was amiss. I turned towards the doctor, who was usually so eager to complain about my behaviour, and saw him simply staring at me. He looked back and forth between my firearm and the dead henchmen, his face as emotionless as their metal masks. Then he dropped his own pistol in disgust and took a step back, which brought him with his back against a column, at which he sunk to the floor.

"Head getting worse?" I asked as I checked my pistol for any remaining heat, deemed it sufficiently cooled down and put it back neatly into my pocket.

"I... Mycroft... What did you do?"

"Lessened our workload considerably. It'll be easier to handle just one person."

"But the others... You killed them."

I cocked an eyebrow and inclined my head to indicate that he had simply stated the obvious. Watson harrumphed exasperated and his expression turned into an angry frown.

"You killed them in cold blood!"

"Do you think they would've hesitated to do the same to us? Any of them?"

"You couldn't possibly know that..."

I looked down at the pile of black and white cloth between us, dark stains spreading along the fabric where the blood oozed from their skulls. We would have to inspect the bodies before we'd move the remaining lunatic to a location more suitable for a proper interrogation. The drapes looked exactly like the one, which the single attacker in Dover had worn.

"You're right, I couldn't. But now I'm one hundred percent sure that they won't. I like these odds much better. Don't you?"

I heard a sharp intake of breath from the doctor. "That doesn't justify your actions."

"Doesn't it? Let me tell you about the situation we're in, because you seem to have forgotten all about it. Sherlock has been abducted by a group of lunatics, who have tried to thwart us at every junction of our journey. All of this -- this whole city -- is a trap, and they've tried to get rid of us every step of the way. I don't know if they want my brother or used him and his letter as bait to get to me, but the fact is that we're out here, exposed and at their mercy... at the mercy of whatever it is that they employ to make nature itself turn against us!" I kept my voice intentionally low and steady, as I just knew that I couldn't let my feelings get the best of me now. "There's no telling what they'll do to Sherlock now that we know their leader's face, and I, for one, am not going to wait around six potential killers. This is not how this works, doctor, and if you're unhappy with my handling of the situation, you're welcome to return to London anytime."

With this I grabbed our would-be informant and pulled him out of the body pile. I ripped a piece of cloth from one of the other's cloaks and tied his hands, as the woman had made off with my only pair of handcuffs. Well, good riddance. Then I threw the man over my shoulder and turned towards Watson.

"Are you staying here?"

"You don't need to interrogate the man," the doctor said quietly and held out a small notebook. "I grabbed this from her pocket just before the explosion happened."

Could we be so lucky?

I dropped the man unceremoniously and received the notebook from the good doctor. It was tiny and grubby, obviously having been carried in the coat for a long time. The edges showed clear signs of repeated use. The pages carried scribbles in several languages, mostly English, but also some in Arabic, curiously. So my theory about her stay south of Turkey held up, but it still didn't connect to a pretty picture. The writing was all very small and meticulous and so impossible to decipher in the twilight. Most of it was numbers, anyway.

On the last page, was a sketch of a rough street layout with an unmistakable X marking a building. Surely the assassin never suspected someone to find it, because even though there were no labels, the street layout looked distinct enough for anyone with half a brain to place with the help of a map. But I didn't need one, because I already knew the place it depicted. It was of a city, whose streets I had learned by heart a number of years ago. There was no mistake and I was confident in my memory.

We would have to travel on to Rome.

The doctor kept quiet through it all, retrieved his own pistol to stow away and stood at a distance from me while I perused the contents of the notebook. I sighed inwardly and felt a sliver of regret as I put the man, who I had wanted to carry away and interrogate, out of his misery. Regret, because it wouldn't be easier to work with Watson that way, and I knew that he wasn't about to abandon the mission to rescue Sherlock, no matter what I had just done. Regret because the man's quick death robbed me of the opportunity for a little payback. And… well, regret because it wasn't my usual style to get rid of potential information sources prematurely.

But somehow I felt that our time was slowly, but surely, running out.

CHAPTER 6

That is what you see. Now, what can you observe?

I didn't speak much to Watson after the episode on the roof. In hindsight I should've just insisted on him going back to London. I couldn't exactly blame him for sticking to his convictions and moral code, because I did the very same, but it was once again clear that we just didn't work well together. Well, I wasn't my brother and I had no ambition to become him, so the doctor would just have to bear with me for a few days longer.

We spent the day on the train to the ancient city of Rome almost in complete silence. With a strange satisfaction I observed Watson grow more uncomfortable and behave awkwardly for the better part of the day. I was reading a book and ignored his squeamish behaviour completely. From time to time I would hold the clay figurine and turn it about, trying to find anything of use about it. But it was just a simple thing, crudely made and absolutely non-descriptive. Like a piece of a board game for children.

Watson couldn't even concentrate on the reading material he had chosen to occupy himself with, but stared out of the window for most of the time. He observed the figurine when I examined it and eyed me nervously when he thought I couldn't see it. I noticed every time. Finally, after almost a day of battling with himself, Watson drew in a big breath and cleared his throat noisily to catch my attention.

"You can refrain from acting so dramatic, Dr. Watson," I said quietly, without looking up from my book, and before he even started to speak out. "I could see you squirming in your seat for the last three hours and working up the courage to address the issue. Incidentally, I have betted against myself how long it *would* take and have to express my disappointment, as I had expected you to speak up about an hour ago."

"Are you *quite* finished?" he asked and pronounced his consonants harshly.

"Yes. And before you ask: I can see your point of view, and while I don't agree, I admit that I acted on instinct. This isn't only my battle, but also yours, and I will consider your opinion should it come to another confrontation. I apologise should I have offended you earlier."

This statement was only partially true. Mostly untrue, in fact. It most certainly didn't excuse the death of six men, at least in in his eyes. But if this little, white lie enabled me to find my brother without any more complications on the doctor's side, so be it. Watson responded with stunned silence and a thoughtful nod as acknowledgement. While it hadn't been a satisfactory apology, we both knew this wasn't the time to fight. Neither of us uttered another word until the train rolled into Rome's main station.

Our progress in Rome was much quicker than in Milan, as we already knew our destination. It was early in the evening as we stowed our luggage at the station, but due to the short winter days, the sun had sunken below the horizon a while ago and the dark brought forth a biting cold. We agreed not to waste any time on finding accommodations, but rather to seek out the location of the church

113

Santa Maria della Quercia immediately, which had turned out to be the X on the notebook's map. After sitting still for almost a day, I desperately needed to move.

In a big city like Rome, there are always people about. Even a cold winter evening did nothing to the hustle and bustle of the city, as opposed to the quiet we had left behind in Milan. As a city dweller, I vastly preferred the noise, as it gave me the comfortable feeling of a big machine running smoothly.

"I suggest we acquire transportation to take us across town," I pointed at the street, where a number of small, rickety cabs were ready to accept customers. Watson agreed without hesitation. Neither of us wanted to walk far through the cold winter night.

The carriage we ended up in was narrow and badly isolated. The driver whipped the horses through the city at a breakneck speed, as I had promised him extra payment should he get us to the church in under half an hour. The passenger cabin rattled over cobblestones and swerved precariously from side to side every time we drove around a corner or circled slower drivers. Our ride was accompanied by loud, colourful exclamations from our driver. You can say what you want about the Italians -- they know how to curse beautifully.

We made good time, but the persistent draft made me feel chilled to my core and my body was constantly shivering. I almost convinced myself that the cold was the only reason I was shaking and once again pushed the worst thoughts out of my head to keep my motivation untainted by fear. The last thing we needed was for *me* to lose my nerve.

This simply wouldn't do.

After I had clung to the seat for just long enough to induce a mild headache, the driver stopped and knocked on the roof of the cabin. We had arrived. I exchanged a few quick words with the man and handed him enough money to make him grin widely. He tipped his head and disappeared into a dark alley. I took a cautious look around. We were standing in the middle of a small square, which featured a large tree in the centre that I recognised to be an oak. It spread leafless, gnarled branches over our heads like twisted fingers. Deserted benches crowded around the trunk, barely visible under mountains of piled up snow, which had been pushed towards them in order to keep the street clear. There were lights in the windows of most houses surrounding us, but only a few people about the street.

The church was barely recognisable as such, jammed between the regular three story houses, with the same yellowish coat of paint. The only thing, which made us realise we were indeed in the right place were the high iron fences put up around the entrance, which kept any unauthorised person from entering the building during the apparent construction work. Snow was also piled in front of the entrance, showing no signs of anyone entering or leaving the premises recently, not even footsteps on top of the white mountains. A sign had been put up a while ago, now barely legible. The renovation had already begun in 1892 -- so they had been at it for almost four years!

"There must be another way into the church," I mused. "It's being restored, so maybe other doors are open. In any case, we can't just walk in through the front door."

115

"Wouldn't they already know we are here?" Watson asked.

"Maybe," I shrugged. "There is a chance that the shooter might've reached this place before us, but it's slim. And if she has, we've all the more reason to hurry. I will go around the houses on the left side to reach the back of the church. You will go the other way, and we'll meet up again on the other side. We need to find another way in."

Watson agreed and we both started our inspection. With every step I crushed ice crystals beneath my feet and the resulting noise seemed to be much louder to my ears than it could physically be. The streets out here, far from the city centre, were narrow and close to deserted. And while I tried to walk as inconspicuously as possible, I still stood out like a sore thumb. The houses around were lined up neatly, without even a narrow alleyway between them, and even on detailed inspection, I couldn't make out a possibility to approach the church from another angle than the front. After turning around the corner two times, I ended up on a rather large square with two fountains in front of an important looking building. I couldn't immediately place it, but it was probably related to a government function, which was obvious from the flags it was flying.

Watson appeared at the corner just on the other side of the block of houses. We exchanged a quick glance, during which I shook my head slightly, and much to my dismay the doctor mirrored my gesture. We slowly walked towards each other, until we met in front of a moderately sized restaurant with well lit, big windows, which let warm light shine out onto the street. Two small tables outside held a few empty wine bottles, some candles and a menu, with which we busied ourselves while we discussed our findings -- or lack thereof.

"The church seems to be completely surrounded by all these buildings. Which means that the front door is the only entrance," the doctor sighed. "Seems like this is our only option."

"Nonsense, Dr. Watson," I smiled. "Look ahead!"

"It's... a restaurant?" he suggested cautiously.

"That is what you see. Now, what can you observe?"

Watson strained his eyes and looked around in a way that was anything but inconspicuous. The restaurant front was large and very well maintained. The decoration could be called classic Italian, if all you knew was the romanticised version of the country. There was a fair number of customers inside, as far as one could make out from a look through the windows. Most of them were still occupied by their dinner. On the whole, it seemed like a respectable establishment. I listened to Watson recounting these facts and nodded my assent, as they weren't wrong, but the one I was looking for wasn't among them.

"All very well. But what's always situated in the back of restaurants?" I tried to coax the answer out of him.

"Usually a service entry for the staff and deliveries."

"Precisely. And judging by the size of the restaurant, I expect them to receive large deliveries. So there must be a way to reach the storage in the back without going through the front door..." I then pointed to the right of the building. "And I believe it's right there."

A few minutes later we had cracked open the lock on the big doors, which covered the entrance to a tunnel in the building. It lead into the backyard of the restaurant, which doubled as a small garden, and conveniently bordered Santa Maria della Quercia. As the temperature was still below zero, none of the staff could be found outside, which meant we could devote our time to examining a sizeable hole in the back wall of the church, only barely covered by several wooden boards.

We cautiously pushed forward into the dark interior of the building. It was even more quiet than a church had any right to be. It didn't look deserted, it looked dead, desolate and abandoned. Dust was everywhere and not even a small sign of activity within the last days... or weeks for that matter. The air was stale, uneasy to breathe in, and my frustration grew by the minute.

Parts of the church had been simply left to decay, whereas others were still wrapped in scaffolding and cloth, as if the workers could return at any second. But there were no tools and the workbenches were empty save for a few small pieces of stonework. One larger statue had been taken down from the wall and stood in the centre of the space. The pews had been pushed to the side and covered with a tarp. Cautious rays of moonlight pierced the darkness and illuminated a few floating dust motes with the silver light. This place hadn't been visited by people in a long time. So why had it been marked?

I turned away from Watson so as not to let my nervousness show. Our logical course of action was to search for a hidden place, in which the woman and her henchmen could've kept Sherlock. There was only one such place in a church like this: The crypt. I turned back toward the altar, as the way below was very likely in the back of the church and closely observed my surroundings as I moved.

Then something small caught my eye: On the scaffolding around the altar, almost invisible against the wood in the twilight of the church, there was a little clay figurine, same as the one in my pocket. A little out of place, yes, but no one else would have given it any further consideration and subsequently ignored it. I picked it up and held it next to mine. They were identical. I called Watson over immediately.

"What's that?" he pointed at a small ceramic plate, lying just where the figurine had been standing. It was painted white and featured a golden ankh symbol in the middle. I made the mistake of moving it.

A sudden rush of wind swept us off our feet. I couldn't hold onto the small objects as I rolled on the ground and tried to protect my head from the impact. Watson landed next to me and released a strained grunt. As I turned my head upwards, a sight that was utterly incomprehensible offered itself to me: A whirlwind of sand, which glowed from the inside out, was quickly building up and tore at the left-over evidence of the restoration effort. Piece by piece, cloth got ripped apart and drawn into the vortex. As even the wood creaked and rattled, I acted. But for once Watson had reacted even faster than I,

119

who had been stunned by the view for entirely too long. He had already dragged me to my feet and backwards, away from the localized storm.

"We can't go through it. The only exit is the front door!" I shouted.

Both of us turned and ran, the path now illuminated in a strange, orange glow. The light cast a false security with its warmth, almost like the setting sun, as the sand cut through air and stone alike, growing ever larger. Then the world exploded. A flash of light, accompanied by an ear-piercing, monstrous sound arrived half a second earlier than the barrage of sand. It hit my back like a wall and I felt like it would rip me apart. As everything faded to black my last thought was dedicated to Sherlock.

I have failed you, brother.

CHAPTER 7

I have faith in your judgment

"Mycroft Holmes, gracing my city with his presence. That I should live to see the day..." a female voice roused me from an unconsciousness that had definitely not been sleep, as I was feeling anything but rested.

I could place the person behind the voice immediately -- a fact that bothered me even more than the pain that flooded my body as soon as I woke up properly. Still, I refrained from stirring and didn't open my eyes. The situation had to be assessed first. I could feel that I was wearing only little clothing and was currently placed in a bed, underneath a soft blanket. My face was warmed by the rays of the sun, the strong light noticeable even through closed eyelids. So I had been unconscious for at least one night. My limbs hurt all over and my head wasn't faring any better. The incident came back to me slowly and as I knew the woman, who was in the room with me, I could deduce everything that had happened afterwards. It was then when I heard someone else clear his throat, cough roughly and gulp down a large amount of water in response. So Watson was in the same room as I.

"We haven't been introduced, have we?" I heard the woman say. "When we arrived at the church you were buried under the rubble together with my colleague, so we brought you in as well."

Ah, there was the confirmation of my theory.

"Arrived at the church?" the doctor asked, voice croaking hoarsely. "How...?"

"Myc..., Mr. Holmes notified us as the pair of you had arrived in Rome," there was a short break, and I didn't even have to open my eyes to know she was looking at me. "Oh yes, I still haven't introduced myself, now have I? How rude of me. The name is Victoria Trevor, agent in the service of Her Majesty, Queen Victoria. Same name, too, so you should have no trouble remembering it."

"My name is Dr. John Watson," he hesitated just a bit before he gave his name, though I was sure she already knew who he was. "I didn't notice him notify anyone, though."

"We have positioned agents at the main station, who relay information to us. Rome is important for the operation of the Secret Service in Italy. If you know how to signal our people, it can be done without anyone noticing, not even someone close by," Victoria explained, the pride in her voice obvious. "But what we do *not* know is why you are here in the first place. We had been notified that Mycroft... uhh, Mr. Holmes would be in the country, but not that he would be visiting Rome."

So they *had* been told of my unsanctioned leave after all. It was to be expected. It had been inevitable to run into Victoria -- a fact that had been obvious to me since Rome had been fixed as our destination. The knowledge didn't make it easier. I had to talk with the doctor alone, first.

"It doesn't seem like Mycroft is waking up," Watson said right on cue, effectively evading Victoria's inquiry, as I had hoped he would.

"His wounds aren't serious. Better to let him wake up in his own time, wouldn't you say?"

"Definitely. Thank you."

"I have to say you're quite lucky. You've emerged relatively unscathed after letting yourselves be blown up in that church."

"We walked right into that…" the doctor said sadly. "I guess we have *you* to thank for getting out alive?"

"Maybe. I think you'd have lived, even if my team hadn't shown up and dug you out of the debris. It was only the wooden scaffolding that collapsed on top of you -- not any of the stonework," Victoria explained.

There was a thoughtful pause, in which we all contemplated how many times each of us had cheated death just by pure chance. I would've liked to have said it had always been due to my superior skills, but in reality a lot of it came down to dumb luck.

"You have to excuse me, Dr. Watson. My agents are eager to take care of the clean-up in the church," she finally said. "And I want to have a proper look at the place myself."

"Of course. I wouldn't want to keep you. Thank you again."

I head Victoria walk across the room, heavy boots audible despite the thick carpet, and expected her to leave. What I definitely didn't expect was the kiss she pressed to my lips only moments later, and it took everything that I had in me not to react. Watson wasn't so skillful in containing his surprise, as I heard a low gasp from his direction, which was quickly stifled. There was no further comment until she left the room. I waited for a little while, then opened my eyes and sat up.

"I would prefer if you could stop your thought process right now."

"The only way for me to stop is for you to tell me how you know Victoria Trevor," Watson grinned, clearly revelling in the fact that I looked very much out of my depth.

"Alright," I conceded immediately. There was no use in avoiding the inevitable. "Just let me…. Give me a minute."

Watson graciously let me have a few seconds to compose a suitable narrative. It took us a while to get out of our beds anyway, as every movement stretched resting skin uncomfortably, brushed cloth against bruises and produced a plethora of different pain points. Watson was still first and foremost a doctor, not concerned about his own injuries, but mostly about mine and he insisted on thoroughly assessing the damage.

As he stumbled over, my eyes fell on the biggest wound the doctor had suffered: a nasty, large gash on his upper left thigh, which had been bandaged tightly to keep the wound closed, but was already bleeding through the cloth. His careful movements suggested a bruising of the ribs and the slowness pointed to what could have been a concussion. I watched him for a while, then I took a deep breath.

"As you probably gathered, Victoria Trevor is an agent in the same organisation as I. Actually, *I* am the reason she joined. Sherlock has told you a story about an old university friend. I remember reading the tale in the Strand Magazine. My brother then brought it to Victoria's attention. She had a good laugh, from what I heard."

"University friend? You mean the one from... '*The Gloria Scott*'? What was his name? Victor... oh..." the realisation seemed to hit Watson like a brick. "You mean Holmes lied to me? He told me a fabricated story?"

"Oh no, doctor. The story is true, all of it. Except the gender of his friend... and he left *me* out, of course. Maybe he wanted to show off his earliest case but protect the identity of Victoria? Or he simply made a joke of it? I could imagine both possibilities," I mused. "My brother can, on occasion, be quite the jester. Anyway, they were quite close for a while."

Close was an understatement, my mind readily corrected me. A surge of pain flooded me, for once not stemming from my injuries. Watson didn't need to know everything.

"Maybe he didn't tell me because I could scarcely believe he had a friend at all, much less a woman," Watson interjected.

"That could also be it. Well, he got to know her through me. The part with the dog is the only small lie, and it does seem rather farfetched if examined closely. Again: Before you ask, we weren't involved back then, and still aren't," I examined the wound on my right hand, squinting my eyes in disappointment, as the movement brought only pain. "She stuck around, learned from us. Absorbed the science of deduction like a sponge absorbs water. A natural intelligence. We made it a challenge to groom her into a capable reasoner."

"You make it sound like she was a pet?"

"I suppose we saw her like that for a while. In the end, she was a good friend to Sherlock, one of the very, very few. But then I joined the Service and she followed me, while my brother stayed behind at the University. When a position opened up in Rome she took the opportunity. I haven't seen her in years."

Yes, a good friend to my brother. A *very* good friend. Silence fell over the room, until I groaned loudly as I stood up, for once wanting to disturb it.

"Would you take a look at my back?" I asked, moving carefully. "It doesn't feel... right."

From what I remembered the blast had hit me from behind. Watson told me that both the shirt on my back and the bedding I had laid on were stained with blood, seeping through the hastily applied bandages. Apparently I had sustained a large, but superficial wound, which meant that my clothing must have effectively been ripped to shreds. I tested my movement range slowly and realised that I could move all muscles, they just hurt something fierce.

"Only this and your hand?" Watson joked while carefully removing the sticky shirt from my wounds. "I need to change those bandages."

We looked around and spotted a box with medical supplies on a nearby table, partly strewn about. Whoever had taken care of us was pretty sure we were in need of further attention. Well, they weren't wrong. Watson tested the strength of his injured leg and retrieved the tools of his trade. I supposed we could've simply called someone to take care of the tasks, but I could see that handling the familiar objects had a calming effect on the doctor and he visibly relaxed as he cleaned the wound on my hand with carbolic acid. It smelled sweet and irritated my skin, but was a welcome pain.

"Thank you for telling me," Watson said after a while. "I appreciate it."

I nodded. While I had omitted a few, rather important details, this would be enough. If there was one thing I wanted to avoid it was talk about the problems of my past. My only hope was that Victoria would see it the same way -- even though I already knew she wouldn't. She had always been so emotional. I winced in pain as Watson removed the bandages from my back, because they had stuck to my skin during the night. Fresh blood ran and dripped down my back onto the bedding.

"You are a lucky man, Mycroft," the doctor said while applying more acid to disinfect my wounds. The way it stung didn't make me feel all that lucky. "For what happened, the damage is quite shallow."

"Shallow?" I huffed. "My shooting hand is injured. A large handicap."

"You are conscious and able to walk. Nothing is broken, and your head seems to have evaded injury, something which mine should learn to achieve. Still, you should take it slow for a while."

Watson's eye rolling at my complaints was almost audible. He took his time to clean the abrasions and then applied a fresh layer of bandages, before I helped him to repeat the process on his own leg. A large gash through the front of his thigh, just as I had suspected. It must've hurt fiercely as the disinfectant ran through it, but the doctor simply gritted his teeth and wiped the few tears that had formed away without comment.

"This was designed to kill us. *Again*," he said after he had regained his composure. "And we walked right into it. So the notebook *was* planted to lure us here. You saw it right away and notified your colleagues."

"I alerted them to our presence in the city, nothing more. They didn't know our exact destination. If I were to guess, I would say they learned of the explosion and deduced the rest. I am prone to attract danger, after all," I shrugged, stating the truth. "I apologise for keeping your out of the loop."

"Working with Holmeses, I am quite used to not getting informed of any plan until it is much too late... but you have some securities, at least, whereas your brother likes to rush into everything, relying solely on himself. It is one of his rather *trying* qualities," the doctor actually laughed where I expected him to reprimand me. "That doesn't mean I'm not angry, but rather at myself for being so blinded."

"The concern for my brother outweighed all reason, and in our haste we both made mistakes. You aren't to blame."

No, *I* was. I could've brought agents with us as support. No, they would've been hurt in the sand explosion just as we had. But how was I to know? Could I have done something different? There had been no other clue to go on... I shook my head. There was no use dwelling on the past.

I was eager to get going, but we were still clad only in baggy nightshirts -- and mine was bloodied so much I couldn't possibly wear it much longer. The remnants of our clothing were laid out on a nearby table, but I ruled them out immediately. My coat had been torn open by the explosion, the suit jacket, as well as the shirt, was ripped in the back, everything stiff from dried blood. The trousers were usable, but looked horrible -- the only thing salvageable were indeed my shoes. I cursed under my breath. The suit had been one of my favourites.

Watson's attire hadn't fared much better. The trousers were torn at the leg, corresponding to the gash he had suffered. He eyed the rest of the garments, but as opposed to my set, not even the shoes could be used again.

"This won't do," I sighed. "Excuse me for a moment."

I left the doctor in the room we had woken up in. Some part of me still wished that he would be unable to walk. Just for a while, so I could leave him behind. Yes, it wasn't a very nice thing to wish for. Quite egoistically, really. But in the end, I worked better alone, and that was a proven fact.

When I entered the hallway, I needed only a few seconds to orientate myself. After all, I had visited the very same building just twelve years and twenty-three days prior -- which was incidentally the same time I had last seen Victoria. I figured she would use her large sitting room as an emergency meeting place and if I hurried she might still be present. I also needed to see the church before the clean-up. As I walked, everyone I passed stared at me either out of curiosity, or simply because I was still clad only in blood stained nightclothes.

At the end of the hallway I descended the stairs and arrived in the comfortably sized entry hall, furnished with only a few low benches at the sides and a decorative table in the middle, which was curiously empty. Just as in the other rooms, the carpeting was elaborate, the colours regal, and the walls were decorated with paintings and banners, which gave the space a dignified feel … that I ruined completely with my disheveled appearance.

My suspicion was right: Voices drifted over from an adjacent sitting room. But I could only take two steps in the right direction before I felt a hand on my arm. I had been so distracted trying to get my thoughts and feelings in order, I hadn't sensed someone approaching me. When I turned around, I was faced with the very same person I had wanted to seek out in the first place.

"Mycroft," Victoria said warmly. My name, uttered in her melodious voice, instantly threw me back in time. "So good to see you, love."

She hadn't changed at all. Well, she had in a way. Her hair was longer and braided, still as auburn as ever, and the laughter lines

130

on her face had started to leave their mark. But her warm eyes still sparkled and her smile was unchanged, showing rather too much teeth. She looked open, welcoming... and her mere presence made me long for days gone by. I mustered my strength and pushed back the feelings that my memory so readily supplied.

"It's good to see you too, Victoria," I said honestly, because it was. "Thank you for helping us out back there."

"You weren't sleeping just now, were you?" Victoria smiled.

"I would appreciate if you could refrain from such... actions in the future."

This earned me a frown, but no further comment. She was still so impulsive. Her carefree attitude didn't match with her high position in the Service at all.

"I would like to examine the scene of the explosion myself," I added.

Victoria paused for a moment, then shook her head.

"And then we go right down to business? Fine. That brings me directly to the most important question: What were you doing in a church in Rome, anyway? If you wanted to see me, there are easier ways."

"It's personal business," I said quickly, even though that wasn't much of an explanation.

"Personal business gets you blown up?"

"... sometimes."

We stared at each other for a heartbeat, then broke into laughter, a familiar warmth, unchanged through all the years, spreading in my chest. *Curses.* That's why I had vowed never to come back here.

"I am here because of Sherlock."

I didn't want to say his name, but there was no way to avoid it. I couldn't keep the matter from Victoria. She had helped me and had a right to know, not even mentioning the history we three had together. Her eyes widened in surprise and shock.

"Sherlock? What's it got to do with him? I didn't know he was in Rome," she asked, uncertainty clear in her voice.

"He was in Milan, where he apparently got abducted. We followed his trail here, but it was a carefully laid trap."

"A trap? By whom?"

I thought of the figurine, left there for us to find, mockingly. Of the masks, the feathers. Of the assassin. No names, no direction, no conclusive clues.

"I don't know. We've captured someone who could be responsible, but she escaped before we acquired any vital information."

"Do you have any theories?"

"Yes. But I won't tell you before we have examined the evidence together. It would be foolish to taint your thought process with my ideas before you form your own."

"You never change," Victoria smiled. "Like Sherlock." I cringed at the way she spoke his name, with a different intonation like all these others -- even mine.

"I can tell you some details on the way to the church. Just… get me some clean clothes first. Ah, and have some brought to Watson, as well," I said flatly and decided not to go into the whole Sherlock-related discussion right now. That never ended well.

So it came to be that I was once again dressed in the Italian version of our agent's uniform, and noticed that they hadn't changed all that much during the last twelve years. It wasn't unlike a dress uniform of the military, kept almost completely in black, mixed with elements that could've been stolen from a riding ensemble. Simple trousers (the same uniform for men and women) were complemented by a black jacket with two rows of small, silver buttons.

I kept my own, comfortable, gray shoes, instead of the shiny, black ones and declined the round hat that came with it. My gun fit snugly under the jacket, and there was even a place for a sword at the side of my belt. I had trained with the weapon, but rarely used in a fight, so I refused the offered, elegantly decorated short rapier and picked up my cane instead, which hadn't deserted me in the explosion. The uniform didn't make blending into a crowd very easy, but it was still better than my torn-up ensemble.

On the way to the church, I filled Victoria in on some of the details, as promised. Since I had woken up, there had been a debate in my head. It was only right and truthful to tell her about the powers we had encountered. I fully expected to find a lot of sand in the church, and there was no other sensible explanation for its presence. I had no fear of being ridiculed for my statements.

No, what irked me was that she *could actually believe me* and thereby validate that everything that had happened was not just a figment of my imagination. Frankly, I didn't know which of those options was worse. Finally, I decided to postpone these details until we found actual evidence in the church.

"I missed you," she said then, as my cursory explanation was over. "All those years…"

"You know the reason for our lack of contact."

"You had always been such a good friend to me, and then you decide to cut off everything?"

Twelve years was a long time, but she couldn't actually have forgotten everything? No, it was likely a ploy to make me talk. So I didn't.

"Do you still…?"

I turned my gaze towards the window. Five years I had waited in her shadow, and now I simply wouldn't give her the satisfaction of the reaction she provoked.

"I guess not. Fine, I get it."

There was anger in her voice, but also sadness. It still made me feel protective and I sighed inwardly. Yes, I wouldn't let myself be drawn into this again, but I couldn't deny her… no, us a chance at closure. It just wasn't the time.

"We can postpone this until after we find Sherlock."

If you will still *want* to talk as soon as we have him back, I thought. I just knew she wouldn't. Still, she signaled her reluctant agreement. We sat in awkward silence, with a notable distance between our bodies in the narrow space, until the carriage arrived at our destination. The only sounds were the rattle of the wheels and the rhythm of horseshoes on the cobblestone streets. From time to time, the sounds of the cityscape filtered through like muffled reminders of the world outside.

I recognised the plaza with the tree in front of the church immediately. Only now, the iron barricades in front of the entrance had been removed and the snow cleared to allow entry into the devastated interior. A large number of footprints showed that the church had seen many visitors that day, and the signs posted on the wall were testament to the presence of police at the scene. I hoped they would not hinder my work and mentioned as much to Victoria.

"The explosion was audible in the adjacent houses. We couldn't keep them from an investigation of their own. But we *could* get them to let us have a look before them, in exchange for help with the clean-up," she explained. Her tone told of countless times where talks hadn't been as smooth.

As I walked behind the woman, who was so familiar to me still, I felt a stab of regret. A reunion should be the cause of joy and fond, nostalgic feelings, while I felt mostly pain and anger. That was no reason for me to start our cooperation on such a bad note, but I needed to keep a reasonable distance between us. Even after all this time, I couldn't trust my heart to not betray me in the most inopportune of moments, but I *could* control my actions.

The inside of the church wasn't as badly damaged as my memory of the incident made me believe. Then again, the sensation of being ripped apart tends to override most other things. It was a wonder that my back was only superficially injured. Yes, it was annoying, but I wasn't physically impaired beyond an irritated feeling. The wound was more of a large abrasion -- and the pain was on the same scale. It was nothing that would keep me from my work. I had performed more strenuous tasks with greater handicaps.

Victoria led me through a group of police officers to the the middle of the church. The wooden scaffolding had broken down completely and was strewn about the place. It covered the altar, pews and much in between. Many decorative items had been crushed by the impact and randomly strewn about the floor, some torn and twisted into a parody of their own self.

Above all there was a layer of coarse, reddish sand. With reluctance I touched the substance and braced myself for the same impact I had felt back at Baker Street. When nothing happened, I rolled a few grains between my fingers and brought them to the tip of my tongue. There was a hint of salt, a sharp and metallic taste that remained. So the initial reaction had been an explosion, which was probably triggered through me as I moved the ceramic tile. That didn't explain the sand, but it brought me back on more stable ground, as at least a part of it was explainable through mundane means.

I stepped cautiously through the rubble, inspecting all parts I could find, but nothing unusual jumped out at me at first glance. No, it was the *absence* of certain parts that was suspicious. Only the wood had been destroyed. If I wanted to kill some people, I would've made sure the ceiling came crashing down on them, at least. Victoria appeared at my side then, the arm of a destroyed statue in hand, pointing its fingers at me with a grin.

"Want to see the exact spot we found you in?"

"It's closer to that door, isn't it?"

"Only you would remember the exact place you were blown up in."

"What can I say? It's what I do. Remembering, that is. Not being blown up." The familiar, light humour came easily. We fell back into the same patterns naturally, and I already knew that every moment shared in joy would make it even harder to say goodbye in the end.

The floor, on the other hand, looked quite serious, as it was bloodstained. I could make out parts of my coat clinging to the splintered wood. The sand grains in the vicinity were soaked in red liquid. Parts of Watson's garments were still stuck under a wooden beam, ripped and crushed together with a statue of an angel, whose face was the only thing still intact, staring at me with dead eyes. It really didn't look like anyone had made it out alive, and I thanked God for having sustained only such a shallow wound.

Now, the work some people would describe as *tedious* began. It was true that this detective work was usually associated with my brother -- but I had always been one step ahead of Sherlock, so why not in this matter? Where *he* needed to see the evidence, *I* could deduce the sequence of events from just the rough details laid out to me. And I was oh so rarely wrong -- which is exactly why my failure in Milan weighed so heavily on my conscience and soul. It forced me to go back to actually applying myself in the field now, testing my own skills to make sure I could still employ them. No one else seemed to realise my internal struggle, but I felt humiliated regardless.

After I took a deep breath and pushed these thoughts as far away as possible, I carefully cleared away the rubble to reach the floor. Plank after plank, ceramic shards and decorative metal wandered through my fingers, none particularly interesting on its own. Then I laid eyes on a sparkling, round piece of metal: A pocket watch with a battered lid, chain torn. It could be opened still and showed a picture of Watson's late wife Mary. The hands of the watch stood still, but I pocketed it regardless.

With Victoria's help I worked my way down to the stone flooring. She hadn't once asked about the sand, but I could feel that she simply didn't want to discuss these details in public. I would have to do my fair share of explaining later. We then moved to the altar, where I had originally found the clay figurine. Shards of some sort of pottery vessel were left on the charred ground, clearly remnants of the small bomb I had suspected to be the cause of the incident, as the material didn't match up with anything else we had found so far. We picked up all the pieces we could find and placed them into a little box one of Victoria's agents politely carried after us.

"I didn't expect this to survive the blast," I mumbled.

With my fingertips I carefully picked up the ceramic plate with the painted ankh, which had been partially hidden underneath a piece of cloth. It was still intact, though slightly scratched, and gleamed as if mocking me.

"I've never seen anything like it," Victoria said.

I agreed. It was an odd thing to leave behind, but it had to be significant. An ankh means life… eternal life? The symbol itself was old, but the plate seemed new. How did it connect with the playing figures… or indeed any of this? I inspected the fragments of the small explosive device for any clues. Burnt cloth, broken pottery shards and twisted metal parts clearly told of the small, round device that had almost been our downfall. There was writing on the shards. Curious. But it was too dark in the twilight of the church to make out much of importance -- for that I would have to clean and arrange the broken parts correctly.

The police force became impatient, voices growing louder by the minute. I turned my attention away from the bomb remnants and took in my surroundings, committed them to memory. The old, deserted church, covered in layers of dust, was now shrouded in an additional layer of sand. The restoration work had been abandoned for quite a while, probably due to a lack of money. There were no valuable items in sight, and what had been decorative tinsel around the altar was smashed by the collapsed wooden planks.

It was the perfect place to lay a trap because you could be sure that no one else would want to enter here except us. And even if anyone did: The clay figurine would have been of no interest to anyone else. So it had *definitely* been set up for us. What a devious and… yes, I admit, *clever* thing to do. I sometimes tended to underestimate the intelligence of my adversaries.

"We have everything?" Victoria asked as she glanced at the policemen.

"Yes, I believe so."

"Dr. Watson is probably worried about you."

I laughed. "He knows that there's nothing to worry about. I am very well capable of looking after myself."

Victoria smiled and gestured to the exit of the church. I went ahead while she gave instructions to some of her agents. The cold air assaulted me as I stepped out of the large doorway and I drew my shoulders upwards to protect my neck from the breeze. How I missed my own coat and scarf. Victoria emerged from the church after a few minutes, and I followed her into the carriage that had brought us here. A tall agent with black hair deposited the box with the bomb fragments on the seat opposite to me and wished us a good return journey.

After we returned, Victoria convinced me to join her for a light luncheon. We fell into a pleasant exchange of information about the last twelve years, in which I learned a great many things about the woman, who was still the subject of my admiration. I wasn't surprised about the fact that she never had a partner during all these years. It only showed that she would never move past Sherlock, and subsequently there would never be a place for me. Now there was a weird atmosphere between us, comprised both of the closeness and trust of old friends, and the heartbreak of jilted lovers -- even though we had never shared that particular bond.

After the meal we sought out Watson. He had fallen asleep and I thought it better to let him rest while we caught up. Frankly, I could've done with some sleep myself, but alas, I had no time to waste on such a thing. That was something you did when the mission was over.

"Ah... there you are," the doctor mumbled sleepily and sat up slowly, after I shook his shoulder to wake him. "I am feeling much better now. That dreadful headache is all but gone. For how long ..."

"Almost four hours, Dr. Watson," Victoria answered readily. "We took the liberty of examining the site of the explosion without you, as you clearly needed more time to recuperate. I wanted to go alone, but Mycroft insisted."

So she was now calling me by my first name in the presence of Watson. Well, if he was observant that should've told him more than I ever wanted. But maybe he simply didn't notice? The doctor carefully swung his legs out of bed and winced slightly. When he lifted the blanket, I could see that blood had seeped through the dressing on his leg.

"I've prepared a change of clothes for you. Take your time to get dressed and meet us in the dining room. We have found some... clues in the church we should look at together," Victoria said and exchanged a glance with me. "I will send one of my men to change the bandage."

We left the doctor to wake up properly and walked together through the spacious villa, towards the dining room on the second level. A number of agents were posted throughout the building -- a smart precaution, but probably unnecessary. And even if we couldn't exclude the possibility of another attack, who could even protect us from these supernatural forces? I didn't voice these concerns and we reached our destination in silence.

Someone had placed the evidence box on a large table in the middle of the room, so we took out the pieces and assembled them as well as we could. There were a lot of parts missing, but what we spread out on a sheet of white cloth slowly painted a picture. The round pottery container had once roughly been the size of two fists and densely packed with a highly flammable powder. I touched the remnants briefly to my tongue and confirmed my earlier suspicion of gunpowder.

The noise of a door hinge alerted me to the presence of Watson. Now clad in the Secret Service uniform, he carried himself... rather differently. With a raised head and drawn back shoulders, motions more controlled and precise, almost all traces of the soft doctor were miraculously gone. What remained was the military man he had once been, surfacing once again in the constraint of the uniform. Enhancing the picture of a veteran was his limping gait -- which was evidence of the large wound he had sustained in the explosion. I wondered briefly what was going on in the good doctor's head at that moment. But if the situation was troubling to him, he didn't give any indication, but joined us at the table to inspect the dusty, dirty assortment of rubble.

"We removed what was left of the explosive device from the church, so the police can get to work," Victoria explained and gestured to the various pieces. "But also so we can examine it properly and get a clue as to who built it."

"I can't believe we know so little about who is behind all this," Watson said bitterly, without addressing me directly, but it stung nonetheless.

"The evidence is inconclusive. We know of the assassin, but she may just as well be a henchman in this. It reeks of plotting and scheming, and she didn't seem the type," I elaborated. "I told Victoria the story behind our journey to Rome and the way forward. You can speak freely in her presence."

"The way forward? But we hit a dead end, didn't we?" the doctor asked confusedly.

"We picked up the parts of the bomb -- everything we could find that had not been blown to smithereens. It leads us to believe that we have to get to Egypt as fast as possible."

Watson looked like he blanked out for a moment.

"Egypt?" he exclaimed. "Please tell me this is a joke! There is no way Holmes is in Egypt!"

"My brother is not only very probably in the country of the Nile, but if the signs on the remnants are to believed, could also be in great danger," I said gravely, the tension and sincerity of my voice leaving no doubt that it was all too real. "Are you prepared to make the journey in your current state, Dr. Watson?"

He straightened his posture, just like a soldier would do before addressing a higher ranking officer. "It sounds... a bit farfetched, I admit. But if you believe that this is the only chance we have to rescue Holmes, I have faith in your judgement."

"Good," I answered and ignored Victoria, who looked at me expectantly. No doubt she expected me to ask her to join us. Well, I had no intention of doing so.

The idea of Egypt always had a slightly mysterious aura to it -- something with which many British were so enthralled lately, they decorated their homes with as many Egyptian artifacts as they could find. I had never understood the fascination, but it also hadn't passed me by unnoticed.

"But even if these objects point to Egypt, it's an impossibly large country. How would we even find Holmes?" Watson asked.

"The bomb has given us all the clues we need. So conveniently even, I am suspecting another trap, but it's the only trail we have, and it would be a folly not to follow it. We'd only risk Sherlock's life," I explained. "I draw your attention to this part."

I picked up a piece of string with a pair of small pliers and held it up to the bright light of a chemical lamp on the table. Watson couldn't see anything out of the ordinary and told me as much.

"This was used to detonate the bomb. I suspect it was secured with the ceramic tile and our actions dislodged it. But the deviousness with which it was set up is not important -- the material itself is." The others listened to my account and eyed the dirty, ragged string I dangled in front of their eyes. "The fibres are exceptionally long and strong. Ordinary natural fibres have much shorter strings, which make them less durable. But this cotton is remarkably solid. Only one type of cotton has these qualities: We call it by its Latin name *Gossypium barbadense* or more commonly 'Egyptian Cotton'."

"Remarkable," Watson whispered reverently.

"Don't thank me. Thank the monograph my brother has written on the strength of natural fibres and their inherent differences. If he knew I had read it and used the information to unravel the clues, leading to his very own rescue, I would never hear the end of it."

Victoria laughed softly in response.

"Which brings me to the second clue," I continued, put the string down and pushed some shards of what seemed to be a broken pot, into the light. "We couldn't find enough to completely reconstruct it, but the parts we have tell a frightening story."

The surface was littered with small paintings, which I knew to be hieroglyphs. They were dusty, but rather new in origin, which made them easier to decipher.

"The writing is not complete, of course. But one name is repeated all over again: *Seth*. The Egyptian God of chaos and war, the desert and storms. They also call him '*The Trickster*'."

"You can read hieroglyphs?" Watson asked in surprise. "But, how?"

"Only rudimentary. A while ago I studied the Rosetta stone and several other texts out of the desire to expand my knowledge," I responded. "It's not a skill I can employ very often, but even though the circumstances are dire, I am nonetheless happy that it could help me now. Though the rest of the text is not as clear, it talks of something happening at the full moon -- which is in two weeks -- and a... *desert wind*, whatever that means. I cannot decipher everything, but *something* is about to happen in Egypt, and I fear for my brother's life -- now more than ever before."

"That might all be logical, but there's just one detail you haven't taken into account at all. The vast amount of sand in the church. There's no way that much could've fit into the bomb, and I didn't find another source."

Why did Victoria have to still be so perceptive? My mind readily supplied a number of excuses, but I just knew they wouldn't be any good. And I didn't want to lie to her either. Then the doctor surprised me by speaking out first.

"Our journey has been accompanied by... strange happenings. Forces that defied any reason. We've encountered one of these incidents in the church," he explained, voice calm but determined. "I know it sounds strange, but ever since Dover these forces have tried to thwart our progress and have made many attempts on our lives. If I tell you that we were assaulted by a small sandstorm in the church, would you believe me?"

I scrutinised Victoria's face for any sign of ridicule, but I found merely disbelief.

"Mycroft?" she asked and turned to me. "Is that true?"

I took a deep breath. "Unfortunately, yes."

She shook her head. "What kind of incidents?"

"Several times we encountered a violent wind or some kind of gale that had no natural origin," I added and intentionally left out the story about my arm. This was unbelievable enough already. I

146

wondered then why the burning feeling hadn't warned me about the trap, like it had in the streets of Milan. But no, that was pitiful. Me, relying on such a... thing?

"I can't believe you would lie to me, but it sounds rather... fantastical."

"Then don't worry about it. We'll leave soon, and then this won't affect you any longer."

"What are you talking about? I'm coming with you!" Victoria announced.

"You will do nothing of the sort," I said icily, having fully expected this turnout. "This doesn't concern you beyond the boundaries of your city."

"You will *not* keep me from Sherlock! No matter the... forces that work against you!" she shouted. "This mission is now mine as much as yours!"

"Mission? Oh, dear..." I laughed bitterly. "Victoria, this '*mission*' isn't sanctioned by headquarters. I already appropriated critical gear, a royal train and convinced an agent to act against orders to get here. Haven't you read the telegrams? They must have informed you by now!"

"They have."

"Well, I guess everything's settled then."

"It is. I'm coming with you," she slammed her fist down onto the tabletop, making the fragments of the bomb jump on impact.

"I won't drag yet another person around, who is only *weighing me down*!" I exclaimed, my head already growing warm.

"Excuse me?" I heard Watson harrumph, but ignored him outright.

"We were never supposed to meet again, so just pretend it never happened."

"I can forget *you*, Mycroft, but I will never forget Sherlock! You can't stop me from helping him!"

It took all I had in me not to take a step back. If I had ever needed any proof of my love for Victoria, I would have found it in the way her words stabbed my heart, cruelly and efficiently.

"Fine. Do as you like. But don't expect me to look out for you. The same goes for you, doctor," I spat, anger colouring my pronunciation.

"Fine," Watson mirrored my tone of voice, straightening his posture, then exchanged a look with Victoria, who just shook her head disappointedly.

"No matter what you say -- you need me. I can secure transport to get us closer to Egypt, which will leave in the morning," Victoria said. "Be assured that I *will* support you to the best of my abilities."

"But only two weeks? We need at least one to reach the other continent, and only if we can catch a ship across the Mediterranean Sea in time. We don't even know the schedules... if they even match up with ours!" Watson let out with a frustrated sigh, the tension in the room now higher than ever before. "This is impossible!"

"Don't underestimate the power of the Secret Service. I can arrange for *something*, I just know it."

"Then get to it," I dismissed her like a servant.

Victoria huffed, but didn't give in to my taunt. "I have sent for a proper dinner. We can figure out our options before then. You should rest while you can. I'm not happy about the fact that you are about to travel with all those injuries, but I won't be the one to stop you."

We stared at each other, not at peace, but in a silence that expressed a temporary truce. I took a deep breath and first smoothed down my hair in a well-practiced gesture, then did the same to my clothes, straightening them in an effort to regain composure. In the process my hand brushed against the contents of my jacket pocket. It contained the first clay figurine, the ceramic plate and another item.

"I pulled your watch from the rubble, doctor," I said and handed the battered piece of round metal to the man. "It's broken, unfortunately, and the chain is torn. But I believe you might want to hold onto it, regardless."

He took it with a smile, expressing gratitude. The metal was dented, but the mechanism to open the lid was still working. The hands of the watch had indeed stopped, but the picture behind the glass was still intact. It showed a drawing of his late wife Mary, fashioned by none other than Sherlock Holmes himself, who had been forced to draw her after Watson discovered his surprising skill with the pencil.

CHAPTER 8

I don't hate him. He's dim and annoys me.

Victoria had indeed arranged our transportation in less than a few hours after the discussion. Our plan was now to travel to the city of Catania by train and then catch a ship on its way to Egypt. If we didn't miss the departure, it would take us to the African continent with some days to spare. If we *did* miss it... well, that just wasn't an option.

I slept through most of the first leg of our travel, which was a clear sign of my body in more need of rest than I was giving it. I knew that if I were to disregard my health further, it would come to haunt me later. My injuries were nothing compared to Watson's, even though I had to sleep on my stomach to allow them to heal. The gash on the doctor's leg flared up briefly and brought only pain and worry. He would carry a scar, there was no doubt. But the doctor played it off -- he was host to so many scars already, it would be stranger to see a part of his body unharmed.

While we were on the train, we had entertainment in the form of Victoria's desire to tell stories from my brother's university days. They included the real sequence of events of 'The Gloria Scott'. Watson had a good laugh on Sherlock's account, and I couldn't blame him, even though I felt old beyond my years hearing my youth recounted this way.

Despite everything that had been said between us, Victoria never stopped her subtle advances. I reciprocated none of her gestures. There was something about the way she tried to keep me close, while I knew she was only with us to rescue Sherlock, which made me feel unsettled, and I tried my best to keep a more professional distance between us. At least Watson made no attempt to inquire further.

Finally -- after two full days -- we arrived. The air in Catania felt almost like spring, with temperatures just above freezing and no snow to clutter the landscape. Still, we were almost too late. After the train drove into the station right by the harbour, I let Victoria usher us through the crowded space, right to the seafront. We boarded the huge, elaborately decorated cruise ship *Aurora*, which departed as soon as we had set foot on its deck.

It was on board the *Aurora* we were looking towards five days of forced vacation, unable to do anything but wait for the ship to arrive in Alexandria. True to the rules of our training, we tried our best to lie low and recuperate as well as we could. But even though I rationally knew all of this to be true, I had a strange, nervous energy about me, which stemmed mostly from my bad conscience. The plight of my brother was always in the back of mind and accused me of relaxing while he could be in mortal danger. It certainly didn't ease the wait, even though Victoria had actually managed to acquire two of the most luxurious cabins aboard. It was a nice change-up from the train benches and it could only do us good.

So it came to be that Ian Ashdown and his wife, as well as their associate Richard Brewer became the most interesting people on board the *Aurora*. News travels fast, no matter where you are, and the community on board a ship is tiny at best. Staying hidden inside our cabins helped our recuperation immensely, but it only wrapped us in a shroud of mystery. As a result, it was impossible to keep a low profile, and we agreed to mingle with the other passengers for the last days of the journey. Rumours were getting out of hand as it was, and our very ordinary presence would hopefully help to dispel some of the more outlandish ones.

On the third day I found myself at luncheon with Victoria and Watson in one of the ship's big ballrooms, amidst the murmuring crowd. It was weird being under scrutiny like this, when I was used to acting from the shadows. Sure, a job sometimes required me to be visible, but there is only so much one can do while being the centre of attention.

The ballroom was a grand thing, used for luncheons, dinners and after-dinner entertainment. As the biggest room on the ship, it was the only one which could hold all the first- and second-class passengers for these occasions, which totaled about 100 people. I estimated roughly 250 passengers to be on board -- without the crew, with which the count should have reached 300 in total. The third class dined on a lower deck, distributed between smaller rooms. I was sure that if I were to have a look at the passenger manifest, my estimations would hold up.

Our chosen table was situated close to a wide door, opened on this sunny day to let the guests enjoy the calm, blue sea and fresh, salty air to complement their food. It did wonders for my appetite, and even Watson seemed rejuvenated after the fight with his stomach for the first two days of our voyage. For such a small vessel, it was very opulently decorated, but you could see the years of service at sea clearly in the washed out colours and worn down wood, bleached by sun and rain. Far from dilapidated, it gave everything a charmingly rustic atmosphere, which I actually enjoyed a great deal.

We fell into an easy chat about the dreadful weather we had left behind in London, happenings in the city and listened to Victoria describing the wonders of Paris, including tips on where to get the best fish should Watson ever visit. We talked about anything and everything except Egypt, Italy and Sherlock Holmes. People, who had been eavesdropping, lost interest when I delivered the final blow and started to recount my mother's best cake recipes. Much to everyone's dismay, we turned out to be perfectly ordinary people.

But some persistent individuals didn't seem to be deterred by our attempts and shadowed us all through the luncheon. Luckily, most of our injuries were easily hidden beneath clothing -- not the agent's uniforms, some more personal, inconspicuous items -- but the bandages on my right hand were not so easily shielded from the inquisitive view. Even though I had been using it to eat and perform other tasks as if it wasn't injured, it didn't help to completely sell the illusion.

After luncheon, Watson excused himself, which was no surprise. He had been a bundle of barely contained energy all day and itched to explore the ship. It surprised me to see such an initiative in him, but I supposed he didn't take well to having been locked in his cabin for a few days.

"Now that we don't have to look after him anymore, how about we enjoy ourselves a little?" Victoria broke the silence that had ensued after the doctor left us to order a drink at the bar.

"I have absolutely no idea what you're on about," I said while swirling the remnants of my acceptable coffee in the small cup.

"Of course you don't. I was thinking we could take a look around the ship together. I'm just as anxious as our friend to see the vessel in detail."

I nodded, as I was feeling ill at ease myself. Improvising one's way out of a tough situation was one thing. Doing so without knowledge of all the options was foolish at best and prone to fail at the most inopportune moment. While I wasn't expecting anyone to get to us here, we weren't safe from everything. So far I had gotten a child killed and the doctor blown up during our short trip, and I couldn't shake the feeling of something else going very wrong, very soon.

Watson had received his drink and raised the glass in our direction before exiting the room. I noticed several heads following him, mostly female. Objectively viewed, he did have his own, peculiar charm... I suppose.

"You think we should follow him?" Victoria mused, observing the way my eyes trailed the good doctor as he exited the room.

"He should be able to behave himself for a while. I don't have the highest expectations, but that, at least, should be manageable -- even by him."

My colleague leaned back in her chair, crossed her legs and made a show of using her decorated hand fan coquettishly. "You don't think very highly of the poor man. Your animosity is thinly disguised, dear."

"I don't hate him. He's dim and annoys me. It's as simple as that."

"Your brother holds him in high regard, though," she continued. "I can see why, too. The way he's hurrying after him all the way to Egypt is commendable."

"Didn't you jump right at the chance to ..."

"Shut up!"

I chuckled softly at her played indignation. But I knew that I was also guilty as charged. There we were, three people stumbling about the world after Sherlock Holmes. Victoria didn't even have to point it out, we knew it to be true for all of us.

A small silence settled over the table as the room cleared out around us. It was the familiar quiet we had always been so good at sharing. From the corner of my eye I watched Victoria busy herself with the table decoration, pushing a piece of tinsel around with her finger. She was clearly waiting for me to make a move, so I did.

"Care to join me for a little walk, my dear? The weather is ever so nice today."

She smiled a genuine smile and took my offered hand, then linked her arm with mine to form the picture of a perfectly happy, married couple. I allowed the fondness that wallowed up inside me to take over for a moment, if only because it helped to sell the illusion.

We walked out into the sunshine, which was blinding after the twilight of the room. The sea sparkled calmly in the rays of the midday sun and the horizon was shrouded in a low hanging mist. Our surroundings seemed so peaceful, I was almost fooled into the illusion that we were actually on a pleasure cruise. We slowly walked down the side of the ship and neither of us broke the reverent silence.

Along the way we passed a number of deck chairs, lined up neatly, following the gentle curve of the railing. Most of them were occupied by passengers taking an afternoon nap after luncheon. Other people were absorbed either in quiet conversation or by the fantastic view. I wasn't searching for anything in particular, but took in all the details of the ship regardless. Some would call it an occupational hazard, but I knew better.

I couldn't turn off my brain if I wanted to.

So I counted the number of lifeboats while we passed them and plotted the quickest way to reach them from a number of places on the *Aurora*. I examined the deterioration of the paint on the ship's walls, noted that it had last been painted over five years prior, but the railing only a few months ago. The sun-bleached boards we walked on had probably never been exchanged, but were well maintained. I absentmindedly counted the passengers we passed to make sure they added up with my estimations.

"It seems like the weather will hold," I said as we reached the front, now standing directly in the rushing air, agitated by the ship cutting through it. I saw Victoria pull her scarf closer around her shoulders. The wind wasn't as cold as on the Continent, but it brought a certain, uncomfortable chill.

"This seems like a dream."

"More like a nightmare," I countered gravely.

"Oh, Mycroft. Try to relax!"

"How can I? This has been one long string of failures."

I didn't turn to watch my companion's face, but I could hear the smile in her answer. "Not all of it was so bad, now was it?"

"I got a child shot and let the killer escape. The only clues we can investigate have probably been planted so we'd find them, and we don't have any option than to comply and follow them. When I finally return to London, the people at headquarters will suspend me for insubordination… or worse. Have I missed anything?"

"You forget the look on their faces when they find out I flagged down a whole cruise ship in the name of the Service -- entirely for personal reasons," Victoria laughed.

"You didn't …"

"Come on! How else were we going to reach Egypt in time?"

A shadow passed over me and for a second all strength deserted my body.

"I am *so* sorry," was the only thing I could say, softly, barely audible over the wind. "I didn't mean for you to get into trouble, too. This could cost you your position in Rome."

157

A couple of people walked by and greeted us in a wary, but friendly manner. We watched them descend the stairs to the lower deck, where there was an open space in which a group had already gathered for games. Their conversations and laughter drifted over to us invitingly.

"I love my work, but …"

"That's exactly why I'm saying."

"Mycroft, just listen. I love my work, but I love Sherlock even more. I know that's not what you want to hear, but it's the truth."

I eyed the gentle waves intently. "What you see in my idiot baby brother is still beyond me."

"Everyone's an idiot compared to you, darling."

I had to shake my head. "Lately I've been feeling like a fool."

"And everyone has these days."

I shook my head. "That's just it. Everyone *else* has them. I don't."

"If it helps in any way, I think you're doing the best you can in these circumstances."

"It helps a little," I admitted.

"Should we join them down there?" Victoria pointed to the lower deck, where some other passengers had started another round of shuffleboard. I watched the teams push around the small wooden disks for a few seconds before I shook my head.

"I'm not really the game type of person."

"Well I am, and you won't leave your poor wife to fend for herself between those strange people, will you?"

Only seconds later, I found myself pulled along into the middle of the fray.

The day passed uneventfully. All too soon the shadows grew longer and night fell quickly. Victoria was occupied playing the darling of the masses and I kept an eye on the crowd, but saw nothing that seemed out of the ordinary. With the sun gone, the surrounding sea had grown dark, almost to a midnight black. Rationally, the water wasn't any different, but everything considered, it was a rather frightful sight. The moon had not yet risen and the winds were growing colder by the minute. Electric lights had been switched on some time ago and illuminated the deck, which made it feel like a warm island within the darkness. The games had been cleared away and tables arranged, so that the passengers might enjoy the night in the open with drinks and music.

We had been invited to join a group of gentlemen at their table, who were on their way to Alexandria to support the British troops. All decorated war veterans, they were amicable enough, but couldn't stop boasting with their war tales. If anything, it made me grow more fond of Watson, who never bragged about his deeds.

What an odd feeling.

Myself, I couldn't stand these men. Ian Ashdown, on the other hand, was fascinated.

"I was stationed in India," one of them with a rather prominent white mustache, little eyes and a strong jaw, said in a gravelly voice. He was clad in his uniform like all of them were -- the only difference being his rather corpulent form. I could've deduced more from the vast selection of medals tacked to his chest, but I refrained. He probably didn't earn them in battle, anyway.

"You lucky bastard. I had to stay behind in London," another nodded empathetically, his stiff beard touching the cloth on his breast every time he lowered it. "My health wouldn't allow me to travel."

"So what about you, Mr. Ashdown?" The first one asked and took a gulp of brandy, so large the glass was emptied, even though the waiter had just filled it. "Did you ever serve in the military?"

"Oh, please, look at me... I could never fight out there. I'm just a tailor!" I took a sip of brandy myself and smiled dumbly, while actually, I had saved all of their asses, while risking my life *repeatedly*.

The fat man laughed and his three friends joined in. "Ah, please do not think me mocking you," he assured me in hasty tones. "I sometimes forget myself when I have too much to drink... my wife tells me every so often. What brings you out here, then?"

"Oh, just some business in Egypt," I shrugged. "Nothing important."

The four veterans exchanged pointed looks. I knew what they were about even before the tall one with the ridiculous haircut opened his thin mouth, which was situated underneath a hawk-like nose, only separated by a rather poor excuse of a mustache. "So if it's nothing important why did you divert the *Aurora* all the way to Catania?"

"And how *did* you do that, anyway?" the fat one added.

160

"I say nothing important, but that's really only because I'm not at liberty to discuss details," I said with just enough authority in my voice. Victoria and I exchanged look, as if we had a shared secret. Well, that wasn't all that far from the truth.

"Well, not anyone can order a course change just like that," hawk-nose mused, to which the fourth man, who had never opened his mouth, just nodded in agreement.

"What does your husband do, exactly, Mrs. Ashdown, when he's not *tailoring*?" The long-bearded veteran addressed Victoria directly because he probably thought it would be an easier way to get to the truth.

My companion let out an amused laugh. "Oh, dear gentlemen, I'm afraid I can't tell you anything. We're under orders from the highest ranks."

"Victoria!" I said loudly, exasperated. "Please!"

"Oh, I'm so sorry, dear. This is all too exciting for me."

The men watched our exchange, which went perfectly, even though we had never practiced it. The mention of *highest ranks* should give them enough vague information to satisfy their curiosity.

"Please don't tell my associate we talked about this," I concluded the talk and waved for the waiter to refill my brandy glass. "He wouldn't approve. I've said too much already."

"Of course," the fat one assured me, after hesitating for just a fraction.

There it was. The cautious respect for the unknown man who could potentially hold a higher rank than you. A total turnaround from the way they had looked down on me for not being as heavily decorated. They realised I had no need to boast to defend my rightful status, because I was still on active duty, whereas they clung to their positions in name only.

Now, that was better.

As if to save the men from the awkward silence, we were interrupted by two people, who rolled out a piano from inside the ship and placed it in the centre of the space. A man in a tuxedo walked behind it with a purposeful stride, upright and proud. Some people applauded as they became aware of him. I took care not to stare at him too closely, even though he was devilishly handsome. It just wouldn't do while my wife was at my side. Not that it would do in any other situation.

"Ladies and gentlemen," the man stated loudly in a voice higher than I'd expected. "I'm afraid I have bad news for you tonight. My dear colleague Georgie has fallen ill and cannot perform for you."

A murmur of disappointment spread throughout the audience, and even the veterans looked sad. My eyes fell on a lone violin case. Ah, so tuxedo played the piano and was usually accompanied by this Georgie character.

"Dear, won't you volunteer?" Victoria said, loudly enough for the surrounding people to hear. "You always play such wonderful melodies for me."

She was as sharp with her eyes as I was myself. Always had been. And her mental capacity didn't seem to have diminished while we had been apart. I didn't know if she had any agenda or just wanted to set me up, but I didn't mind. Contrary to what my fellow men might think, I enjoyed a performance in front of an appreciative audience.

"You flatter me. But I really don't think I'd be up to the challenge."

"Nonsense. You'll do just fine," Victoria encouraged me.

"Right. Go on and play for us," hawk-nose smirked, evidently seeing my reluctance as fear to embarrass myself. "A piano by itself is nice to listen to, but a duet is always preferable."

"Would the gentlemen care to join me then?" the performer asked, well aware of what had transpired.

"I couldn't…"

But then he winked at me, and I had no more reason to keep up my false modesty. "Oh, alright. If you want me to embarrass myself so thoroughly, I won't deny you the pleasure, my dear."

I rose to the audience applauding my courage and walked the few steps to the middle, where the piano player handed me the violin. I tested the sound quality and coaxed a small melody out of the instrument to test it.

"I see you weren't just talk. Anything in particular you can play well?"

"Oh, play whatever you want. If I don't know the tune, I will improvise."

The man laughed and took a seat in front of the large instrument. "I hope you know what you're getting into… Ladies and gentlemen! May I present…"

"Ian Ashdown," I introduced myself and did a little bow and winked in Victoria's direction. "It's a pleasure to perform for you. I hope I can be an adequate replacement for tonight."

"Just don't play *too* well. You'll put poor Georgie out of a job," tuxedo remarked and lost no time in starting the first tune.

I closed my eyes and concentrated on the notes. Ah, I knew that one. He had started me off easy with a very well-known tune. After a few seconds I fell into the rhythm and accompanied the slow melody, swaying softly with the music, eyes closed all throughout the song. When it ended and the piano started a more lively tune, I did what I could do best: improvise. The happy melody floated through the audience into the mist, and from the ship's deck out onto the open sea.

While I *did* enjoy the performance, it also gave me a perfect opportunity to observe the crowd. I counted the passengers while I turned to the music and made note of the seemingly more important faces. All while Victoria looked at me adoringly, like I was the only person in the world that mattered to her. If only.

As Watson appeared at the railing of the upper deck, I spotted him immediately, but didn't let it interrupt the performance. He watched me finish the current song and another two, before I declared to have taken up enough of everyone's time already. The pianist thanked me dearly and shook my hand with both of his. I returned his smile genuinely, because who doesn't enjoy the attention of a handsome man?

I returned to the table, where the veterans stared at me with a mixture of admiration and disbelief. Many people back in London knew my little brother to be the extraordinary and enthusiastic violin player in our family. But what only few were aware of, is that I was the one who taught him. And as with everything else, I was better at it.

Much better.

"Marvelous performance, Mr. Ashdown," hawk-nose exclaimed and raised his glass. "That a tailor should know how to coax such harmonies out of this fine instrument!"

"You flatter me," I answered. "I merely dawdle in my free time to entertain Mrs. Ashdown. Think nothing of it."

"Nonsense," a familiar voice then sounded from behind me. "Very impressive. I have never heard you play like *that* before, my friend."

"Ah, there he is," I let my features light up as Watson stepped next to me. "My associate Mr. Brewer. I would be lost without him. He's keeping track of all the pesky numbers you need to keep a business afloat."

The other men laughed and we exchanged a few more jokes before they politely excused themselves. Watson took a seat at the table and we were alone at last.

"Thank god they're gone," Victoria sighed as soon as they were out of earshot. "How could you stand them?"

"I couldn't," I answered truthfully.

The waiter started to serve the soup on my order. That would keep other, curious people away from our table for a while, as it would have been exceedingly impolite to interrupt us during dinner.

"I haven't heard you play in such a long time, darling," Victoria smiled, her delight not even one bit faked. "Thank you for the performance."

I cleared my throat. "You are most welcome. But you must be aware that this wasn't for *your* benefit?"

"No need to be so unromantic," she laughed and took a sip of wine.

We had finished with our soup and were served a pasta dish complete with seafood in a creamy sauce. While I picked at the clams, I let my gaze wander. The piano player finished his performance for the night and the other tables had already cleared out, as the night air was fresh and chilly. After the climate we had endured in Italy, this felt more like a spring breeze to me, but other passengers were not so resilient. A few polite nods were given into our direction as some of the guests departed, but no one else attempted to talk with us beyond a few words of praise for my violin performance.

"Who are you looking for?" I asked Watson, who almost dropped his fork out of surprise. "You observe the other passengers attentively."

"Oh, I made the acquaintance of an elderly couple yesterday -- James and Agatha Hill -- and wondered if I could spot them in the crowd," he answered innocently enough.

"You left your cabin yesterday?" I asked.

166

"I… yes. I know we agreed not to go out on our own, but I felt so sick, I had to get some air. They approached me because I was apparently as white as a sheet. We talked about everything and nothing -- but mostly about Egypt. They had learned much about the country from a friend who is an aficionado of Egyptian culture."

"That's most helpful," I nodded. "And maybe too great a coincidence?"

"Is it really? We are on our way to Alexandria, after all. There are bound to be a lot of people interested in all things Egypt on board," he countered.

"Still, it's always wise to be careful, doctor," I insisted while he frowned at my patronising tone.

"Anyway, my thoughts drifted back to our conversation. And then I finally remembered where I'd heard the phrase *Desert Wind* before," he explained.

"Please, do elaborate," I urged him.

"I didn't think much of it back then, but about two years ago I treated a group of people in London, all with the same symptoms of sepsis," he recounted. "They had all cut their right index finger with what they called a *hallowed* knife… that turned out to be the cause of their sickness, because it had been ancient, rusty and incredibly dirty. Of the group of eight people, two ultimately died from the infection, which wasn't the proudest moment of my career. But what is important is that they were in engaged in a ritual of an *Egyptian* cult. One of the women told me the name as she teared up over her foolishness and warned me to never get in contact with the people of the *Desert Wind*."

"A most singular incident, doctor. You have done well in remembering the details," I commended him on his account.

"I could've done that sooner...," he said apologetically, but I waved his concern away.

"This is exactly the kind of clue we need to give us a starting point for our investigation in Alexandria." And maybe we wouldn't stumble about like headless chicken.

"Do you recall more about the cult?" Victoria asked.

"Unfortunately, this is all I know," he shrugged. "When the woman realised what she had told me, she seemed frightened to death. She pleaded with me not to tell anyone about the information she had given me, especially not that it had been she who told it. I didn't want to pry any further."

"That in itself is already suggestive. We shall endeavour to find out more about this *Desert Wind* group when we are on the southern continent. Well done, doctor."

Watson grinned proudly for having contributed to our investigation. The only thing missing from the picture was a wagging tail, as I could see him quite clearly as a dog, who brought a particularly large stick to his master, and wanted to be praised for it. But I had no time to dwell on this for long, because a high-pitched scream resounded through the ship and ripped everyone on deck from their thoughts. We jumped up, the cult and our dinner all but forgotten.

"The starboard side!" A man shouted and pointed into the direction. We followed the crowd -- myself with a mixture of curiosity and uneasiness in my heart. Why couldn't I go *anywhere* without a potentially dreadful incident in my vicinity?

Well, probably because I was usually the cause of it...

As we neared what seemed to be the centre of the commotion, the space became too crowded to go on. Victoria pulled us towards the stairs, so we could have a look at the scene from the upper deck. Luckily, only a small group of people had the same idea, which enabled us to get a good view.

A woman sat on the floor on the deck below us and held onto one of the maintenance staff's arms, sobbing violently. From up here, her words were unintelligible and almost immediately swallowed by the winds, which had picked up over the last hour -- coincidence or not? The scene was cast in a harsh illumination by an emergency spotlight, just now hastily carried over by another staff member. Half hidden beneath the tarp cover on top of one of the lifeboats, which flapped in the breeze, I could see the reason for her agitation: The bodies of both a man and a woman were lying lifeless in a pool of blood.

"She must've noticed the tarp, which had come loose in the stronger wind and during the process of inspection, she has found the bodies," I elaborated, listing the obvious facts. "It seems like whoever hid them there didn't fasten the ropes securely enough, so when the breeze picked up, it unraveled the knots."

"I can see even from here that their throats are slit. This wasn't a crime born of impulse, but a planned murder," Victoria added. "It must have happened inside the lifeboat. There's no other way to explain the amount of blood underneath them."

"Agreed," I nodded. "And there is no blood on the deck. The murder must have happened during the morning hours of last night. It would have been impossible to carry it out while everyone was awake and the winds only died down around 4 o'clock in the morning."

"So... do you think we have been followed?" Watson asked. "I don't know how anyone could've made it in time."

"You think this connected to us, do you doctor?" I raised my eyebrow.

"I... well, I can't discard the possibility," he shrugged.

"I didn't notice another person as we boarded the ship. It was a quick affair," Victoria mused. "Though they used the opportunity to restock their fresh produce for the kitchen."

I agreed, as my observations were similar. It wasn't completely impossible for anyone to follow us, as you could never dismiss even the smallest chance, but it was highly improbable.

"Shall we aid the investigation?" Watson wondered. "If this is even remotely connected to us, I wouldn't feel right to just ignore it."

"No, we cannot make ourselves known in that way," I answered.

Watson's shoulders sank. There was a murder and he could no nothing, which very clearly disappointed him. Maybe it was his sense of justice, or maybe he had just been around Sherlock for too long already. I wagered it was the latter.

"We can't do anything officially, but we still have a few days left on board the *Aurora*, and I intend to find the culprit before we land in Alexandria. I believe the captain will be glad for our help. We just can't reveal ourselves to anyone else."

"I understand completely," Watson was quick to assure me. "We shall get to the bottom of this murder!"

"The game's afoot then," Victoria added with a grin.

I simply shook my head.

CHAPTER 9

Not as preposterous as you might think

The crew had a hard time getting all passengers away from the location of the murder, and it took even more effort to convince everyone to return to their cabins for the night. We stood in the shadows and waited for the bulk of people to clear out before approaching the captain. He beckoned us to his office, and it was immediately clear that he was out of his depth with the current development.

We entered the small, cluttered space, which was almost completely occupied by a worn-out desk that had been screwed to the floor, and countless cabinets covering all walls, filled to the brim with books, documents and various exotic decorations. The man himself -- greying hair, a well-maintained full bread, strikingly blue eyes, corpulent form and short stature -- was sweating despite the chill of the night. He took a seat and gestured for us to close the door behind us. All three of us had barely enough room to stand in front of the desk without hitting anything off a shelf. The air was thick and uncomfortable.

The captain eyed me warily and I could see that he already held us accountable for the murder on *his* ship. The three strangers that had been forced upon him by a higher power. It was no surprise that he was cautious, and I couldn't blame him. We already suspected that the murder was indeed connected to our presence, after all.

"Captain Fraser, we would like to offer our assistance with the investigation," I opened the conversation as no one else made an attempt to. "While we can't do so openly, I believe we can still help you."

"How?" the small man asked and leaned back in his chair. No acknowledgement, no sign of gratitude, just doubt. Something in the diversion of the ship must've angered him greatly. I was just about sure that he had been pressured into making for Catania by a superior. That would explain why he hadn't welcomed us when we boarded. Well, that wasn't my concern right now.

"The culprit can't go far. We need to corner them sooner than later, but for that we need the cooperation of your crew," I paused just briefly, because what I was about to ask could very well be taken as an insult. "Do you trust every worker under you?"

Just as expected, the first reaction was a sharp intake of air. Fraser looked ready to launch into an argument, but then he just shook his head.

"This is... I might not like you, but if you can help me to lay hands on the murderer I will aid you. Yes, I *do* trust my crew. There are a few new faces in the kitchen this time around, but they're vouched for by older crewmen. They wouldn't be here otherwise."

I felt some of the tension dissipate from the room like smoke clearing the air. A reluctant cooperation was still better than none at all.

"If you can say so with conviction, we will assume that the culprit isn't among the crew, but rather one of the passengers. The

173

couple was in first class, but we can't exclude the others, as everyone can basically roam the public areas freely. I already have a plan to flush the murderer out of hiding."

The others eyed me with curiosity, the unspoken questions obvious. I chose to answer without them having to be posed.

"Tomorrow night after dinner, we will bring passengers of all classes together on the entertainment deck for an announcement regarding the murder. Attendance will be mandatory. You will tell this to your crew at the morning assembly and then again to the people present at breakfast. The message is clear: We will reveal who the murderer is."

"But you haven't even looked at the bodies... or their cabins!" Watson exclaimed. "How can you *already* expose them?"

"Doing so would only be excess work to confirm unimportant details," I countered. "But I suppose we will have the whole day tomorrow, so it can't hurt to examine them, if that satisfies your curiosity."

Watson shook his head. "So you know who the murderer is, then?"

"No."

"But then ..."

"Not *yet*, in any case. They will be at the announcement, both because they can hide in the crowd much more easily and because they want to see whom we condemn."

"Then *who* will you blame?" the captain asked.

"No one," Victoria said. "You will make them reveal themselves."

"Exactly. And that is because the killer is neither part of the crew nor the passengers. They are most certainly unplanned additions, just as we are. Subsequently they are much more likely to be connected to *us* than to the victims, which eliminates the need to investigate them further. I am already certain that the dead bodies belong to the very couple my associate interacted with yesterday."

Watson jolted in surprise, which only made him back into the shelf and push a ledger over the edge. It landed on the wooden floorboards with a resounding thump.

"I can tell you that their names are James and Agatha Hill. A wedded couple from Glasgow. That much is apparent from the passenger manifest and the confirming statements of some crewmembers," the captain explained.

"How did you know?" Watson asked me.

"I should've never let you people board my ship," Fraser interjected. "My gut told me not to, but I obeyed orders. Now there's two innocent people dead. Ah, don't look at me like that. They ran an agency for governesses, for god's sake! Who in their right mind would go to all the trouble and go after them on the ship?"

I appraised the captain once more. He wasn't as limited in his thoughts as I had assumed. Although he *did* hold the highest rank on a reputable vessel, that really wasn't conclusive evidence for anything. I had superiors with less brain capacity than a horse.

"Captain Fraser is right. Also they were left in a location that was easily discoverable, when the murderer could have just dumped them in the sea. It was a greater effort to arrange them in the lifeboat than to simply let them fall to their watery grave," Victoria added. "So someone made sure we'd see the bodies…"

Then it hit me.

"Where is the woman that found them? The one that cried out?"

"I had the ship's doctor accompany her to his rooms to give her a sedative," the captain answered. "Why? Do you think …"

I turned immediately and forcefully pushed the door open. The wood hit a man behind it, who threw some curses after me, but I already turned my back on him. Now I was glad for my previously pointless exploration of the *Aurora* -- because I was able to take the shortest route to the doctor's office. I sprinted through the narrow service corridors and dodged the occasional crewman, strafed one of them with my elbow and left many more angry words behind me. With a last burst of speed I reached the doctor's room at the other end of the ship.

The door was open. That wasn't good at all. Still out of breath I stepped through the doorway, the pocket watch with the wire ready in my hand as it was the only weapon I carried with me at the moment. Careless, utterly careless, I chastised myself in my thoughts.

There was no noise and no movement. The place seemed deserted, even though a yellow light bathed the room in a warm, welcoming glow, indicating a human presence. Either the doctor had left or… I had no need to elaborate further, as my eyes fell onto a person lying behind a desk on the floor. Before I knelt down next to him, I surveyed the rest of the room and inspected all corners as to not be ambushed, but there was no one else present.

"Doctor?" I asked after I confirmed that his heart was still beating. "Doctor, can you hear me?"

After a few gentle shakes, the man blinked his way back into consciousness. Shortly after he winced in pain, and as he sat up I could see why. The back of his head sported a large wound. Blood dripped down through his greying, dirty blonde hair and onto the white shirt, staining the fabric a deep red. His glasses lay on the floorboards next to his legs, crushed as if someone had stepped on them. He tried to say something, but his words only emerged as a pained groan. I stashed my pocket watch and helped the man to lean against his desk.

"This probably feels worse than it actually is," I explained to him, as he seemed to hear me despite the pain-induced daze in which he floated. "You're going to be okay. Let me clean this up for you, while you tell me all about what happened."

"My head is killing me," he mumbled.

"I would hope not," I heard Watson's voice from the door. He paced over and did his own assessment of the damage. "I can take it from here."

Grateful I backed up and focused on getting sensible information out of the victim. "Doctor…," I paused for him to fill in the gap.

"Gains, sir. Albert Gains."

"It's good that he remembers his name," Watson said.

"Dr. Gains. Do you recall what happened that made you end up on the floor?"

"Yes, I think so. I accompanied the woman to my office. The captain ordered it, but I would've done so anyway. After that dreadful find, you know, she seemed agitated and shaken. I can't blame her. So I thought I'd give her a sedative to help her sleep, but…"

Gains held his head briefly and shook it like in denial, which elicited a short noise of annoyance from Watson, who had to pause in his cleaning efforts.

"I turned my back to retrieve the pills from the cabinet. You see, the one behind my desk? That's where I keep the medicine, you know, where I can keep an eye on it. Then something hit me and I woke up with a terrible headache and you, sir, talking to me."

"So it was the woman who hit you?" I asked.

"I couldn't tell, sir. With my back turned and all," his words didn't come fluently, but there was no reason to doubt him. In my mind I cursed, but on the outside I bestowed a gentle smile onto the bleeding man, who had been injured through my inaction.

"Can you describe her, then?" I asked further, as I had only seen the woman from a distance. "Anything that struck you as odd, maybe?"

"She had long, brown hair. Wore normal evening attire… something in black and white. I couldn't really say…"

"Her face?" Victoria added.

"Ah, she was crying all the time, shivering, you know? I had to practically carry her along. Kept her face down and in her hands, so I didn't get a good look," Gains shrugged and looked apologetic. "Was she of any importance?"

"Good man, it was probably she who struck you down!" Watson exclaimed.

"Me? Attacked and defeated by a woman? Preposterous!" The ship's doctor laughed, but regretted his actions immediately as the motion agitated the wound on his skull.

"Not as preposterous as you might think," I remarked with a glance at Victoria.

A little while later, Captain Fraser joined us in the doctor's office, just as we put the man to rest on his own bed. Watson took care of his colleague dutifully, who drifted into a deep sleep as soon as his head touched the pillow, aided by a generous dose of sedatives.

"Now what happened here?" he asked wearily after he closed the door behind him. I quickly recounted the facts.

"...and I suspect the woman to be the culprit -- or at least in league with them. She alerted everyone to the presence of the bodies while we were present and disappeared conveniently afterwards," I closed my explanation.

"I can't very well round up all female passengers on such a vague assumption," Fraser sighed. "What happened is bad enough. The reputation of the company, and my own, will suffer badly if I openly suspect all women of murder."

"I won't ask this of you. We will go with the original plan," I assured him.

"How will an assembly help?" Watson asked.

"By bringing everyone together. I mentioned earlier that my plan is for the culprits to reveal themselves. We will achieve this by telling everyone the following words tomorrow night: The ship is to be searched from top to bottom, except the passenger cabins. We tell them that we're sure that the murderer is a stowaway and everyone has to remain in their cabins, to be identified upon request."

"That brings us no closer than we are now," Victoria remarked.

"Don't you see? The culprit has no place in a cabin -- and if all of them are occupied, they won't find one to hide in as soon as the passengers have settled. Though they could squeeze into somewhere before everyone returns to their quarters. Our cabin, for example, is large enough for someone to hide in a closet without us ever noticing. It would be an uncomfortable night, for sure, but still preferable to getting caught. Alternatively they might try to hide in the engine room or similar, but all of that doesn't really matter. We will have crewmen positioned at all paths leading away from the deck -- and whoever tries to leave early will be apprehended."

"That might just work," Watson nodded. "But what if it doesn't?"

"We have one last bottleneck: As soon as the ship anchors in Alexandria, we can check every passenger against the manifest one last time. But I'd rather lay my hands on them as soon as possible."

180

We all turned our heads to Captain Fraser, who held the ultimate decision. He let his gaze linger on Gains for a few seconds while he pondered the options, but I could see in his eyes that he had already decided.

"Let's proceed as you suggested. The thought of a murderer running free on my ship is enough to induce nightmares. If we don't catch them with your trick, I will order a search of the ship anyway, and include the cabins as well. It'll take longer and put more people at risk, but I don't see an alternative," the captain leaned against the wall as he talked, as if he were tired of it all -- which was probably more than true. "I can brief the crew in the morning, if you tell me what I should say."

I admit that I was slightly surprised to achieve this level of cooperation so easily, as his initial demeanour had been rather icy. Still, I wasn't about to complain.

We oversaw the transportation of the corpses into a room adjacent to the doctor's office for an examination the next day, when we'd have the benefit of sunlight and not just a flimsy electrical bulb.

I slept uneasy that night and woke to a dull ache in my arm, which mirrored the anxiety I felt about another possible encounter with the strange powers that had accompanied us. But this time we had a plan, and bar any complications during the day, I was sure it would prove fruitful. I was determined to be one step ahead. It just *had* to work.

After breakfast in our cabins, we adjourned to Doctor Gains' office to examine the Hills more closely. It wasn't important to our plan, but Watson insisted on a contribution, so I let him have his *fun*. The bodies were no longer under rigor mortis, so he carefully lifted their limbs and examined any and all places that could've been hurt in a struggle -- but there was nothing to find.

They clearly had been sedated and carried to the boat one by one. Agatha Hill first, her throat already slit when her husband was brought along after her. I pointed out that her nightgown was only partially sullied by blood on her back, whereas all of James Hill's clothes were soaked, which meant he was put down after a sizable amount of the red liquid had time to collect in the bottom of the boat. A very sharp blade had been used. There was only one, deep incision. It was all that had been needed. The air supply was immediately cut off, which hindered the victim from screaming and thereby alerting anyone.

The examination brought no new clues. I had looked out for any... odd marks, but if there had been foul play, it wasn't visible. Watson was irritated by the lack of evidence and Victoria shared his agitation despite my reassurances. They led me to the victims' cabin to continue the search. I knew that Watson forced himself to keep going mainly out of denial. He blamed himself for leaving his room without permission and subsequently getting to know the couple who had then been killed -- likely only because of the contact they had. He was determined to do everything in his power to contribute.

I indulged him this time. I knew all too well how he felt.

"Now I *know* there was no struggle," Victoria mumbled as she entered the room behind me.

It had the same layout as my own cabin with a bed that's just slightly too narrow, a low side-table, two chairs and a dressing table with a big mirror. What I could see of the luggage was neatly arranged on various surfaces, a stack of cases in the corner. The dressing table held a few commonplace items, but nothing more.

I didn't need to be in the room. Nothing in this cabin would've made any difference to the plan we had to carry out. Sure, I could now tell you more about James Hill's tendency to favour his left foot while walking or Agatha Hill's unhealthy obsession with mint-flavoured candy, but that didn't help me in any way. The course of action had already been clear, and all that was left was to fill in these boring details my brother called clues.

Still, I took pity on Watson, who did an admirable job of a proper investigation, and so I looked around the room for anything that might strike me as out of the ordinary. The couple wasn't connected to us by any means other than their unfortunate encounter with Watson, so there was no reason to examine their personal items too closely.

"They were abducted in their sleep, right?" Victoria asked then and pointed at the bed.

Surrounded by orderly objects, the neatly made up bedding didn't stand out at all -- but it was clearly left like that intentionally. Why else would the murderer have bothered rearranging the cloth after they dragged the victims out of bed, if not to direct our attention to it? I felt a peculiar chill as my eyes fell on a little bump in the middle of the bed, cloth tenting just barely. It could've just been a coincidence, maybe the murderer just had a strange sense of humour, but something in me knew that wasn't the case.

I raised the sheet carefully and laid my eyes on yet another clay figurine of the same type I had already seen twice. And underneath it another small ceramic plate.

"I'd like everyone to leave the room *right now*," I said calmly, but with emphasis.

Victoria didn't hesitate; she grabbed Watson by the arm immediately and pulled him out of the cabin into the hallway. We exchanged a glance, and after I gave her a subtle nod, she closed the door behind them despite Watson's vocal protest. There was no warning feeling in my hand, but there hadn't been for the last bomb either. This time I was prepared. Never say I don't learn from my mistakes.

A thorough investigation of the bedding and frame revealed nothing out of the ordinary. But as I couldn't move the cloth directly underneath the tile in fear of setting off another explosion, I wasn't yet assured of my safety. From a small sewing set on the dressing table, which had evidently belonged to Agatha Hill, I pulled a length of string and fastened one end into a loop. I put it around the figurine and partially under the plate, then carefully stepped back until I had reached the door of the cabin and joined the others in the hallway.

With a protective layer of wood between me and the present that had been left for us, I pulled at the string to dislodge it. Where I had expected the roar of a localised storm to greet me just like in the church in Rome, there was only silence. While it was lucky to remain unscathed this time, I wasn't too fond of this irregularity.

We entered the room together. The clay figurine had fallen over and the little ceramic tile turned on its face. I picked it up and found it painted with a simple picture of three circles that were crowned by a cross each. A religious symbol then? I had to find out more about the *Desert Wind* in Alexandria before I could be sure. Solemnly I handed the evidence to Watson.

"So there's no doubt," he stated.

"None at all."

CHAPTER 10

What are you implying, Mycroft?

When Watson arrived on the deck that night, Victoria and I had already taken our respective places near two of the five main exits. Most people were still dressed for dinner, and I too was clad in a tuxedo for the occasion, as anything else would've made me stand out. Victoria had chosen a simple, but elegant dress in shades of aquamarine that still gave her enough freedom to run after our suspect. It was a nice change to see her in such a feminine attire, but I much preferred her wearing her agent's uniform. It just felt right.

During the day, the captain had briefed all of his crew about the real goal of the evening. There was a chance that the culprit would find out about our plan this way, but it was slim and in no comparison to what we could gain. Under the pretense that the announcement was also meant for the working people, they would mingle with the passengers and monitor the passageways that we couldn't cover. They knew the ship much better than we ever could.

As the space filled up, the atmosphere grew nervous. People were anxious to be in such close contact with others, while the murderer was still at large. All through the day there had been fewer passengers in the common areas, and the ones that did venture out, stayed in groups of familiar faces. Everyone eyed everyone else suspiciously.

Victoria motioned for me to focus my attention on a lone man, leaning against a support beam. He seemed bored by the proceedings and didn't share the nervous feelings of his fellow shipmates. But I shook my head. This wasn't the person we were looking for -- I could feel it in my gut. I saw the pianist close by, and he nodded a greeting at me, amicably despite everything.

The voices around me grew louder as we waited. Electric lights cast their yellow glow on our heads and were reflected in the sequins of many accessories, making the mass of people sparkle like the sea in the midday sun. A thick fog was building on the water and slowly rose upwards, as if the ocean extended its arms to embrace the ship.

"Ladies and gentlemen, fellow passengers on the *Aurora*, my crewmen. Thank you for attending this announcement regarding the incident that took place yesterday. Firstly, I would like to let you know that we are one day behind schedule, but will reach Alexandria on the day after tomorrow. As an apology, we will offer you the return journey to England at a reduced rate. Visit my office during the day tomorrow, and I will personally hand out the signed vouchers."

There were appreciative murmurs among the people around me as Fraser mentioned the vouchers. He held the attention of all passengers on deck. I attentively searched the crowd for anyone who deviated from this pattern, but came up with nothing. My only hope was that my companions would be luckier as the most important part of the speech was still ahead.

"And that brings me to the reason we're all gathered here. As you all know, there has been a tragic incident yesterday, as the both James Hill and his wife, Agatha, have been found dead. There is no doubt that it was malicious violence that brought about their end, which means that there is a culprit, who is still among us. All lifeboats are accounted for and there is no other way they could've escaped."

The crowd grew agitated. It was one thing to suspect it, but having been told that they could, at this very moment, be in the same place as the person who slit another's throat, was something you couldn't just ignore. My gaze fell on several people, who kept to themselves, but none of them were women. No one had moved yet, either.

"We will not stand by quietly while a murderer is at large on our ship. Tonight we will perform a search of the entire vessel from top to bottom. If you don't want to be caught as a suspicious person, I strongly advise you to remain in your cabin, to be called upon only if needed. Everyone outside their assigned living quarters will be subjected to an inquiry. I apologise for this drastic measure…"

On the other side of the deck, a woman, adorned with a violet hat, detached herself from a group of people. In these close quarters it had been easy for her to blend in, but now she had broken cover and pushed through the bodies to reach the edge of the deck. And she was heading directly into the direction of…

"Watson!" I exclaimed loudly, without any regard for the captain's speech, and pointed at the woman. "Hat!"

Captain Fraser halted his words, much to everyone's confusion. We held eye contact for all but a second before I dived into the churning mass of people. Heat enveloped me as I pushed through the passengers sideways, one arm ahead to scout the way. People around me shouted and stumbled as I left a veritable chaos in my wake. A scream rang out, followed by the turning of the tide. Suddenly the passengers ran towards me, and I felt as though I were swimming against a strong current. Then I stumbled out into the open, and right onto the scene of another imminent murder.

Watson lay spread out on the floor, like captured prey underneath a predator, which had taken the form of a woman in a shorter, white dress. Her shawl had fallen to the ground, where it fluttered in the rising wind, which made a thick bank of fog roll across the deck. I was only a few feet away from the pair as she raised her arm, brandishing a golden knife, which glinted in the light.

There was no time to lose, and no indication that she might've seen me approach. I grabbed my walking cane and lashed out in a wide swing that came crashing down on the woman's hand. She gasped in shock and released the blade, which was flung far from her by the strong impact and landed at the feet of the passive onlookers. Quickly I twisted the handle of the cane just so, to release the long, elegant blade contained within -- but I wouldn't have needed to bother.

The good doctor bolted upright, threw his attacker off. In a blur of action he grabbed his very own pocket watch and pulled the deadly string from it, laying it neatly around the woman's throat and drew her back. They were sitting back to front on the floor, almost in a loving embrace, were it not for the threat of death hovering between them.

I stepped closer while I retracted the blade, sheathing it neatly back in its hiding place. The woman hissed, but didn't dare to speak against the tightly held wire. Her eyes, gleaming furiously at me like burning emeralds, left no doubt: It was the very same person who had escaped us in Milan.

There was much I wanted to ask her, but I settled for just one word.

"Why?"

She grinned and kicked my leg, which I ignored as if a mere fly had landed on it. If anyone were to dictate the course of action, it was me. She narrowed her eyes.

"Why? For the master of course," she squeezed out and laughed despite the string around her throat. "All for the master!"

Now that the situation seemed to be under partial control, the curious passengers flooded the space again and crowded around us. This was not something that should be done publicly. The masses soaked up any and all information -- rumours that we could never get rid of were already starting to make their rounds. Any more time out in the open would be a plain nuisance to me.

"Victoria?" I asked loudly.

"Almost there, just …"

I could see her fall to the ground in the crowd. A collective gasp of surprise went up along with her pained groan. Did the woman have an accomplice? I dashed forward. This time the people parted in front of me and I found my companion on the ground, holding her right hand close to her chest.

"What happened?" I asked as I fell to my knees beside her.

"The knife... I wanted to pick it up, but it was as hot as fire!"

The accursed piece of metal lay in front of her. There was nothing to indicate the heat that it had radiated. Cautiously I wrapped my hand in a handkerchief and tried to touch it, but to me it did nothing. It was of the same make I had previously seen in Dover, golden and coarse, decorated with symbols -- hieroglyphs!

"Show me your hand," I asked Victoria and held out mine. Carefully she placed hers on top, palm upwards. A pattern had been burned into her skin, which matched the one on the knife's handle. The same way it had been back at the beginning of our journey. As we both looked onto the damage, it faded right in front of our eyes, until only healthy skin remained.

"It's witchcraft!" a man shouted and veered backwards. Others followed him. "She's a witch!"

"There's something wrong with her!"

"A witch!"

I shook my head, despite the knowledge about the powers that had followed us. That was one thing. Superstition another. I exchanged a glance with Victoria, making sure she was alright.

"Listen to me, everyone," Captain Fraser walked into the middle of the commotion. "Please return to your cabins for the night. My crew and I will handle this. You can all sleep safely, knowing we have apprehended the culprit."

"How can you be sure?" one woman asked loudly.

191

"I'll burn your eyes out, then you *will* ....," the woman on the ground replied, to which Watson responded by pulling the wire tighter.

It took the captain and his men a while to clear the area, but finally the passengers had all filtered out. It took even longer and involved a lot of strong words, as well as advanced diplomacy, to convince the man to leave the interrogation of the woman to me. He didn't know who she was, or how she was connected to us, and I wasn't about to reveal any of it to him. In the end he only permitted us to have an hour with her before we'd had to hand her over. There was nothing more we could do, but make the hour count -- the captain's word was law on board his ship.

The room they had provided us with was small and badly lit. At least we were away from prying eyes. The woman didn't let herself be tied to the low wooden chair without protest, but as soon as she was secured her demeanour changed completely. I was almost compelled to wonder why we had taken so much precaution to detain such a dainty lady.

Her black hair pooled around her shoulders, lowered in defeat. Eyes, previously sparkling a vicious green were now lowered and filled with tears, their shine dimmed to just a fraction. Her dress was in disarray and torn at the sleeve, the shawl lost somewhere in the proceedings. I could see feelings of compassion rise in Watson's eyes, so I motioned for him to stand down. Victoria moved behind the woman as I straightened my posture and brushed the creases out of my suit.

"This time you won't get away so easily," I opened the interrogation. "Even if you manage to escape us now, the ship won't be in harbour for another day. Your only means to evade us is to commit yourself to a watery grave."

"Sir, please, why am I here?" she asked, her voice already broken from crying. "Why are you doing this to me?"

"Don't play innocent. Do you think I wouldn't recognise you after our encounter in Milan, brief as it was?"

"I'm scared…"

"As you should be. Now, you have just a little time to provide me with the answers I need, before we move on to more drastic measures."

The woman stared at Watson, but the good doctor just averted his eyes. I put the dagger onto the table, which I had carried with me in my handkerchief.

"This is a similar weapon to the one the doctor and I were attacked with in Dover. Unfortunately the last one was lost to the waves together with its owner. It would be a pity to have the same happen here," I continued, but there was only silence in the room. Our captive didn't even look at the piece of metal. "These are hieroglyphs. I am almost certain that you are in league with the *Desert Wind* cult, who abducted my brother to perform a sacrificial ritual."

The last words had never been uttered before. I had read them partly on the bomb back in Rome, but never told the others about it, as to not worry them even more. So the ones recoiling in shock were Watson and Victoria, and not the unknown woman.

"These symbols read 'Seth, God of the Storm. Calamity, Curse, Death.' It shows a picture of Seth killing Horus -- a piece of the Egyptian mythology. Is that what it is? Are you sacrificing my brother to Seth? Why?"

I slammed the dagger down onto the table, which made the woman jump in surprise, but she stayed silent. Still, her act was gone. She stopped crying and drew her shoulders upwards in a defiant posture. My accusations must have hit upon some sort of truth.

"Victoria, her purse."

The small, dark, plainly decorated bag that we had brought along with us, was emptied upon the table. A silver flask fell out, sounding hollow on impact. Empty. A few coins, red feathers, a pair of small spectacles. All dusted with a fine layer of sand that clung to fabric on the inside.

I stared at the small flask, which was engraved with the initials "S.M." and the name of a club that was all too familiar. My eyes darted back and forth between the woman and the singular item, and then, just like that, all fell into place.

"You're far from home, Moran, very far."

Her eyes widened in shock and then narrowed in anger. At me for figuring out her identity, or at herself for giving her confirmation so quickly, I didn't know. But now I knew just how this was all connected. Oh, it was so simple, I almost wanted to cry.

"You lost me, Mycroft," Watson interjected.

"Surely you remember Sherlock's return to Baker Street, Doctor? How you waited in the empty house for Sebastian Moran to appear and catch him?" I held out the flask with the initials. "The man has a younger sister named Elizabeth, who made a brief appearance at court, and I chide myself for not recognising her earlier, as she's sitting right in front of you."

"Moran?" Victoria asked cautiously. "Sherlock mentioned the name while he... resided with me after the fall."

"Sebastian is locked away for good, but it seems like another of his family has taken it upon herself to carry out an elaborate revenge plan. Tell me, have I always been on your list as the one who enabled Sherlock all those years? Or did you just want to get rid of Watson?"

"I don't have to answer to you."

"No, you don't, but that doesn't mean I won't be able to get to the truth. The letter was designed to lure me out specifically. It was a riddle only I could solve, and you knew that Watson would turn to me for help. But *you* couldn't possibly know of my involvement. No, that particular fact could have only come from a *very certain professor*..."

"What are you implying, Mycroft?"

"That Moriarty has simply switched from one Moran to the next to do his dirty work."

The room fell silent. I knew exactly what went through their heads, because the same was swirling around in mine. It was the only thing that made sense, as the longer I observed her, Elizabeth Moran seemed less and less capable of planning out this operation on her own. Maybe I just underestimated her, but my guesses were rarely wrong.

"You made a deal with the devil to help your brother, is that it?" I asked the assassin and brought my fist down on the table for emphasis. "And somehow the devil supplied you with the occult powers you need to take us down."

"Right. Occult powers," Elizabeth laughed haughtily. "Has the worry about your brother eroded your mind?"

"So you finally admit in having a hand in his abduction?" Watson exclaimed and ignored her taunt outright.

"I confess to nothing."

I released a drawn-out breath and pushed the desire to simply make the woman talk through physical means deep, deep down. That wasn't my style. Well, at least not in front of my companions. Yet.

"Your possible connection to Moriarty is reason enough for me to condemn you, Elizabeth. I wouldn't even need to draw attention to the red feather tufts still clinging to your unwashed hair and the abrasion on your hands I recognise from the examination of my own body after the explosion in the church."

Watson and Victoria were as quiet at the culprit as we all waited for her to react. There was no way she could still believe that there was any possibility for her to get out of this. She was involved with everything -- possibly even the mastermind behind the operation, as I couldn't yet be sure that the math professor was indeed still alive.

"You're right," Elizabeth then mumbled.

I raised my head in astonishment. I had expected her to speak out, but never so quickly.

196

"Yes, you're right about one thing. I have access to powers beyond your understanding. I *will* curse you and your friends. You shall never reach Egypt, I will make sure of it. Even if I die in the process!" the assassin hissed and twisted in her bindings.

Victoria was quickly upon her to restrain the movement, but Elizabeth showed no sign of stopping. Her face was split by a grin so wide it was almost unnatural. Watson instinctively took a step back, but I willed my body to stay, and so it did.

"You know about the church explosion and how it came to be," I stated quietly. "You've experienced the very same phenomenon recently, otherwise your fingers wouldn't be in such a bad state. Tell me, what do you mean by powers beyond my understanding?"

"I've told him that *you're* really the one to look out for, not your brother. But he wouldn't listen."

"Him? So you *are* working for Moriarty after all?" Watson asked. "Who else could bear such a grudge against Holmes?"

The woman averted her gaze, stopped her movements as if her strings had been cut, and sank into herself, head low, her chin almost touching the torso. At first I couldn't make out that she was talking to herself, as the noise of the waves crashing into the ship's hull and the rising wind overpowered her speech. But then I heard her mumbling rough words, breathily and continuously. I shook her shoulder but that didn't interrupt the flow of syllables, if they even were words that had any coherent meaning.

Then I saw her wince in pain and not a second later the regretfully familiar odour of burnt flesh permeated the air. I grabbed

197

her hair with my right hand and pulled her head back, only to reveal the most startling sight I had ever laid my eyes on: The front of her dress, just in the hollow of her neck, was singed, embers still glowing and ill-smelling smoke was rising.

I lost no time to confer with my companions, but reached for what I could make out through the burnt holes in the white cloth to be an amulet around her neck. The force I employed to pull it away was considerable and the lack of resistance I received from the damaged string made me stumble backwards. The hot metal burned my hand and I let it fall to the floor with a colourful curse.

"Mycroft!" Victoria exclaimed and was immediately at my side as I clutched my hand tightly. Despite the brief contact, it felt like the metal had wormed itself into my very flesh, making not only my palm feel like burning hot magma, but sending a heat radiating through my body that was like nothing I had ever experienced.

"Destroy that infernal thing!" I yelled and pushed her away. "Quickly, before it burns a hole into the floor!"

She whirled around to see the amulet already starting to set the carpet on fire. The wind outside had picked up to a frightening degree and roared fiercely. I hoped I had only imagined the ship tilting ever so slightly. Watson and Victoria had picked up heavy objects and brought them down on the piece of metal while I sat frozen, despite the agonizing pain.

Finally there was no denying the obvious, horrible truth any longer. We *were* facing powers beyond our understanding -- something I had never thought possible. Time and time again I had pushed the facts out of my mind, but they always came back, stronger and more menacing than before. I could always rely on my wits and vast knowledge to make sense of everything that life threw at me, and my mental faculties had never once deserted me. But these... happenings had no logical explanation, no sensible root. I didn't... simply couldn't predict or use my intellect to work against them.

It frightened me like nothing else had in my life. There and then the reality of my situation sank in: I was on a ship, locked in a room with a woman, who could summon up the very forces of Nature itself to kill us all at any moment -- possibly even sink the ship. How was I supposed to fight against... *that*?

A loud noise brought me back to the present and I saw Watson bring the handle of his pistol down onto the amulet repeatedly. He dented the metal and made parts of it fly into all directions. With a fierce determination he kept on hacking away until the amulet was all but a twisted, dented piece of metal. The smell of charred fabric mingled with the sweet aroma of burning flesh and made me feel sick. The cabin air was saturated with a thick, black smoke, which made it hard to breathe. As Victoria flung open the door, my gaze wandered automatically to our captive, but she was unconscious and unable to flee.

My arm was burning from the inside and the pain was too much for me to bear, so I followed her into the darkness.

CHAPTER 11

This isn't a game!

The world was still dark, but there was a cool wind on my skin. There was the salty smell of sea water, but also a trace of rotten wood and curious spices. I blinked into the cautious light of the day, which filtered through a thick fog reluctantly, and felt the light rain on my face, slowly soaking the cloth that had been put on top of me as a blanket. The rays of the sun seemed to make the haze glow. The atmosphere was eerie, almost serenely quiet.

"Where am I?"

"Mycroft!" Victoria appeared in my field of view and fussed over my hair as she smoothed it back, out of my face. I felt that the strands were already damp. "You're with us again!"

"Took you a while," Watson added with a smile in his voice.

I summoned my strength and sat up, which made the flimsy wooden stretcher underneath me creak in protest. A look around confirmed my suspicion: We had almost arrived at the harbour. Even through the uncharacteristic fog I could make out the stone buildings in the distance. We were positioned on the upper deck, above the bulk of the passengers. Next to me was another stretcher, with a person bound to it.

Elizabeth Moran!

"Is she…?"

"No, she's just unconscious. Just as you were," Victoria shook her head. "We couldn't wake either of you, so the decision was made to take you to headquarters. Well, it was made *for* us, really. Captain Fraser wants none of us on board a minute longer than necessary."

There was a spot that remained uncrowded on the lower deck, as everyone kept a respectful distance. Two crates stood at the railing, ready to be brought ashore. It felt like a funeral, and in a way I suppose it was.

"Did you alert the people here?" I asked Victoria.

"We had no way of getting a message to them, so we have to drop in unannounced."

"As if the higher-ups don't love me enough already."

This earned me a smile and a friendly hand on my shoulder. "Don't worry, I'll explain. You keep on resting."

"I feel fine," I answered, and it was the truth. My head was clear and my body rested. The right hand was bandaged, but I flexed it and felt only a little pain.

"You've been out for over a day," Watson countered.

"I can't very well be carried into headquarters and then waltz off again. No, I'm walking," I insisted.

My companions knew it was futile to argue with me, so they didn't even try.

The headquarters of the Secret Service in Alexandria was housed in a wing of my homeland's embassy. During the British occupation of Egypt, they had appropriated so many buildings and stationed so many soldiers, that no one thought twice about the additional operatives. Since the British still managed Egyptian affairs,

201

their presence in the city had been heavy for a few years now -- which was at present very much to our advantage.

Elizabeth was subsequently incarcerated at the branch office and left in capable hands... well, at least in hands I could trust. She never woke up, so we couldn't interrogate her and had to resort to old-fashioned research.

The worship of the deity Seth, long ago practiced even as far north as the seaside city of Alexandria, was now all but forgotten. His temples lay far south, further than we could have ever traveled during the remaining time. Newer cults tend to flock to places that have a history and provide the right setting for their followers. You'd much more likely find an occult seance being held in a derelict church than a colourful garden. And we were looking to stop an *actual* ritual, if the clues were anything to go by.

If the *Desert Wind* followed this ancient cult, they would flock to these sites, but they would also have easily accessible places in larger cities to attract followers. No cult was without a bulk of exploitable members. While there was an old, small temple of Seth in the city, it was unused and had only been discovered a few years ago. The god had been demonized even during the ancient Egyptians' time, which erased him not only from the temples, but also from most recorded history. So we did what we had to do: Follow the only clue we had, which lead to the underground site in the middle of Alexandria.

But *of course* there had been another problem on tap. While the agency had no qualms with detaining Elizabeth, to let *us* proceed was something that didn't come lightly. I had to discuss my recent behaviour with the branch leader, an uncompromising Scottish woman by the name of Marigold Bates. While her name would let one think of a charming person and her appearance was just as gentle, behind the glowing blue eyes and auburn head of wavy hair was a cunning reasoner, with a confidence rivalled only by my own.

Of course she had been notified of my -- and by extension Victoria's -- deeds, and the liberties we had taken to come this far, but what she hadn't been informed of was the real reason. And so I found that the name of my brother opened doors even in this distant, exotic country, where no one should have a reason even to know of him.

How elated I was and how furious it made me feel.

The discussion had taken up most of the night. After only a few hours of sleep, we were on our way in the early morning hours, fueled by a few cups of very strong, Arabian black tea, flavoured with an unholy amount of brown sugar.

It was a mild winter day in the oriental coastal city, and despite the early hour it was already packed with people. Luckily, the freezing cold of Europe didn't reach all the way to the continent of Africa. As the haze of the morning cleared, the blue sky promised a beautiful day of sunshine. If not for our rush and the general uneasiness, it could have been a pleasant day for a holiday. While we walked in silence, I once again found the envelope in my pocket, which contained that fateful note, and caressed it almost nostalgically.

"This is it," I pointed at what seemed to be a small park in the middle of the city, after I confirmed our position with help of a map.

The buildings around us were not higher than two floors, rather dilapidated, but still inhabited. It had a more rural feeling to it than the city centre we had just crossed, with a lot of storage buildings around, market carts parked next to half destroyed walls and only a very few people walking about, minding their own business. The area was overgrown and not at all cared for, except for a herd of donkeys keeping the grass down to a minimum. They grazed in and around the low ruins which were spread out through most of the park area.

"I expected a building, not... rubble and donkeys," Watson admitted.

"Who would build a ritual altar in a place like this?" Victoria was clearly annoyed, and I couldn't blame her.

"It's alright," I put a hand on her shoulder. "The place is supposed to be underground, so it doesn't matter what the surface looks like."

We explored the area as if we were clueless visitors to the city -- which, if you think about it, described us pretty well. This way, we hoped to catch some unusual details, anything hidden in plain sight, something to show us we were indeed in the right place. At first we walked around and chatted idly. None of the local people paid us any mind. Watson had his doubts about their allegiance, but I laughed and remarked that the most suspicious people around were probably ourselves.

After a while, I found a hole in the ground, covered only by a lid that could be lifted easily. Surrounding it were stacks of material and some tools that could've belonged to a carpenter. I took in the scene for a few seconds, then brought over my companions.

"This is it," I stated.

"Are you sure?" Watson asked, and I shot him a silencing glare.

"What you can see is an abandoned excavation site. There was a layer of sand on the lid, which had built up over time, and the materials to reinforce the structure haven't been moved in at least five months. The tools belonged to the workers and for a time there were people going in and out of here with heavy carts, still visible in the grooves over there."

"But if it is abandoned, it's certainly not the place were looking for!" Victoria said.

"So it fooled you too, didn't it? The path' surface is too uniform to have been lying barren. With this many free-roaming donkeys around, you'd expect at least some hoofprints. Furthermore, the layer of sand on the lid was recently put on by hand, higher in some places than others and not aligned with the wind direction. As for the material, it's probably just a front. No one would pay any mind to a group of archaeologists going in and out of a ruin."

"But what if it's another trap?" Watson asked nervously.

"You talk like we have a choice," Victoria stated. "Though we could split up. Two go down, one returns to headquarters to see if Elizabeth woke up."

"No. Either way, I have a bad feeling," I shook my head. "I say we all go together."

We lifted the lid made of old wooden boards, which were haphazardly nailed and bound together, off the hole in the ground. The smell of stale air and ancient rot drifted upwards -- one you would normally associate with old cellars or deserted castle dungeons. That particular scent promised cold and dark rooms with little to no light, wrapped in eerie silence. I have visited my fair share of these rooms during my lifetime, and had no desire to do so again, but at least it made me able to anticipate what could possibly lay ahead.

"After you," Victoria smiled and motioned gentlemanly into the direction of the hole in the ground.

"Ladies first?" I suggested with a smirk on my lips.

Victoria let out an exasperated sigh, but it sounded rather more fond than annoyed.

"Alright, then," she said and pulled a small box out of a pouch at her belt. Inside the box was a silver object which looked a bit like a pen, but the top was made of a metal ornament with inlaid glass. The agent twisted the two ends of the object into opposite directions, and with the sound of cracking glass the top started to emit a white light.

"Chemical lamp," she explained to Watson, whose face had taken on an expression of surprise. "Will not last all that long, but I hope they have some sort of illumination down there at the excavation site."

"Or secret hideout," Watson supplemented.

"Yes, or that."

So Victoria went first, as her light illuminated a comfortably large area, despite being so small. The stairs went straight down into the pitch-black darkness. I was the last to enter the subterranean corridor and let the wooden lid fall close behind me. We wanted to avoid anyone following us, even though I knew that we had probably long been revealed, as on every step of our journey so far. But somehow, in my single-mindedness to find Sherlock, I wasn't even worried about that any more.

I just wanted it to be over.

"There's a horizontal tunnel straight ahead, but it doesn't seem to be all that long. I can hear our steps echo differently," Victoria said as we stepped into the long hallway behind her. "Is it just me or is there a smell of water in the air?"

"No, not just you. But there are traces of burnt oil, as well. Someone has indeed been down here recently," I added.

Watson inhaled deeply, trying to detect something as well, but the stale air just made him cough. Bless his effort. We carefully walked along the hallway until we reached something that looked like a portal into another world. The corridor opened up into a small room, which contained a doorway twice as high as the previous space. It was flanked by two columns with reliefs of Egyptian gods to either side. It was clear that this had once been the official entrance, and the hallway we had just progressed through had been dug later.

"What are those?" Watson asked reverently.

"They are depictions of the gods Seth and Horus... two gods, whom the Egyptians believed to be locked in an eternal struggle," I said, glad for the hour I took brushing up on Egyptian mythology the night before. While my brain had the capacity to hold incredible amounts of information, it was never a bad idea to refresh your memory. "Seth represents the desert and Horus the water of the Nile, as far as I remember."

"So that means we *are* in the right place?"

"It seems to be connected, at least. At some point Seth became demonized and many of his likenesses were erased from temples and other places of worship. The fact that this is one is still intact is what I'd call a good sign."

"Demonized?" Watson shook his head. "Sounds about right."

We continued through the doorway into another short hallway. The walls here were decorated by hieroglyphs and other depictions of Seth. It was an ominous feeling to enter what felt like a grave to me, even though I wasn't prone to believe in superstition. My companions had slowed their steps, their bodies expressing a healthy amount of fear. Then we arrived at the end of the corridor, where the space once again opened up considerably. We were standing at the top of what seemed to be a large, cylindrical cistern. The stairs continued down in a spiral on the inside wall. The light wasn't bright enough to illuminate the opposite wall or the bottom of the structure. I picked up a stone fragment from the floor and threw it down into the darkness. After three seconds I heard a splashing noise.

"The water is about fifteen meters down," I commented. "It might go deeper still -- but I suspect the structure hasn't been built to collect water, but rather happened to fill up over hundreds or thousands of years of neglect."

Victoria knelt down, shone her light on the ground and carefully inched forward. "The stairs seem fine. Someone has cleaned them recently. If we keep to the wall, we should have no trouble on our descent."

"What do you think we'll find?" Watson whispered nervously. The vast space and the darkness below made him feel visibly uneasy.

"I could only speculate…"

Even I dreaded to think of what would happen to me, should I trip and fall down into the dark waters, but it was most definitely beneath me to reveal any such thoughts. One of us had to keep a clear head, and I was always that one. The wall was wet and just a bit slimy, but I put on my leather gloves and kept my hands to it anyway. Rather ruin a pair of good gloves than fall into the abyss.

We descended very slowly, everyone carefully placed their feet one at a time. The stairs were not connected, but rather just coarse stone slabs sticking out of the walls in a downwards spiral. The only confidence in their integrity came from the knowledge that other people must have walked up and down here not long ago. As we arrived at the side opposite of our entry point, a hole opened up in the wall, like a small doorway, but missing its door. It was constructed in the same way as the main entrance, only with some additional statues of the gods instead of simple reliefs. There was another hallway leading away from the cistern, though much narrower and with a low ceiling. A recess right at the entrance contained a stash of items:

Lamps, rolled up parchments, drawing supplies and some wrapped up parcels.

"So there are *actually* archaeologists down here?" the doctor said in surprise. "It might still turn out to be just a normal dig site."

"Never jump to a conclusion before you know all the facts, Dr. Watson," I rebutted. "Come on."

"I will stay here. Signal me if *anything* goes wrong. You have a whistle?" Victoria asked.

"Of course," I answered readily and patted the breast pocket of my jacket.

Watson picked up one of the oil lamps, lit it with a matchstick and handed it to me. The light was not as bright as Victoria's chemical device, but in the narrow passageway it sufficed. As we inched forward, we encountered more recesses on each side. Some of them were empty, but the farther we walked, the more clear it became that the place could be labeled a catacomb. Scenes from the Egyptian Book of the Dead were painted on the walls, giving the place a sinister feel. Still, they were beautifully rendered, and I regretted not having enough time to examine them more closely. We were surrounded by securely wrapped-up mummies tucked into their low stone graves, and almost all sarcophagi had been opened, lids on the floor. The air grew staler by the minute. I held a handkerchief in front of my nose and mouth to avoid breathing in the dust of millennia.

"I can see signs of *actual* archaeological work, although they are few and far between... and rather sloppy," I said and my words broke the absolute silence, which reigned down here. It made Watson jump a little, which I could feel even though he walked behind me.

"I don't claim to be an expert on these kind of excavations, but other than rather little work being done, I don't see anything suspicious? If it's privately funded, maybe they ran out of money or are working with a skeleton crew?" the doctor wondered. "What makes you think the work has been carried out sloppily?"

"The places, in which the graves have been disturbed do not follow any pattern. This seems to me like they just placed some objects here and there to evoke the feeling of work being done in case anyone would want to inspect the place," I explained. "And if it is indeed privately funded, I would expect to see a lot of workers slaving away down here. These projects run on tight budgets. If you'd given money to run a venture like this, wouldn't you want results fast?"

"Yes, I guess you're right."

It was a curious feeling to have a supportive person accompany me... but not so much it made me want to repeat the effort.

The hallway was a dead end. I heard Watson grumble as we turned around and made our way back towards the central cistern. But something was off, as I couldn't spot Victoria's light at the end of the low tunnel. Then I heard my agent companion click her tongue twice in quick succession and immediately ordered Watson to stay behind with the lamp.

I drew a gun and doubled my speed to reach Victoria's position, which was now shrouded in darkness, as she had retreated into the corridor and thrown away her light so as to not give away her location. A few seconds later I joined her on the ground of the corridor, half hidden behind a pile of deserted wooden planks.

"What happened?"

"I heard footsteps at the top," she answered in a low voice.

I strained my ears to make out a sound, signaling to the doctor to stay quiet. A few heartbeats later we were still sitting in silence. The weak light of the oil lamp flickered and cast the shadow of Watson's gun onto the ground in front of me.

"You both stay here. I'll go check it out," I whispered then. "No one leaves the corridor and there's to be no light in the cistern. Understood?"

They both looked like they wanted to complain, but acquiesced quietly. I stashed my gun and advanced towards the doorway. My eyes were used to the murky light by now, but beyond the faint shimmer of orange behind me, there was nothing to see, nothing to make out in the total darkness of the underground graveyard. I cautiously shimmied along the wall and onto the stone slab right outside the corridor. Still there was no sound, except the occasional splashing noise of tiny water droplets merging with the pool below.

I went down on all fours, feeling my way through the darkness, back up the disjointed stairs. On my hands and knees, I made slow progress, painfully aware that a misstep could send me down into a watery grave all too quickly. Because I couldn't see, my other senses were heightened and I acutely felt the chilliness of the air and the freezing stones even through my leather gloves. It felt as though there were always one more step on an endless spiral, even though I had counted the steps and knew exactly how many I would have to climb. Then, finally I had reached the top.

No light, no movement, no person. The way to the surface lay in shadows. Had Victoria imagined it? Did someone flee after seeing her retreat? Had we alerted the cultists to our presence? I took a few more moments to wait, but there was no sign of anyone except us in this uncomfortable place. From my pocket I pulled one of the candles I had snatched from the archaeologist's stash and lit it with a match. Just then I smelled something strange, just for a second. It was like sugar and caramel... almost like treacle. It was gone as quickly as it appeared, but I knew I hadn't been mistaken and filed the information away in the back of my mind.

By the light of the candle, I rejoined my companions, and together we ventured further down into the belly of the structure. This time, Watson took the lead. I followed behind and Victoria provided the rear guard as we walked in silence. I estimated another two full turns of the spiral until we would reach the water surface, and cautiously placed one foot after the other to get there in one piece. Down here, the steps were less heavily used and caked with dirt that had accumulated over a long time.

"There is another tunnel!" Watson said then, his voice echoing in the chamber. "But it seems flooded. No, the water covers merely the bottom of it, but someone has laid out wooden planks to make a dry path," Watson held out to illuminate some of our findings. "Looks like someone doesn't like wet feet."

Due to the raised walkway, there was even less headspace inside the low tunnel compared to the previous one. Watson asked to go last. Even though I didn't know him to be claustrophobic, it was obvious that the mixture of tight spaces, anxiousness and lack of knowledge about the place made him afraid of going on. Admittedly, I could empathise, but it was no reason to stop. Not yet.

The water beneath our feet was still. Tiny splashing noises could be heard when dust and little stones came off the walls as we scraped by them. The air grew heavy with the smell of mold and decay. I was just wondering about our next steps should this turn out to be another dead end, when a sudden draft carried sweet, unused air past me, making the flame of my lamp flicker.

"Something's up ahead," I said, for once unable to hide the excitement in my voice. I don't think any of my companions minded. "I think I can see light. Don't be alarmed -- I will put out our own lamp now."

"Hold on to me, Dr. Watson," Victoria said encouragingly. "Don't fall behind."

He did as he was told and grabbed the cloth of Victoria's jacket just as the light went out. Our surroundings became as dark as a moonless night in an instant, and I had to place my feet carefully, so I would remain on the walkway and not immerse my shoes in the dirty water. But with every step it grew just a bit lighter and I was able to step more confidently.

"We should move quickly," I said as I almost immersed my shoe in the water on a particularly shaky stretch.

The ceiling of the hallway wasn't lower than the above, but on top of the walkway, we all but had to crawl to go through it on dry feet. Finally, we reached a doorway with a few steps leading up into a room from which the light emanated. The space behind it surprised me in more ways than one. It had access to fresh air, even though it was at least ten meters underground. You could breathe easier here than in the rest of the catacomb, and even though it still smelled like something had died in there, it wasn't as unpleasant as what lay behind us. The space was huge, at least three meters high and felt like a room inside a mansion rather than an underground hiding place -- except the windows were missing.

If the altar in the middle, surrounded by statues and candles, had not been there, you could have easily mistaken the space for the study of a very untidy scholar. Shelves at the walls housed books, scrolls and various other curios I partly recognised from my own occasional research work. A big desk in one corner was overflowing with papers, stacked high. I could even see a small chemical lab on a table on the other side of the room, complete with a cupboard filled with all kinds of equipment and ingredients.

You could've almost called the atmosphere homey. It undeniably had a certain, peculiar kind of charm. I tried hard not to look baffled. This was the last thing I had expected down here, even though we had, in fact, been searching for a hideout, which this was.

"The candles are lit," I remarked, as none of the others seemed to give them any mind. "Someone has been here recently. They are rather fresh, too. So that someone could still be in the room."

"If someone is indeed here, this is your chance to come out before we have to find you. And you *don't* want that," Victoria said loudly.

We had already drawn our weapons upon entering the room and held them out into different directions, covering the space around us. Even Watson had grabbed his pistol and for once reacted correctly -- even though I was sure he wouldn't be able to pull the trigger.

"Come out, we know you're here," I added in my best threatening tone, which made clear that I wasn't about to negotiate anything. "Alright, if you don't come to us, we'll come to you."

I nodded at Victoria, who took the left side of the room, whereas I moved away to the right. We slowly walked around piles of books and other objects on the floor and monitored every corner carefully. Watson proceeded to the altar in the middle of the room and kept a watch on the entrance. A few tense minutes later, we lowered our guns.

"If there's no secret passageway we have missed, I regret to say that there is no one else in this room," I sighed. "But that doesn't matter. We have to examine the objects for clues. There *must* be something here, which could lead us to Sherlock, if this place is really part of the *Desert Wind's* operation... which seems very likely."

Thank the stars for the predictable behaviour of religious cults.

"Look at these shelves! When Holmes was proclaimed dead, the Yard turned to me to help them sort out some of Moriarty's things. I recognise a lot of the book titles I saw in his study," Watson said nervously.

"That's a very good observation, doctor. I had the same feeling," I nodded and then turned to Victoria. "When Dr. Watson sorted these things out, he asked me to assist him. I unveiled many of Moriarty's plans and thinned out his web in England considerably."

"*We* unveiled them," Watson said with emphasis.

"You took on the duties of the detective, doctor?" Victoria asked.

"I felt like I owed it to Holmes. I couldn't prevent his death, so I wanted it to mean something. Pick up where he left, so to say," he shrugged, his voice already partly lost in nostalgia. "It was rewarding for a while, but it's not my calling. I returned to my practice as a doctor soon after."

"Nonsense, Dr. Watson. You performed admirably during those days. And in the end, all the credit *did* fall to you, if you remember," I added.

"Only because I could tell no one of your involvement, Mycroft!"

There was much I could have said then. But mine had never been a work of public recognition, and I would rather die than being seen as petty. We searched the remainder of the room in a companionable silence. It was so quiet that every action resounded so much louder than it should. I turned my attention to a pile of very old looking scrolls next to the altar, as Watson called me over, to ask for my help deciphering some hieroglyphic texts.

"This is it, doctor! These scrolls tell of a ritual sacrifice, of a person that functions as vessel for Horus. A killing to be made in honour of the god Seth. It even says where the deed should be carried out. Let me see..." I mumbled excitedly and perused the rest of the parchment. "Aha! Judging from my estimations, I think we can make it to the described place within two days, but I would have to check against official records to make sure."

"And you are certain we can find Sherlock there?" Victoria frowned.

"Yes. This place here is some sort of meeting point for the *Desert Wind*, there is no doubt. And we know of the ritual. This must be it," I nodded.

"What's this, then?" Watson pointed at a stone slab on the altar, inscribed with a mixture of hieroglyphs and ancient greek. "Does it describe the ritual in detail maybe?"

"Let me see," I said and placed my right hand on the stone to trace the indentations.

In that instant the same electrical current I had felt back in Baker Street shot through my hand and up my arm, only many times stronger. I tried to pry my hand away, but it was stuck to the stone as if it was made of iron and the altar a powerful magnet. The symbols beneath my hand flickered as if illuminated from within, and for a second it felt like my hand was being ripped off, then I stumbled back onto Victoria and fell with her to the ground.

I breathed fast and heavy, and held my hand in expectation of pain, but there was none. On the contrary: My hand and arm hadn't felt this unburdened at any other time during this journey. Watson opened his mouth to say something, but was immediately interrupted.

We all jerked up in shock as the sudden noise arrived at our ear. Merely a slow clap, the sound echoed through the space like thunder. In the doorway back to the cistern, which was our only way out, stood a figure wrapped in a wide, white robe, which looked almost like a caricature of a priest. The light from the candles was strong enough to illuminate his face. My eyes widened in horror. Within seconds my gun was back in my hand, as I reacted automatically to this presence. But the vile person in the doorway moved his hands in a soothing gesture.

"Please, please. No need for this. Must we resort to violence every time? Can't I invite you to talk first? Over tea, perhaps?"

I took the opportunity to observe what little I could see of the man. His left hand was missing the pinky finger and over his palm ran an ugly scar. The hair on his head was even thinner than before and a patch covered his right eye, under which a big red blotch stained his cheek. He had certainly taken a lot more damage in the fall than my brother, who had miraculously escaped almost unscathed.

Still, James Moriarty smiled like a cat.

"Ah, the good Dr. Watson," the fiend continued as he scrutinised him. "You don't look much different at all. I must say the uniform of the Secret Service suits you well. Have you been recruited? Congratulations, if so."

"Where is Sherlock?"

"You come into my house, draw guns, answer my question with a counter question... Where are your manners, good man?" he laughed and pulled a mock-disappointed face.

"We have no time for your games," Watson said tensely.

"Games?" he shouted. "Well, if you have no time, why are you participating?"

He threw a little object towards us, and I flinched instinctively. It fell to the floor right in front of my feet. Another small, ceramic plate, painted white with three blue, wavy lines. It was of exactly the same make as the other two in my possession.

"What house are we in now? The House of Water?" I asked, looking up again.

"Oh, very good Mycroft, very good. The waters of chaos and humiliation are the only bad square in the whole game. Such bad luck..."

"Explain," Victoria demanded.

"There's really nothing to explain. Let your dear friend tell you about the rules later, I've no time for that now." Moriarty made a dramatic pause, in which he eyed me intently, then righted himself up as well as he could. "My friends of the *Desert Wind* believe me to be the reincarnation of the god Seth and that your dear detective is the vessel of Horus. Our eternal struggle is divine to them, and they are *so* right. They want to help me to get rid of him and honour Seth at the same time. It's one of these great situations where everybody wins!"

I held my gun higher and pointed it squarely at Moriarty's head.

"You will *not* shoot me. Any of you. Our dear doctor is too polite -- don't look at me like that, you know it to be true. And, after all you all need me to find your precious Sherlock," he spat out my brother's name as if it tasted horrible. "And you will never make it out alive if I *do* get shot. The catacombs behind me are now full of my own agents. Which is also why I can tell you all of this without problem."

I narrowed my eyes and sniffed the air. "Sugar…" I whispered. "You reek of sugar. That's what I smelled up there at the entrance. You let us walk into this trap."

"Only because you so rudely interrupted my breakfast earlier. I had to flee my cozy office and eat in a hurry," the professor shook his head.

My patience with the man ran thin. In one way, I felt incredible anger towards him, but in a weird, perverted way I was also glad to have finally encountered him in person, and thereby confirmed all of our hopes and fears. Watson grabbed the scroll from the altar and held it up next to his gun. I groaned. Improvisation had never been one of his talents, and he should really stop attempting to be clever. Hopefully…

"We don't need you, Moriarty. We have already figured out the place of the ritual," he said triumphantly. "What stops us from shooting you right here? Your agents? Surely you know us better than that."

Never mind.

"Indeed, Dr. Watson. Admirable observation. Someone is using their head, I see. On that note, let me thank you for bringing dear associate Elizabeth back to Egypt. I would have hated for all that training to go to waste. Once I take care of you and Sherlock, I may even let her walk free," he did a little bow into Watson's direction. "As to what stops you from shooting me: Would you believe me when I told you that the catacombs are riddled with explosives?"

"What?" the doctor exclaimed. "That's madness!"

"And also untrue," I said assuredly. "If there had been any explosives hidden here, I would have detected them by their smell."

"Are you really so sure? I expected more of the elder brother of my archenemy. Use your head, Mycroft Holmes," Moriarty still didn't waver from his spot in the entrance of the room. "Where could I have hidden them?"

"The mummies! Theirstink masks the smell of almost anything!" Watson shouted.

"Another point for Dr. Watson. I'm disappointed, dear so-called agent first rank," Moriarty shook his head. "It's true. Should you shoot me, my associates will detonate the mummies and bury you alive. You see, they really *did* excavate and examine them – they just put them back with a little something extra."

How could I have missed this? How... I wavered and involuntarily took a step backwards. Victoria seemed to realise this

222

and in turn took a step up. She held out the gun straight at Moriarty's head.

"Cease your rambling and stop with those cheap tricks! If we *do* shoot you right here, we can save Sherlock, even if we die in the process," she stated. "I, for one, am willing to risk that."

The accused threw his head back in laughter and put one hand to the wall to keep himself upright. His action bothered me much less than it should have, but I was still on edge, disappointed in myself. The professor was not the calm and collected person, the quiet and rational mathematician we had known in London. This was a disfigured, madman in the service of a cult to the Egyptian death god Seth. Hell, he may have even believed himself to be a god! I was betting on the fact that he had even more injuries hidden underneath his white robe... and in his head.

"I'm sorry, but this is delightful. Yes, sacrifice. This is good. Unfortunately it won't do you, or your precious Sherlock any good. I am not the leader of *Desert Wind* -- merely a very enthusiastic supporter. They will go through with the ritual whether I am there or not, even though they might not be as happy. As long as I can keep you here, there will be no one to stop it."

"Keep us here? Not kill us?" I asked, frowning.

"Oh, yes. The *House of Water* has a special role in the game. I really thought you studied it? But I can tell you. Anyone who visits this House gets thrown back to the beginning of the playing field. And while I can't send you back to London, I can inconvenience you long enough to make it count."

"You're sick," Victoria spat. "This isn't a game!"

"Now, now. No need for this," he tutted again, even had the audacity to raise his finger in a reprimanding fashion. "I'll tell you now what's going to happen. You lot are staying right here. There is enough reading material to keep you occupied for the next few days. As soon as Sherlock is dead, I will come back and kill you too. It's as beautifully simple as that."

"And what makes you think we would agree to that?" Watson said through gritted teeth. "This doesn't sound like a very fair offer to me."

"Oh, because the only alternative is my agents detonating the explosives while we are all in here," Moriarty shrugged. "I'd be killed, as well, but this would eradicate all chances for your precious Sherlock instantly. Your call. Please, take your time discussing. I will be right here."

He raised part his robe to reveal a bag hanging around his shoulders under the cloth. From this he produced a small package made of paper. We all braced ourselves, but felt a bit silly when all the professor pulled out of it was a pastry dusted with sugar. He bit into it with vigour.

"Anyone fancy a bite?" he held the baked good out to us. "No? Fine. More for myself."

We turned towards each other, but I still kept an eye on Moriarty while we talked. Watson was of the opinion to take the chance. The explosives weren't directly above us. If we could take out Moriarty, we should try our luck. Victoria was cautiously agreeing, but not quite as sure about the placement of the explosives. Myself, I wasn't sure about anything, but least of all I wanted the catacomb to crash down on us.

"I do have to thank you, Mycroft," Moriarty smiled then. "The curse was meant for your brother only, but it seems it worked just as well on a person sharing the same blood."

"Curse?" Watson asked.

"More of a... tracking spell. It fell on you when you touched the sand in London, so we could always know where you are. Don't worry, it was canceled out when you touched that stone before. But that doesn't matter, because I'll know where you'll be until the end of your life: Right here."

I bristled at the notion that I should've been under a spell, but it explained so many things that I couldn't find the words.

"Liar," Victoria spat.

"It doesn't matter if you think me speaking lies. I have bent ancient magic to my will, and it will only be a matter of time before I bend you as well. Oh, talking about ancient magic, do you have any wishes for your last meal before I kill you all? When I come back, I can bring you your last supper."

I stayed silent while Victoria and Watson discussed our options. Both brought forth good arguments, but I had never been the person to listen to the opinions of others. We had to get out of here, and there was only one way, I was sure of it.

"No need to watch out for your figure anymore, either. Eat whatever unhealthy things you want. That is the privilege of those about to die," the professor continued.

He seemed intent to throw us off at every corner. Watson became visibly annoyed by Moriarty's comments.

"If it's quite alright with you two, I think I'd prefer an afternoon tea spread," I said then and made the decision for us all -- doing what I always did best: improvise.

"Excellent choice, my dear Mycroft. You should expect me back in about... well, let me see... a week?" Moriarty smiled like a cat who got the mouse and the cream at the same time.

I ignored the disbelieving stares of my companions and returned the professor's expression. "A week it is. See you then."

"Wait!" Victoria shouted. "What has gotten into ..."

I grabbed her arm and stared into her eyes with silent emphasis, then shook my head. Watson was silenced much easier with just a glance, telling him to refrain from contradicting me or trying anything. He was conditioned to listen to the orders of a Holmes -- it didn't seem to matter which one it was. But then something surprising happened. The good doctor visibly steeled himself and turned towards Moriarty, smiling.

"If I might... could you look into some strawberry jam? I can't have my scones without a bit of strawberry jam," he added.

"Indeed, indeed. Absolutely fantastic," Moriarty clapped his hands excitedly. "I will send out my associates at once. We should be able to find some strawberry jam in Egypt."

I had to suppress my laughter at the doctor's performance. Victoria wasn't as happy. "Are you all mad?" her shoulders slumped and she put her face in her hand. All of us looked at her, including Moriarty. Then she broke out into a nervous laughter.

"How wonderful to see that we are all on the same page now," Moriarty nodded and popped the last piece of his pastry into his mouth, which was now also dusted with an obscene amount of sugar. "I will be leaving now. Just to remind you: My agents are still inside the catacombs. Trying to come after me would result in an ugly death." Moriarty turned around with a flourish, which made his robe fan out like a cloak. Within seconds he had disappeared into the darkness behind the entrance of the room.

We waited until the sounds of Moriarty's footsteps on the wooden planks disappeared completely. Victoria sank to the floor, head in her hands, and Watson seemed like he wanted to do the same. Instead he looked to me, waiting for an explanation of my plan, silently hoping I had one at all.

"If all fails, we'll at least have a nice last meal," I offered.

"What were you thinking?" Victoria sighed.

"That's not the man, who left London all those years ago. His injuries, the years watching his network being dismantled and the influence of this dreadful cult have made him a different person. I could see only a small spark of the rational math professor underneath it all," I shook my head disappointedly. "If he was dangerous before, he was at least predictable to a certain degree. You could reason with him, if only within a small margin. This man is crazy. These people are the most dangerous, because you can never predict their actions."

"So all that talk about keeping us here was a lie?" Watson asked.

"No, I think he intends to keep us alive, at least for as long as the sacrifice hasn't been made. He is going to great lengths to make sure Sherlock's death is benefitting him by making sure all conditions that the cult requires are perfect. And these conditions seem to include following the rules of this dreaded game. *House of Water* indeed." I spat.

"I don't care why he does it. Just what do we do now?" Victoria groaned. "This is nothing like I've ever encountered before."

I took a seat next to her on the floor. "I can now understand how he might have threatened Elizabeth into working for him -- why she was frightened enough to perform these abominable tasks. For now, agreeing to his plan was the quickest way to get rid of him."

"You are right, of course," Watson nodded. "But we need to get out of here quickly. If we really need two days to get to the sacrificial site, we cannot afford to waste another hour."

"We need to scout ..."

CHAPTER 12

I saw the face… of a demon

I couldn't finish my sentence, because we were interrupted by a loud, echoing noise and a strong vibration in the ground and walls surrounding us, which knocked Watson off his feet. He stumbled and fell between Victoria and me. We immediately grabbed him and dragged his body underneath the large desk to seek shelter. It hadn't been a moment too late, as the shelves started collapsing and a large number of books and various other objects fell around us as the ground continued to jerk violently. The cacophony of breaking glass and metal instruments hitting the stone floor told me that even the chemical instruments were being destroyed by the shaking.

I closed my eyes to protect them and so the only things I could sense were the noises of rumbling stones, that rubbed against each other in the walls, splintered wood and fractured glass. Years of dust were disturbed and flared up, filling the air with the particles of ancient things and made it hard to breathe. I covered my head with my jacket, hoping to avoid breathing it in, knowing it could prove hazardous, should I even survive this whole ordeal.

After what seemed like a small eternity, the stones stopped their vibrations and the dust started to settle again. I opened my eyes to behold the devastation around us. The room was utterly ruined. Like a small miracle, a single candle was still alive in the middle of the rubble, illuminating a small radius around it and the dust particles floating in the air.

"Do you still have the lamp?" Victoria asked and the question seemed so normal in the midst of this destruction, I had to huff with a small bout of laughter, but then shook my head.

"I left it near the candles. Sorry."

"No worries," she nodded and got up from underneath the desk to search for the lamp, as if nothing had happened.

"Are you alright, Dr. Watson?" I asked the man, who was still holding onto my jacket, which he quickly remedied with a muttered apology.

"I don't seem to be hurt. Thank god for your quick reaction."

"This is what I warned you about -- he's completely unpredictable! He detonated the explosives anyway!" I shouted as soon as I emerged from the space under the desk, then punched the wall accompanied by a rather violent shout. "I should never have tried to reason with him, just shoot him right there and then. Now he walks free, Sherlock will be killed and all we can do is sit here and die slowly!"

Victoria had found the lamp and lit the wick on the small candle. She turned around to us and frowned. "Mycroft, stop this right now. There is no time to wallow in self-pity, so don't even start. As you might have noticed, the fresh air supply has been cut off, so we need to act quickly if we are to have even half a chance of ever getting out of here."

I turned around, still breathing heavily. My eyes were narrowed and there was no mistaking my expression for anything but barely restrained wrath. 'How *dare* she talk to me like that?' my mind readily supplied, but through years of practice the words didn't leave my mouth. I clutched my fingers tightly in order to regain some resemblance control, but knew I would fail if pushed any further.

"Give me a minute," I managed tensely and closed my eyes.

"One minute," she replied and turned around.

I sat, willing the heat in my heart to go away and return to rational thought. Watson had the good sense to stay quiet and busied himself by searching through the scrolls. Then the room turned brighter and I and opened my eyes to see Victoria emerge from the doorway again. Her shoes and trousers were dripping on the dusty floor.

"I have good news and bad news," she said.

"There is good news?" I answered in a sarcastic tone of voice.

"Stop that infernal attitude *at once*, Mycroft Holmes. I gave you your miserable minute! You're insufferable once you get like this, and I won't have it. Not right now!" Victoria shouted with a vengeance, almost throwing the lamp to the floor in the progress. "If your inactivity is what leads to us dying down here, I will personally bring you back to life and kill you again with my bare hands!"

We locked eyes in a silent dispute -- one even the doctor dared not interrupt. I had half a mind to start up a fight, but by now my own fiery anger had burned down to just a little flame, and I made a conscious effort to extinguish it for good. Then I rose carefully and righted my clothing, getting rid of creases and patting dust from the surface. Finally, I smoothed down my hair in a gesture familiar to my companions.

"The detonation happened in the upper levels of the cistern. It seems that Moriarty wasn't lying when he told us that the explosives were hidden inside the mummies. Most of the stone slabs, which served as stairs, are also destroyed, so I regret to say we don't have the option of climbing them to get out," Victoria explained. She held the lamp into the doorway, and we walked closer to see that the water level was now much higher. "The rubble of the collapsed stairs has accumulated in the water and made it rise, but we can still walk through the tunnel."

"We have to leave before we run out of air," I frowned. "There is no telling how much longer this chamber will hold up. Moriarty might have let the explosives go off to trap us here, but this is an old structure and even he couldn't know what the consequences of his actions would be."

"I trust your judgement, Mycroft," Watson said calmly, and it felt strange for him to sound so sincere just after he had seen me acting badly, but I could detect no lie in his voice. Victoria put a hand on my arm and nodded at me with a smile. I nodded in response and motioned for her to show us the way out of the ruined room, but not before I stopped and picked up some of the candles.

With my face turned away from the others, I closed my eyes briefly and took a deep breath in an effort to compose myself. This wasn't me. It couldn't be. I'd get them out of here, and if I was to die in the process, so be it.

To immerse myself in the water, which reached up to my waist, was an expectedly unpleasant experience -- made even more so by the knowledge that I wouldn't be able to dry off until I'd reached the surface again. Icy cold and dark, the water sloshed around as we carefully waded through it. The explosion had agitated the foul air and made the rotten smell even worse. I held my arms high and kept both hands on the ceiling of the tunnel to keep them at least a bit dry. The collapsed walkway lay strewn around on the bottom of the tunnel and we cautiously inched forward so as to not misstep and fall completely into the dirty liquid. It was impossible to see through anything in this murky atmosphere. Even though I was walking right behind her, the light of the lamp in Victoria's hand only reached me partially, and I had to fumble through the darkness, more feeling than seeing.

Oh, Sherlock would pay dearly for making me go through this.

We reached the central cylinder, and while there were enough steps left for us to all stand inside, the way upwards was clearly cut off. Victoria examined the remains of the fewsteps still left embedded in the wall and the holes left by other, completely collapsed ones, while I observed the water in the light of the oil lamp. Watson did his best to illuminate the wall for Victoria with a candle he had lit on the lamp wick.

"We might be able to climb this," Victoria shrugged. "But there is no telling if the upper tunnel is collapsed or not. I don't know if we should risk it."

"Do we have another option?" Watson asked. "If the tunnel is open, one of us could lower a rope to help the others."

"I should do it -- I'm the lightest. If we are to take the chance, we have to do it now while I still have my strength," Victoria offered.

"That might not be necessary," I interrupted their discussion. "Do you see the water level?"

They turned around to see me point at the wall next to me, where the water now stood about half a metre above the platform in front of the doorway. Then I pointed to the stones lying in the water behind me.

"The stone stairs were about a metre wide and I counted forty-eight of them, roughly forty of which could be down in the water right now. Given the volume of stone, the water level should be much higher, but it has only risen this little," I explained. "There must be a way for the water to escape, and we could take the same route."

"But how can we tell where that is?" the doctor asked nervously. "We would have to dive, but it's pitch black down there!"

"The staircase goes all the way to the bottom. I believe there was never supposed to be water down here, but it filled up over the centuries. It would have risen further if not for a possibility to escape somewhere else. There may well be another tunnel down there, that we are missing," I explained. "And, yes, the only option to find out for sure is for one of us to dive into it. I will do it."

"That sounds dangerous, Mycroft. We don't even know if a person can get out that way," Victoria said. "I wouldn't …"

"No, I *have* to do it. The only other options are to climb or starve. Climbing will most certainly lead to injury, and to just sit here isn't really an option at all. If I find nothing, we can look to other possibilities, and you can do what you like."

She nodded reluctantly

"The doorway can only be beneath us, following the progression of the steps and the remaining height of the space," I sighed inwardly. "Hold this as close to the water surface as you dare while I dive."

I handed Victoria the same silver device she had previously employed to light our way through the catacombs. It was a standard issue item for the Secret Service and would provide a much brighter light than the oil lamp, but only for a few minutes. I strapped all clothes tighter to my body, before slowly I descended the steps that were still immersed in the water. As soon as it reached to my shoulders, I took the plunge and swam over to the platform the other two were standing on. Victoria, also in the water up to her thighs, smiled at me and twisted the little cylinder, which immediately started to emit a light so bright it was almost blinding in contrast to the dim, flickering fire.

"See you in a bit," I smiled and took a deep breath.

The cold assaulted all my senses at once as my head was fully immersed in the murky depths. Since the water was still partially clear, I had a bit of vision, and I carefully kept above ground to avoid stirring up any more mud.

House of Water, indeed...

As expected, there was another opening right beneath us, and I dove straight down to examine it. The platform above had protected it

235

from being obstructed with debris, but while I could make out the rough shape of objects in my vicinity, what lay behind the door might as well have been a bottomless abyss in pitch black darkness. There was still air in my lungs, so I opted to swim into the tunnel. My eyes took a few moments to adjust, but as they did I could make out a partly collapsed hallway disappearing into the distance. My first thought was that the explosion made it collapse, but on closer inspection I could scratch years of sediment from the rocks. Well, if it had held out that long...

Now my air was running out. I turned around and swam straight towards the single light above the surface, almost bumping into the lamp that Victoria drew back at the last second. Gasping for air I managed to position myself sitting on the platform, head just above the water surface, shivering. Still, there was no reason to leave it, as I would have to dive again. My skin was red from the cold and I wiped my eyes, blinking into the bright, artificial light of the small cylinder.

"There is a tunnel, but it's partly collapsed. The damage seems old, though, and not a result of the explosion," I said in between heavy breaths. "But I couldn't tell anything more than that. The light doesn't reach into the tunnel. I could use the emergency strip, but I only have one on my person. Victoria?"

"Also only one. But if this doesn't qualify as an emergency, nothing does. If our only other feasible option is to climb, I say we take the chance," she shrugged.

"Emergency strip?" Watson asked.

"A small amount of magnesium in an airtight vial. We carry it as means to create an emergency signal, but it will also burn on contact with water and should provide a burst of light even underwater, when I break it," I explained. "It will only shine for a few seconds, and then it's gone forever."

Watson looked up into the darkness, but even with the brighter light, he would've not been able to tell if the topmost tunnel were collapsed or not.

"I agree with Victoria. If I can avoid climbing... even if it means diving though the water," the doctor concluded.

"Then it's decided," I slid off the platform once more and fully back into the water, then produced a small glass vial from one of the many pouches on my belt. "Here's to hoping I can bring better news this time."

The faces of my companions disappeared from view as I once again slipped into the black body of water. This time I knew my heading and dove into the tunnel directly. But after only a few strokes the bright light source behind me flickered out of existence. I was swallowed by the darkness, which made it impossible to tell left from right or up from down. A curse escaped me despite it making no sound and there being no one hear it. How could I've been so foolish not to secure myself with a safety line?

I had no choice but to use the magnesium strip now, praying to God it would make me able to find the way out. Consciously I kept my eyes open, made as little movement as possible and cracked the vial. Just as expected, the magnesium burned rapidly and enabled me to survey my surroundings for all but three seconds before it was used up. But they were sufficient. Immediately I pushed my body forward with a few powerful strokes and breached the water surface once again. Watson reached for my hand and pulled me up, almost dropping his lamp.

"The water may be troubling us now, but it might also be our salvation," I said, now shivering in earnest but shaky voice. The cold sapped my strength rapidly. "Some people seem have to built a well all the way down to the tunnel. It looks like it's still in use as the catacombs have apparently functioned as an actual cistern over the years. It's some way down the tunnel, but we should be able to reach it. I could see light above."

"So we get to climb a well instead of a cistern?"Watson asked. "Lucky us."

"Lucky us, indeed. It will prove to be much easier. But don't worry... I volunteer to climb it first and get some sort of rope to help you two," I added. "I will be glad to exercise the muscles to get some warmth back into my body. We will need a flash of light to find the right direction again, so I'll need the other strip."

"This time I'll go ahead," Victoria offered and I took her up on it.

"So much for storing my gun where it doesn't get wet," Watson mumbled under his breath. In an effort to preserve both his weapon and the paper with the instructions of the ritual, he folded it neatly and tightly, then put both into one of the inside pockets of the jacket, which was made of leather and could be securely closed. I had

238

taken similar precautions before my dive, but now there was nothing about my person that wasn't soaked through and through. Still, I left the doctor to his preparations, knowing they were also a form of bracing himself for the ordeal yet to come.

We placed the lamp on a step above the water line and lit all remaining candles to provide as much light as possible. Then Victoria and Watson carefully slipped into the water alongside me. Watson was already nervous and shivered.

"Please, relax, Dr. Watson. You will go directly after Victoria and I will be behind you to make sure nothing goes awry," I reassuringly placed a hand on his shoulder. "It's not far. Alright?"

"Sure," he nodded. "Lead the way."

"Victoria? The opening is about twenty feet into the hallway, more to the right side. I can still go ahead ..."

"See you on the other side," she grinned, took a deep breath and was gone.

I did the same and dove down behind her and Watson as fast as I could. All I had to do was sink to the floor and then follow the doctor's form while he was swimming through the doorway. But it seemed I had overestimated his courage, because being confronted with the black hole in the wall and the person in front of him being swallowed by it, he hesitated instinctively, which cost us vital seconds of air. But I didn't hesitate and applied a gentle push to the doctor's back, which ripped him from his stupor.

The tunnel was wide enough for me to pass him, so I grabbed his arm to pull him along. This didn't only assure I wouldn't lose him, it would also make it impossible for him to desert us and return to the catacombs. I could feel him flail a few times as he bumped into the tunnel walls, but kept my grip steady and my bearings clear.

Then, suddenly, a flash of light illuminated our surroundings. I felt the doctor jerk in my grasp and move erratically. In his panicked state, the doctor opened his mouth to scream, which only depleted his precious air reserves further. I pulled him away horizontally, then finally ever upwards, as I followed Victoria. It was a chore to hold on to the doctor, who by now struggled to escape my grasp in the quest to reach the surface -- his distressed mind not realising that it was only my action, which would ultimately save him.

This way I found myself squeezed into a narrow well, which was barely wide enough to fit us three, with the promise of freedom delivered by rays of sunshine, illuminating part of the topmost wall. I breathed heavily, as did my companions, but in a stroke of luck, we had avoided injuries -- or worse.

"What spooked you so?" I asked hoarsely while I patted Watson's back to assist the vigorous coughing.

"I... the light..." he huffed. "I saw the face... of a demon."

Victoria and I exchanged a glance. She had already regained her composure.

"A demon?" I asked.

"A distorted face," he confirmed.

"It was a stone statue."

"Whatever it was -- the shock punched the last air out of me. I owe you my life, Mycroft."

"You owe nothing to anyone. But if you insist, give your thanks to Victoria, as she led us through the well to the surface," I said with emphasis. "And now I'd better move. Every second spent in the water will make it less likely for me to be able to climb this."

Supporting myself with my back on one side of the well and with my feet on the other, I found that the wall was indeed stable enough for me to climb. I slowly inched upwards for what must have been very well over thirty feet. The walls were comprised only of compacted earth, which meant that the pair beneath me had to endure a shower of dust and stones until I was clear.

As I reached the surface, I was glad to stretch my legs out of the hole and roll myself to the side. The well was positioned in the corner of a derelict building and the opening cornered by low walls on three sides. While it provided cover, it also prevented me from seeing anything beyond a small path, some bushes and a tree spreading out its branches over my head. There was a rope fastened to one of the building's wooden beams, with a hook to attach a bucket, so I knew it would be long enough to reach the water surface. I cut off the hook, slung it around a beam and tested the strength of both the knot and the wood. It seemed to be sufficient.

"Be careful, I'll throw you a rope," I let my voice echo through the well. "And be quick. We seem to be alone for now, but it's only matter of time."

Victoria insisted on Watson going first and secured the end of the rope around his waist in a way it would carry most of his weight.

The doctor started his ascent much slower than I had done without the rope. His sluggishness made me nervous.

And then I made a stupid mistake. Cautiously, I stuck my head around the corner of the building to get a view of the entrance to the catacombs and assess the situation. Of course I was immediately spotted by a guard, undoubtedly left behind by Moriarty. He drew his gun and started shooting at once -- and while I had retracted my head in a timely manner, it didn't bode well for our chances overall.

There was shouting in both English and Arabic and I could make out at least three different voices among them. In reflex, my hand flew to my gun, only to find it had been soaked completely. It would work again eventually, but only after a thorough cleaning. Brilliant. As if to hammer the point home, a bullet hit the wall behind me with a loud impact noise.

I couldn't defend myself, so the only option was to flee. There was a low wall that reached into the bushes on my right. If I could use them as cover, I could make for the building. I didn't need to escape, I merely had to draw the attackers away from the well so that Victoria and Watson would be able to reach the surface safely. I grabbed a large stone from the partly collapsed ruin and threw it in the opposite direction. It would take them a while to aim again after being distracted and I could make those seconds count.

The shots rang out and I jumped. Adrenaline flooded my system and gave me the boost I needed to get my muscles going after the whole ordeal underground. There was no time to think about the consequences of my decision, and so I flew and didn't look back. I skipped, ducked behind the next wall and threw myself directly into the greenery. My wet clothes squelched and transformed the dust beneath to me into mud, which left a clear trail to follow. Perfect.

My adversaries ceased their fire and shouted again. Then I heard them run. Their change of position meant a window of opportunity, though to get back up wasn't as easy as it may have seemed. My clothes dragged me down by their added watery weight and the liquid in my boots sloshed around. Still, I summoned up my strength, made a dash for the wall of the building and trailed along the side until I reached the corner. The guards were still running. Good, so they hadn't lost me. A shot ricocheted off the wall behind me and gave me a very clear incentive to move.

Neither doubt nor fear entered my mind as I ran toward the door of the building, even though a mortal threat was just behind me. This was what I lived for. If the other two hadn't been with me, it would have been easy to escape, but for now my first priority was to procure a weapon and either take out my pursuers as quickly as possible, or lose them.

I ducked into the building -- fate had it that the door wasn't locked. But there was no use in hiding, so I slammed the rickety wooden door shut behind me with such force I feared it might break, but it held together valiantly. The noise should attract them. They would think me foolish, producing such an obvious clue to pinpoint my location, but underestimating me would only work in my favour.

Now, the building seemed to be a storage facility, maybe a barn for the donkeys, but it was deserted at the moment. Two galleries of wooden floors were above me, at the walls all around the room, reachable only via stairs in the back. The whole place was curiously empty, except for the straw on the ground and a few nondescript crates on the upper levels. It gave off the impression of a place that had seen better days. Well, in that way we were completely alike.

But there was no time to linger. I had but one chance to get out of this on top. The door could be locked from the inside, but the key was missing, as was the wooden beam that could've been used to block it. Still, I positioned myself behind it and waited for the first guard to show. I didn't have to wait long.

The voices grew louder. I could make out the command to enter the building and braced myself. The door flew open. I caught it with both hands and pushed back, made it fall shut again as soon as one of my pursuers had entered. He was caught off guard by my action and whirled around. But it was too late for him to shoot, as I had already kicked the gun from his hand, sent it flying into the dust and at the same time reached for the one weapon the water couldn't have put out of order: My pocket watch.

A forceful pull extracted the thin wire. I threw myself at the staggering man and wrapped the deadly string around his neck in a fluid motion. The sudden pain induced a panic in him, and he moved jerkily. We collapsed together in front of the door -- not a moment too soon. Both of our bodies combined were enough to block it as the remaining guards started their assault. As the wood shook and splintered above me, I was acutely aware of my position: My back was against the flimsy wood. Should they choose to shoot at it, I wouldn't be protected.

Just then my assailant ceased his flailing motions and sank fully to the floor. I didn't bother to check if he were only unconscious or worse, and it didn't matter to me anyway. With an effort I pushed myself along the floor, feet against the door for leverage, to reach the dropped gun. As soon as my fingers were on it, I turned around and pulled the lifeless body of my attacker in front of me, as it provided the only cover I could achieve.

The blocking weight was gone and door burst open.

I lay on the floor, which was unwise in the long term, but provided me with the much needed element of surprise, as the guards, falling into the building, didn't bother to observe the ground. Their loss. Three people entered and fell one after the other, stumbling over their collapsing colleagues, as I shot them, so neatly lined up for me.

The shots had been deafening in such close quarters, but I had no time to wait for my ears to adjust. The body across my torso was rolled to the side and I snatched the wire from his throat, stored the silver watch into one of my pockets to reassemble later. As was my custom, I collected all guns from my attackers -- it's not like they needed them anymore.

Some agitated voices resounded through the narrow alleyway in front of the building, and I jumped up, threw the guns to the other side of the room as I made my way toward the stairs. There was no way I could escape through the front door, and I couldn't close it either, as the pile of bodies blocked the entryway.

The drying cloth and leather started to chafe my skin as I moved, while my boots were still filled with so much water I might as well have still stood in the depths of the cistern. Stray strands of hair fell into my face as I ran, itching and irritating. I wasn't going to lose any part of my protective uniform just because it felt uncomfortable, so I gnashed my teeth in order to calm my growing anger and pushed my hair back with one hand, hoping it would still be wet enough to keep some semblance of form and not distract me any further.

There was commotion below me as the dead bodies were discovered, but I didn't look back. Now that there was something to properly occupy my pursuers, I made it my new goal to reunite with my companions. I escaped through a latch in the storage building's roof and left the battle behind me.

The cautious sunlight of the day, reminded me that even though we were in Egypt and the air was dry, it was still winter. I wasn't going to be warmed up by those rays any time soon. A big tree indicated the location of the park, and I ran toward it, then fell down on my knees at the edge of the building and stuck my head out cautiously. From above, I could spot Watson and Victoria, as they crouched behind a wall, close to the point from which I had started my run. There was no time to lose.

To get their attention, I let a shot ring out. Watson turned his head up in an instant and surveyed the rooftops. As he spied me, I could see his eagerness to shout even from the distance, so I motioned for him to stay quiet. The main commotion was still happening around the corner, so I made a quick decision, put away the gun and swung my legs over the edge of the building. With an effort I pushed myself off the roof and into the tree, barely catching one of the thicker branches and cursed quietly as my hands were cut, despite my gloves, from holding onto the rough bark to decelerate my fall. But it was of no matter. The tree was easily climbable, and after only a few moments, I was on the ground, reunited at last with the others. We eyed each other, and I searched for signs of injury, but the only thing that seemed to trouble them were clothes even wetter than mine and a visible tiredness in their features.

"This can't be yours?" Watson asked and pointed at the gun, which I drew.

"No, I snatched it from one of my attackers," I grinned despite my state and pointed up. "Those fools followed me all the way into there. I could corner some of them in the building and silence them for good. But even if they are idiots, it won't take them long to realise I have disappeared through the roof. Follow me."

They nodded and fell into step behind me, as I lead them along the side of the ruins and between two buildings on the other side of the plaza, behind a group of donkeys. We moved at a fast pace, which made my body ache from exhaustion and drew a lot of attention to us when passing other people in the narrow streets.

"Where are we going?" Victoria asked.

"Does it matter? Anywhere is good as long as it leads away from there," Watson said.

"We are going to the Nile to charter a boat to take us upstream, south of Cairo," I answered. "From there it's a journey of about half a day into the desert to reach the ritual site."

"I put the instructions into my jacket, but I am afraid they are quite ruined now," the doctor stated sadly.

"No worries, doctor. I have committed them to memory. Through here, now," I pointed into the direction of a very small alley, just as I heard people shouting behind us. "And hurry, please."

"If I trust anything in this world, it's your memory, Mycroft," Watson said in a rare declaration of faith in my abilities, which I had absolutely no mind for properly processing at that moment.

We might as well have stepped into a separate world as soon as we turned the corner. A market, though small and constrained, presented itself in front of us. It was a curious thing of little booths, set up in a way they presented their wares from windows and boards tied in front of them. It was impossible to run straight through the corridor, which was indeed no wider than the arm span of a grown man. One would have to perform a slalom run to avoid bumping into anything -- or anyone.

I congratulated myself on my rapid deduction of our surroundings, as this was exactly the type of place I had wanted to find. Waving for my traveling companions to follow after me, I ducked and ran away beneath the wooden boards in a crouched position, as though through a very low tunnel. I trusted the others to follow suit as there was really only one way to go from here. Indeed I reached the other side of the market quicker than they could hope to achieve and saw them both dodge, duck and scramble along behind me.

But just as they caught up with me, two gunshots rang out in a quick succession from the other end of the market, and as if they had practiced it, all traders and visitors immediately filtered out of the space into the buildings, in what seemed to be just an instant. Boards retreated into the houses, windows closed and merchandise was dragged to safety. I saw Moriarty's henchmen on the other side, now with easy access where I had hoped to lose them for good -- all the advantage we might have achieved through our shortcut melted to almost nothing. Without hesitation, I produced my weapon, aimed and shot at our pursuers. The fact that we had a pistol at our disposal came as a surprise to them, as one was hit and fell to the floor, while the others took cover behind and inside various buildings.

More shots rang out as soon as they had positioned themselves. I couldn't pinpoint who had fired them, as the noise echoed in the narrow passage and made the very air vibrate. I didn't have much ammunition left, even counting the pilfered bullets, so we wouldn't be able to hold this position for long. I took a look around.

We were crouched in the space between two high buildings, and at the end of the path I could see a busy street with many people passing by. The noise of the street life seemed to overpower the gunshot echoes, because no one reacted to the fight. We could have made a dash for it and tried to disappear within the crowd before Moriarty's men could reach us, but I would've rather gotten rid of them before that. Then I spotted what could be our salvation.

"Watson, Victoria," I hissed between my teeth, addressing them without taking my eyes from the corner. "Kindly join me."

Watson approached my position cautiously, as I pointed my gun into the alley with a motion that made it clear to look for what I had seen. He drew back a few steps to the opposite wall and walked out as much as he dared, so he could follow my line of sight without being in danger of getting shot.

"The bags up on the balcony?" he asked as quietly as possible and flinched as another shot rang out just then.

I returned the shot, not with the intention to hit anyone, just to make clear that we were indeed still able to defend us, then nodded. "Their shape suggests that they are filled with a substance like flour or spices. I have three shots left before I have to reload. When I stop my responses to their shots, they will realise that and take the window of opportunity. You two run ahead and I'll shoot the bags. With the powder in the air, it will be very hard to see and breathe … which will hopefully incapacitate the bastards for a while. And if not, at least I will have given you a head start," I returned another shot. "Two now. Turn left at the end of the path, follow the street until you see a large column, wait for me in its shadow. Don't worry about me, I am much quicker than you are."

Victoria grabbed Watson's hand without waiting for his response and they were off, jumping over heaps of garbage and unidentifiable objects to get away. I watched Watson almost fall head first into a puddle, but he managed to catch himself at the last second by grabbing the wall on each side. Finally, they emerged onto the street, and I turned my attention back to our pursuers and returned yet another fire.

One shot left. I angled my gun around the corner and knowingly exposed my position while carefully taking my time to aim. The response was instant: Shots rang out, deafeningly loud, piercing the corner of the building I had taken cover behind. I wanted to flinch, but I didn't. With one eye closed, I held my breath to eliminate any quiver in my hands and pulled the trigger.

A cloud of yellowish dust exploded in the street as the bullet of my gun ripped through the bag and exited on the other side. I didn't stick around to witness the result of my actions, but noted that the shooting of firearms had ceased and been replaced by angry shouts, interrupted by frequent coughs and the crashing of some objects. I followed the same path as Watson and Victoria, made an effort to avoid the puddle that had almost been the doctor's downfall and emerged on the broader street into the blinding light. My eyes had trouble adjusting to the strong rays of the midday sun, but I couldn't afford to wait for them to catch up to me, as my appearance on the street wasn't only very sudden but also very unusual. My clothes were ruined and soiled, my hands bloody and I had no illusions about being able to blend into the crowd like this.

With limited vision, I pushed my way forward and elicited angry comments in a language foreign to me. With all the noise, colours and the strong light assaulting my senses, I almost missed the pair I tried to find near the column, which was exactly where I had pictured it to be.

251

"They are incapacitated for now," I said as I dragged them along through the crowd and didn't stop even for one second. "Quickly now, through here. Follow me closely."

We stopped in front of a narrow building in an even narrower street, almost hidden behind a mountain of crates and other storage containers. I produced a small key from my pocket -- sent a quick thank you to any deity responsible for keeping it safe during the ordeal -- and opened the door, which seemed to lead into a derelict place. But as soon as we entered the space, we were pleasantly surprised by the complete opposite. A well-furnished, albeit very small, house welcomed us -- something which you would have never guessed given the looks of the building from the outside.

But then again, that was clearly the point of it.

"We can clean up here and change clothes into something more inconspicuous," I explained after I had securely locked the door behind us. "If Moriarty didn't infiltrate the agency, his thugs don't know about this place and we should be safe here. The Secret Service has safe houses all over the city, located in strategic places. A heightened safety measure, following the British occupation of Egypt. Still, we're lucky this one is located within running distance."

I couldn't miss the surprise, which was still written on Watson's face. He nodded mutely and moved in the direction I indicated as the location of the washroom -- it was in a back room of the ground floor. But after only a few steps, he stopped and shook his head.

"Please, Victoria, after you," he said and inclined his head slightly.

She raised one eyebrow at me, daring me to step in front of her, then moved past the doctor in the narrow hallway. "I won't decline such a generous offer."

Watson and I were left to sit down at the table in the only other room big enough to fit two people. The noise from the street filtered dampened through the walls, much like the little sunlight illuminating the room through barred windows. We exchanged a glance, and it took only seconds for us both to break out in senseless laughter. I knew it was only compensation for the tense minutes we had just endured before, joy about a successful escape without bodily harm, but I relished it regardless.

It was rare for me to share these moments with another person.

"Wait here, I will bring you a change of clothes," I said before I stood up and walked in the direction of the narrow stairs. I left him behind, slightly dazed from the dissipating rush of adrenaline. Any moment now the fatigue would set in, which would definitely make him feel his years. It was no different for myself, but I had learned to disguise these occasions with grace.

The damp clothes had started to dry and were clinging uncomfortably to my body. I had planned to wait until I could use the washroom, but there was no time for all of us to clean up properly. As I reached a small room on the upper floor, a large wardrobe greeted me, in which I knew I would find a replacement set of clothes for all of us. The used clothes could be left here and would be collected at the next convenient time. There *were* advantages in working for a large, influential organisation.

I picked sand-coloured linen suit pants, complemented by a vest on top of a blue shirt, which would enable me to pass easily as a British visitor to the city. For Watson, who was a lot shorter than me, I picked a similar combination, but in darker colours. With a set of matching shoes each, we were well-equipped to make our way back to the embassy, pick up our luggage and procure a boat to take us upstream along the Nile.

As I peeled myself out of the ruined uniform, I made sure to transfer all items to the pockets of my new suit -- first and foremost the silver pocket watch, which I gave a cursory cleaning and rewind, so it would be usable again. The acquired gun and remaining ammunition found a place under my jacket as well. Dried off perfunctorily, I slipped into the new clothes and longed for a hot bath to be properly clean. A comb made sure my hair was neatly aligned, and I finished off the picture with a burgundy coloured scarf around my neck. No need to be careless with your look, even if on the run.

After I had tied my new shoes, I grabbed the clothes for Watson and made my way back down the stairs. I found the doctor at the table in a state of partial undress. The items he had salvaged after our dive spread out on the table. I could make out a ruined cigar, the scroll he had tried to save, and his waterlogged gun. As I moved around the man, I saw the small pocket watch he clutched in his hand.

The front of the watch was open, and I could see him gently caress the picture of Mary, which had miraculously escaped any watery damage.

I politely cleared my throat to indicate my presence and he closed the watch, put it onto the table next to the other items. "Here is a towel and a change of garments," I said and let a bundle of clothes drop onto the table next to him.

"The Secret Service is well-stocked," he remarked, but I just shrugged.

"It might seem like it, but that's only because we had a lot of trouble in the city in recent years, which resulted in a higher count of agents and more supplies for the area."

"Ah, not everyone is happy with the British reforms of the country, I take it?" Watson asked rhetorically.

"Believe me, these houses are not as well-maintained in any city we operate in. Sometimes they are missing altogether. This was a lucky circumstance," I explained. "Almost so much, I am afraid we have used up our luck for the coming days."

"Please, Mycroft, I don't want to hear things like that," Victoria emerged from behind me. "We'll save that stupid Sherlock. We've come so far already."

I smiled at her and made way for the agent to join us in the tiny kitchen space. She wore a set of clothes consisting of light brown trousers, a patterned shirt and a pair of dark boots. Her long hair was still wet, and she kept drying it with a towel as she sat down on a small chair.

"I suggest you change into some more suitable clothes, doctor," I grinned and pointed at the stack still lying on the table. It was only then he realised that he was sitting next to us in what were basically his undergarments, clinging wetly to his body. With haste, he grabbed the pile of dry clothes, rushed off to the bathroom area and closed the door behind him fast. Victoria laughed brightly at his actions, which made me smile as well. Somehow I was glad that despite the grim situation, we could still enjoy ourselves at least a little.

"Are you alright?" Victoria asked as the doctor was gone.

"Only scraped my hands. A few bumps here and there. I've had worse."

"No need to play tough with me, Mycroft."

I shook my head. "That's not it. It's really nothing to worry about."

Victoria inclined her head as we locked eyes in an inquisitive gaze. She stood up and proceeded to search the cupboards for what I knew was an emergency stash of medical supplies. Sure enough, she pulled a couple of bandages and some disinfecting alcohol from a small box. I willed myself not to flinch as she cleaned the wounds on my hands, one after the other, and we sat in silence, both simply staring down at the damage.

"Sometimes I wish I had never met your brother," she said quietly, as she was finished.

"You always know just how to push the metaphorical dagger deeper into my heart."

256

She opened her mouth to retaliate, and I could see her posture straighten in protest, but then Watson opened the door in the noisiest way possible.

"My apologies, I didn't want to disturb you," he lowered his head apologetically. "If you have something to discuss, I can give you some privacy."

"Very kind of you, Dr. Watson, very kind," I interrupted him. "But not necessary. We should leave here as soon as possible."

I glanced at Victoria. There was no room to argue needlessly, as we both knew the subject matter only too well and had iterated on it *ad nauseam*. We gathered our personal things, left the soiled clothes in the bathroom and returned to headquarters in record time, where, once again, nothing went as planned.

CHAPTER 13

I swear to god, I will find you

We arrived at headquarters to find the place in disarray. From the outside, nothing was apparent, but after being let into the heavily guarded fortress, we fell into a cauldron of chaos. There was shouting, people running about, but most important of all: large blood stains on the floor. Even -- or rather especially -- the quarters that had been given to the Secret Service were wasted. A chill ran down my spine as I thought of the implications this could have.

I found myself alone in the office of one, Marigold Bates. Victoria and Watson were being held in the hallway for further questioning -- because that was exactly what this was: an inquiry. The brilliant, blue eyes of Bates gleamed with anger, barely restrained, until she closed the door behind me and finally exploded.

"You come here against all orders, convince me to support your foolish quest and after only a day of your presence in the city, three of my agents are dead and several more severely wounded!" she shouted and brought her fist down on the broad wooden desk for emphasis, which made her writing pen fall from its stand.

"If you tell me what happened, I can try to explain..." I responded calmly.

"What happened? I can tell you what happened: You are a walking liability, Mycroft Holmes, inviting the enemy into our home by simple carelessness. I should've known when I saw the corpses that accompanied you into the city," Bates was not about to back down, and even though I felt the subconscious need to retreat, I knew that every concession would potentially cost us the valuable time we needed to reach Sherlock in time.

"With all due respect, the victims were *not* my responsibility. And we brought their murderer …"

"Yes! You brought that woman here. Assured us she would stay put until your return. And what good did that do us?"

"Wait!" I exclaimed. "This is about Elizabeth Moran?"

"What else did you think?"

A number of conflicting emotions coursed through me. Contempt for the Moran woman for making my life so hard. Shame, because I allowed this to happen to a branch of the Secret Service. But most of all anger toward myself for being so utterly stupid. Again. In my single-minded pursuit, I had not properly assessed the situation and felt responsible for the deaths of my fellow agents.

My emotions must have all been visible on my face, as Bates graciously let me regain my composure before she continued talking. "I'm sorry, Holmes. But in light of these developments I have to do what headquarters told me to: Detain you and your friends."

"But my brother …"

"Is not of international importance, despite what he means to you personally. I cannot stand by this reckless behaviour anymore," the branch manager said gravely. "You will be able to defend yourself when the time comes, but right now I won't allow any argument. Please leave this room and send in your companions."

In any other case I would have started to argue right away. I was confident in my ability to wrap everyone around my finger. But that would take time, because the moral high ground was on Bates' side. I didn't want to waste any time. No, there was only one option. We would have to run once again.

I nodded curtly at Bates, who narrowed her eyes at my silent acquiescence. We had crossed paths before, and it had never been this easy to get me to agree to anything. But her feelings were of no matter to me. I turned around and left the room without uttering another word, only to find my companions had deserted me.

When I entered the room, which an agent indicated to me, Watson was in the process of stitching up a leg wound on an unconscious man in front of him while he sat on the floor. His clothes were bloodied, but he didn't seem to realise this, as he looked to his work with an expression of utter concentration. Two other men lay on improvised bedding on the floor of the small chamber, bandaged haphazardly.

"The blade used on them was serrated and the wounds are still bleeding. The doctor has offered his expertise to patch them up properly," Victoria explained, as she was leaning against the window -- the only place with a bit of fresh air.

"I see," I just said mutely. There was much we had to discuss, but the image of Watson jumping into the fray like this made a bigger impression on me than I would've liked to admit. He didn't rush, but worked diligently along the edge, pressed the flesh together with his hands, without regard for his own cleanliness.

As he knotted the last string and proceeded to pick up some bandages, I stepped next to him and offered to hold up the leg so he could bind it properly. He thanked me with a weary smile and quickly wrapped the leg tightly in clean cloth. As all was done, he sank back and wiped his hands on the already ruined trousers, uttering an apology, which I immediately refuted.

"Thank you for your help," I said as I carefully put down the injured leg, then offered Watson a hand to stand up, despite the state of his. As he had risen to his feet and proceeded to the table to wash his hands in the water bowl, I cleared my throat once to get his attention.

"Elizabeth Moran has been freed."

He dropped the washcloth and had to hold onto the edge of the table to stabilize himself. His expression was one of despair and nausea.

"*More* deaths connected to us," he sighed, let himself fall onto a nearby chair and put his hands over both eyes. "No matter where we go, people fall around us. Is this really worth it?"

"I understand your argument, Dr. Watson. But we have to arrange our transport *now*," I explained. "I'm very sorry, but we have to leave immediately."

"With Elizabeth on the run?"

"While this is regrettable, she is not our priority. She is no threat to us now," I said calmly. This was a blatant lie, but I needed to get him to move. Watson eyed me in a way that openly expressed his doubt in my words, but didn't comment further.

"I didn't expect Moriarty to place such value on her," Victoria placed a hand on my shoulder. "She must be more important to him than we thought. But why?"

"Does it matter?" I asked in a strained voice. "Agents are both dead and wounded. Not to mention the security breach to this building and the implications this carries. I am in no mood to discuss this woman any further. We really need to go before Bates detains us."

"Detains us?" Victoria asked.

"We walk in here unannounced, get several agents killed, and you expect them to let us go again? They will keep us for the investigation of this security breach and that will void all chances for my brother to see another day. It was a mistake even coming back here."

"Our supplies are in a storage room down the hall," Victoria said.

"There might already be agents outside this very door," I added. "We can try to pick it up, but there's no guarantee."

"Can't we leave through the window or something equally underhanded?" Watson asked as he rummaged through the cupboards of the room for a new shirt and trousers to change into. He found a non-descript combination of beige clothes that suited the occasion just fine and did his best to remove the blood from his skin before changing into them.

"No, they will have heightened the security after the breach. It'll be as hard to break out as it is to break in now. Our one chance is the possibility that Bates hasn't informed her staff of our new status as detainees yet. We could just walk out."

"That'll never work, Mycroft," Watson shook his head.

"Oh, you might be surprised how many people don't recognise you as a threat if you just walk as if it's your god-given right to pass through," I answered. "But we can't leave as group. You two go first -- and carry the bloodied cloth and the washbowl. Those will make it less likely for people to want to speak with you. I will meet you outside."

"Where are you going?" Victoria asked as she picked up the bowl.

"To get our things."

"Leave it. We can get them when we return."

"I am *not* coming back here. Ever."

She shook her head, but I could see an understanding in her eyes. I watched the pair depart from the room and cautiously eyed the corridor. There was no sign of a guard. No one was watching. I waited for my companions to disappear behind the corner and immediately proceeded into the opposite direction, where I knew our belongings to be stashed. Unfortunately this brought me by Bates' office again. The door was still closed, so I wandered by undetected to the storage room - only to be caught by the arm and dragged into the small space. The door slammed shut behind me as soon as I entered it.

"Not a sound," I heard a female voice hiss. "Don't you dare say anything right now, Mycroft Holmes."

I nodded mutely and turned around to stare into the face of an enraged Marigold Bates. She had a death-grip on my arm, and I felt her nails digging into my skin even through the fabric of my shirt. This wasn't good… at all. I wanted to talk my way out of it, but her demeanour made it quite clear that I wasn't allowed to do so.

"First you bring death into my house and then you want to steal yourself away?" The head-agent snarled. "Is this how you were trained? How you were raised?"

I opened my mouth to reply.

"Quiet! I will get you for this, Holmes. I will. And I trust you won't try to run away from a proper investigation."

I was well aware of the depth of my actions and lowered my head in defeat, indicating that I wouldn't impair the proceedings. There was no way I could get out of it, in any case. Victoria had been right… had I never searched out the luggage, we'd all be on our way out of here. My only hope was that companions might realise that they should carry on without me.

"So if I don't find you back here right after you go gallivanting off to save your brother from whatever danger it is that he finds himself in, I swear to God, I will find you. And you will regret the day."

"But you…"

"I said *not a sound*," she released my arm, which hurt fiercely where she had grabbed it. A hand-shaped bruise was sure to bloom a

264

the spot later. She held out our meagre luggage with the other hand. "Take it and go, before I change my mind. If anyone asks me, I'll pretend you made your escape."

"I don't know what to say... Thank you."

She huffed a laugh. "Thank me by getting Sherlock out of his mess."

With a motion that dismissed me as if I were a servant, she indicated me to leave. I performed a short, but sincere bow and closed the door behind me after I left the room. With a dazed expression I walked through the embassy and out of the front door without anyone to block my path.

CHAPTER 14

It's a wonder he survived at all

In the evening of the same day I found myself in an Egypt very different from the hustle and bustle of the city. It was just as you heard about it in the tales being told by Egyptophile Londoners, who filled their homes with real or fake artifacts from this strange, ancient land. From my vantage point on the small ship, which slowly, but steadily worked its way upstream from Alexandria, I observed the passing landscape. This was a vision of the wealthy and prosperous empire this country had once been. The reeds on the bank formed a sea of green, flowing gently in the wind above the great Nile and the horizon opened up to show a vista of the desert. We passed small settlements in the midst of generously proportioned fields, and while I eyed my surroundings with curiosity and wonder, no person on the shore paid any attention to our ship.

The weather was mild, and even though the sun was already low, I didn't feel cold at all. How odd, thinking back to our journey through the Alps right now, like a thing out of a fairytale story. But no matter how much curiosity I had for the land, there was only so much energy in my body, and it had run out long ago. So only an hour into our day-long journey, I excused myself to lie down in the small cabin I had been given, grateful for a proper bed and a small amount of peace before our ordeal would start again. Soon I had drifted off into the arms of Morpheus, even before the sun had fully sunk in the West, and I have been told that I missed one of the most beautiful sunsets I should be able to imagine.

I woke to a dull ache in my skull. It was already morning, but the gentle motion of the ship told me that we were still on our way. I sat up and massaged my temples. Even though I should have had sufficient sleep, my muscles ached and my joints creaked as I stood up and selected my clothes for the day. The temperature was mild, but I suspected it would grow warmer during the day -- we were supposed to head out into the desert after all -- so I chose a light combination of outerwear and some parts of the uniform I had worn back in Italy, carried all this way.

Outside my cabin, only the crew of the small ship was up and about. No wonder -- after the strenuous activities of yesterday, my companions also needed every bit of rest they could possibly get. I moved around the vessel once, which was only big enough to accommodate six cabins in the back, a small room for captain and crew, and an open area to sit and enjoy the landscape in front. A gentle breeze was blowing, still strong enough to counter the heat of the sun, but not for long. One of the crew members approached and greeted me politely before I was informed that we were not far from our destination of Faiyum -- one of the oldest cities in Egypt. It was time to prepare.

But first I had something to set right that had been weighing on my mind for days.

"May I come in, doctor?" I asked from outside the thin door of his cabin.

"Yes, of course," he answered.

I opened the door to find Watson already dressed in the same set of stolen clothing as the day before, blinking into the sudden brightness.

"How did you know I was awake?" he wondered as he sat down on the small bed and pointed me to the tiny chair, in case I would want to take a seat, as well.

"A magician never reveals his tricks," I smiled and took him up on his offer. "Frankly, I heard you groan when you woke up, because you realised that your arm hurt. And before you ask: You are still shaking it a bit now and then, as if the blood flow still isn't quite sufficient."

Watson nodded in acknowledgement. "Have we arrived already?"

"Soon," I said and cleared my throat, paused just a bit, because I was about to do something that only happened once in a decade. "And before we continue, I believe I owe you an apology. I treated you poorly on this journey, while you have been a support to me. Please don't confuse my usual manner with ungratefulness."

"Mycroft, please," he answered with a smile and leaned forward. "Think nothing of it. We're simply going to fetch Holmes, return to London together, and all will be forgotten. Then we will bind him to his chair, so he can never do stupid things again."

"My brother would be out of his locks within seconds."

"And berate me for whatever type of knot I used."

"Then go into a lecture about proper binding techniques."

"Before lighting a pipe, shushing us out of the house and shouting for a cup of tea from Mrs. Hudson."

We joined in a hearty laugh, which must have been rather loud, as Victoria soon appeared in the doorway to see what all the ruckus was about.

"What's so funny?" She grinned as she leaned against the door frame. I could see the rough desert landscape passing by behind her.

"Sherlock," we both answered simultaneously.

Victoria laughed brightly in response and shook her head. "I'll be the last person to deny that. Come on now, we will be arriving shortly."

"Leave your things on the ship, doctor," I advised as I rose to my feet. "We will take only weapons and the most necessary items. Everything else will slow us down. If we move quickly, and without any hindering baggage, we should be able to reach the ritual site before nightfall."

The doctor nodded his agreement and I left his cabin together with Victoria. We entered our individual cabins and gathered what little we would take with us on the journey through the desert. This was a highly irregular venture, and I had never walked into the Sahara like this before. I couldn't deny the anxiety that spread through every corner of my mind, but I could perfectly well ignore it.

Victoria was in conversation with the captain of the ship in the front of the boat as I joined her. We had arrived, but just as planned, we weren't in any port.

"Dr. Watson, are you ready?" Victoria asked him as he approached us. "We will use the boat to reach the shore and go on from there. As this expedition is no longer under the protection of the agency, we are on our own. The ship was chartered privately by Mycroft and will remain here until we return."

"And if we don't return?" Watson asked.

"They will wait for three days and then they're free to go."

"Don't worry, doctor," I smiled and put a hand on his shoulder. "Even without the support of the Service, we'll still be able to do our best."

"Is Sherlock Holmes worth nothing to them?"

I refrained from commenting, as I was sure that Bates wouldn't take kindly to me telling everyone about her insubordinate deed in favour of my brother.

Victoria shrugged. "If we were in London, I believe you would find enough supporters to help us out. Maybe even in Belgium or Norway."

"Ah, yes, Norway. That would be possible," Watson nodded. "I guess you're right. Egypt is too far away to have been touched by his influence. Even the illustrious detective has places where no one knows of him. If only they would sell the Strand Magazine here."

Victoria laughed. "You should suggest that to your editor."

"Are you two ready?" I asked curtly.

They turned to me with both hope and distress on their faces and accepted the small backpacks I handed out, as well as a big piece of cloth, which was to be used as a cloak, with a hood attached.

"It may be winter, and the temperatures are not as high, but the sun is still relentless in the desert. I suggest you wear the cloak to protect yourself," I explained. "The backpack contains water and some rations, though not much. I don't expect us to be in the sandy expanse for more than two days."

"Do you have any idea what we might find?" the doctor asked, while he shouldered his pack. "Not that I don't trust your memory of the description in the scroll."

"I have been asking that myself. I searched all the maps I could lay my hands on while we were still in Alexandria, but the place described in the hieroglyphs is in a rocky, lifeless area, in the midst a hilly region with no discernible features. There is not an oasis or similar landmark even close to the spot. No special place recorded in any archaeological records, nothing mentioned in the few descriptions of the *Desert Wind* cult or the temples of Seth that I could turn up."

"That doesn't sound very promising," he countered.

"Indeed, it does not. The only way to find out is to go there ourselves. I have a compass and can find the right coordinates with the help of the sun," I assured him. "The only problem is time. If I have deciphered the ritual description correctly, the *sacrifice* will be undertaken when the moon rises above the horizon, which happens very early tonight and should give us only roughly twelve hours to find Sherlock."

"Child's play," Victoria joked and I just shook my head.

We all boarded the boat, but none of the crew would join us. They would wait for us here until we returned. It would cost me extra, sure, but that little money was nothing I was concerned with now.

"The workers refuse to set feet on the eastern bench of the Nile here. There are stories of evil spirits that cling to you and bring misfortune," Victoria explained as Watson asked why we were left to our own devices.

"We can take this as a good sign that shows we are on the right path," I shrugged. "Seth is the god of calamity. Maybe some old knowledge transformed into this superstition."

"I'll take it as encouragement then, and not as a vision of doom," Watson sighed.

"Why, doctor, you're being quite dramatic today," Victoria said as she took her place opposite to mine and grabbed an oar.

"We're about to venture out into the Sahara to stop a cult from using my friend as a ritual sacrifice. This is plenty dramatic already."

And just like that we were all on the shore, checked our equipment one last time, dragged the boat to land and concealed it between the reeds just in case. I pulled out the compass to find the right direction for us to start off in and then took a last look around. Behind us flowed the Nile, the majestic river, which had built the Egyptian empire and sustained it for hundreds, if not thousands of years. On the other side, I could see fields of green and small houses shielded by large palm trees. On our side, there was only a small band of vegetation, which terminated all too soon and gave way to a rocky plain with light sand and dark rocks, looking every bit as unwelcome to life as possible.

"This is the way, if the hieroglyphs are to be trusted. If not, we'll walk into the desert for nothing and will likely never see Sherlock again."

"No need to be so cheerful, Mycroft," Victoria snarked. "I am aware that Moriarty gambled on us finding his hideout in Alexandria, so the instructions might be falsified, but they looked proper to me."

"No way to find out now but to go in," Watson sighed.

I handed each person piece of paper, inscribed with an identical map of the region, the ritual place marked with the unambiguous X -- in case we got separated. Then I made a show of double-checking our water supplies and clothing status. My nervousness showed during the process. Victoria grew silent and adopted a faraway look in her eyes, stared into the direction in which Sherlock was supposedly being held. Watson seemed to have sunk into himself.

Our tentatively cheerful mood was replaced by a grim determination as we began the trip through the rocky plain, towards the low hills in the distance. The sun was not yet at full strength, but it already promised to be a hot and uncomfortable day. I had volunteered to take the lead, with Watson right behind me and Victoria at the rear to make sure he wouldn't get lost.

We walked until long past noon. The sun was already on its downward path towards the horizon, but it would still be some hours until it disappeared completely. Walking, stumbling, across the uneven, hard ground had left me breathless, exhausted and aching. The stress of the previous day caught up to me, the mental taxation from being thrown from one place to the other, and traveling across two continents in only two weeks had me in its grip and wouldn't let go. Normally I'd have no problem with this, but the worry about Sherlock amplified all other feelings. My wounds made themselves known again, and my head pulsed with a dull ache every time I took a step. The only thing I could do was walk ahead as well as I could, as I knew that every break and every delay could mean the end for my brother.

If I ever lay my hands on him again, I will have to restrain myself not to kill him.

Except for a short confirmation of my companion's continued presence every half hour or so, I didn't talk, and neither did they. The day wasn't overly hot, but we had covered our heads with the cloaks regardless, as it wouldn't do for any of us to be sun-struck right now. While the heat was bearable, the exceptional dryness of my surroundings caused me considerable distress. No matter how often I took a sip of water and kept it in my mouth, it always felt like I had inhaled a handful of sand only seconds after the precious liquid had dissipated.

I continuously surveyed the horizon, but couldn't make out anything but bluish, hazy skies over a rocky landscape, in which bright sand and dark stone where the only inhabitants. With every step, my melancholy grew, with every misstep my annoyance grew even further. Not only about my surroundings, but about everything that came to mind, which was a lot when you walked silently through the desert for hours.

My companions must have been equally lost in thoughts, as Watson all but ran into me when I stopped in my tracks. He had to catch himself on a bigger rock to regain his balance. I took out my compass and by angling it correctly with the help of my watch and the sun, checked our current direction. The doctor slumped down on a low, rock as I meticulously repeated the measurement three times to be extra sure. There is never room for error in the Sahara.

"If I estimate correctly, we should be less than two miles from our goal," Victoria said, as she sat down next to Watson.

"You are almost correct," I mumbled.

She busied herself and dug a handful of dates from her backpack. Watson joined her and consumed some of his own provisions. I snatched a date from Victoria's hand, which was met with an expression of surprise from her side and an eyebrow raised in challenge from mine. I felt delighted by the sugary juices of the date, which stayed in my mouth far longer than the occasional sip of water had.

"Over there," I interrupted the two and pointed to a very low hill in the distance, from which we were separated by a shallow, wide valley. "Can you see it too?"

They visibly strained their eyes to discern what I had pointed out, but even though I heard a surprised gasp from Victoria, the doctor just shook his head.

"There is a column of black smoke behind that hill. But it *is* very faint. Not from a big fire," Victoria explained to him. "I am surprised you could make it out through the haze, Mycroft."

"Only after I confirmed the exact direction. But it's definitely where we should be heading," I explained and stashed my compass, as well as the small map I had perused. "I had already begun to think that the instructions were fake."

"The longer I thought about that, the more I believed them to be absolutely genuine," Watson added. "There was really no reason for them not to be."

"What makes you think that?" Victoria asked with a hint of disbelief in her voice. "Moriarty might as well have left the plans there to lead us astray, or into a trap."

"But that is just it. Moriarty left them there," Watson countered.

"I don't understand," Victoria shook her head.

"Well, Dr. Watson, you can use your head after all. I am beginning to see why my brother keeps you around," I mused. "Of course, because the madman left them there, they had to be very quite genuine."

Victoria still frowned.

"He has been leaving clues for us along the way. Easily findable breadcrumbs, to point us in the right direction at every step of the way, always making sure we would continue to go on," I elaborated on my statement. "Everything was designed to keep us playing his game."

"But we escaped his trap in Alexandria," Victoria shook her head. "If he meant for us to die there, why give us a very accurate map?"

"I suppose he never expected us to leave that place," I answered gravely. "He probably delighted in the knowledge that we had the correct map in our hands but could do nothing to change Sherlock's destiny."

"That's just... wrong," she said tensely and rose to her feet. Then the agent extended a hand to help Watson stand up as well, which he took gratefully. "He must have hit his head harder than I thought when he tumbled down that waterfall in Switzerland."

"It's a wonder he survived at all. And an even bigger one is that my brother emerged not only with his life intact, but with his faculties working as intended. We may never know what exactly happened on that fateful day, but I do know that Sherlock is behind that hill, and I will stop at nothing to get him back to London alive. We have roughly three hours left before the moon rises, and I suggest we make good use of them."

The other two indicated their agreement and we walked down the slope, not with a spring in our step, but with a strong resolve in our hearts that gave us the strength to carry on. The valley was wide, and we covered ourselves with the cloaks in an effort at concealment. Still, if anyone had watched the space, they would have spotted us sooner or later. But there was no sign of any human on the horizon.

As soon as we had reached the next crest, we dropped to the ground and positioned ourselves behind some low, dark rocks. There it was: A small circle of tents with a platform made of stone in the middle, which looked like a pyramid with the top cut clean off. From the distance, I couldn't make out individual items or people walking about, but my heart sank as I realised that the size of the camp hinted at a rather large number of enemies for us to overcome.

CHAPTER 15

It appears we are at an impasse

"The rocks are arranged in several circular patterns around the centre, throughout the depression," Victoria pointed out, while examining the surroundings of the camp with a small spyglass. "This hasn't been constructed recently, either. The whole place seems ancient."

"Like the priests of Seth have been using it for a long time," Watson speculated. "And now they have recruited Moriarty into their ranks. It still feels... unreal, even though I am *actually* sitting crouched in the Sahara, breathing in so much dust my throat feels as though it's lined with sandpaper."

"Believe me, I don't feel much better, doctor. But it doesn't matter, because somewhere down there is my brother, and he had better be alive -- otherwise I will make sure that those cultists' holy site will also be their final resting place..." My voice grew gradually lower, until the last part was accompanied by a threatening growl.

"Have you spotted Holmes yet?" Watson asked hopefully, but Victoria just shook her head.

"If he even *is* in the camp. I've spotted neither him nor Moriarty. Well, their weird regalia looks right from what you told me, but that's about it," Victoria shrugged. "It feels... off, somehow."

The distance we would have to cross without cover was considerable. The depression was wide and flat, probably measuring almost half a mile across, looking like a very shallow impact crater.

"We'll wait until the darkness falls," I decided. "They won't be able to spot our approach then. Even though that leaves us with a much smaller window of opportunity."

My companions had no choice but to agree, as there was no other feasible option. The next half hour was one of the longest I ever had to endure. But even though this was as close to the situations I had encountered in my work for the Secret Service as it could be, I was feeling rather anxious. Nervous. Even shaky. It was clear why I felt so untypically unnerved. Not because of the unknown, which I encountered frequently. Not because of the danger, which I had ceased to faze me long ago. And certainly not because of the location, which, though unusual, wouldn't prove an insurmountable obstacle. No, it was simply because this time, the life at stake was that of my *exasperatingly* beloved brother, and for once my emotions wouldn't stop surfacing. Watson had talked about tying him to a chair upon our return, and the longer I pondered my situation, the certainty of it being a joke grew smaller and smaller.

While we waited, the sun sank lower, and the landscape was bathed in a golden light, which made the sand and even the dark stones glow as if hallowed. The atmosphere morphed into something out of a fairy tale as the very land seemed to shine from the inside. I could see why they would worship the god of the desert in a place like this.

"The men in their monochromatic robes walk around the camp and flaunt their red headdresses made of feathers, which bob with each step they take," Watson relayed the pictures he saw. "But there is no purpose to their movement -- they walk aimlessly and in circles, much like the drunkards stumbling through east London late at night."

"An apt description, doctor," Victoria commended him.

"There is some black smoke rising from a platform in the middle," he continued. "And a bowl with something burning in it. In front of …"

Before he could continue, a high-pitched scream drifted from the centre of the valley to our ears, just as the last rays of the sun disappeared behind the horizon. I jumped up, ripped the spyglass from the good doctor's hands and took a look at our place of interest myself.

"Was that Sherlock?" Victoria asked with a shivering voice, just as another painful scream erupted.

"No, it sounded rather like a woman," Watson said quickly. "Holmes' voice is too deep to produce these sounds, I hope. Something is starting down there, now that the sun is gone."

"We should now be able to walk across under cover of our cloaks," I stated and stashed the spyglass in my pocket.

"I suggest we approach the first ring of stones. They are the biggest and should provide some sort of cover while we wait for the night to fall properly. The air will soon be too hazy for them to see us in the distance," Victoria explained and pointed at a group of stones to our right, roughly a third of the way into the valley.

"I trust your judgement, Victoria. No time to lose now."

I stood up and drew the sand-coloured cloak closely around my shoulders to conceal any recognisable form that might give me away, just as my companions did the same. Crouching low, we fell into single file and tried to get across the distance as fast and as inconspicuously as we could manage. And with every purposeful step I kept my head a bit higher and left a part of my anxiety and doubt behind me.

As we had almost reached the stones of the outer ring, I was startled by a low rumbling, which seemed to permeate the very ground as well as the air surrounding us. It didn't last all that long, but when I exchanged glances with the other two, I knew I hadn't imagined it. Then, despite every precaution, Victoria emitted a squealing noise of surprise and pulled us down to the ground before she pointed upwards, to the sky.

I will never forget the sight that lay before us that very moment.

Above the featureless, flat ground, standing out against the darkening sky, already tinted in an inky blue, a bright wall of clouds stood upright and proud. It was like a monument in honour of the day, which refused to fall into darkness, glowing yellow and gold in the setting sun. There was no way to judge just how high the clouds reached, but they covered almost half of the heavens and made me feel rather insignificant.

"That's impossible," I uttered with a shaky voice. "We should have seen this coming. There should've been signs! How can it appear just like this?"

"The clouds?"

"Dr. Watson!" I shouted, slightly panicked, all caution forgotten. "By god man, look closer! Those aren't clouds! We need to get to cover *now*."

I had never been exposed to a sandstorm before, but I instinctively knew the danger it meant for us. It was almost impossible to comprehend the sheer size of the wall of sand in front of me. All the horror stories I had heard about this natural phenomenon played in my head simultaneously.

We watched the camp, but no reaction to the storm was visible. In fact, there were more people outside the tents now than before, gathering around the central structure. They seemed to gather, all faced towards the central point. I could only barely make them out now, as the light faded rapidly. The only things to stand in defiance of the night were the wall of sand above us and the rekindled fire in a bowl in midst of the group I suspected to be the actual *Desert Wind* cultists.

"The density of tents seemed to be a bit higher on the left side, and we should be able to hide somewhere," Victoria suggested and I agreed readily.

The wind had already picked up and the first particles of sand were flying through the air, not yet painful when they hit my skin, but uncomfortable enough that I dreaded being out in the open much longer. With the threat looming, we approached the camp even faster, if only to seek shelter in one of the tents. As I looked up, I could see that only the topmost part of the sandstorm was still illuminated by the setting sun and the lower part had morphed into a threatening, swirling black mass, about to swallow us whole. As we reached the camp, I let myself fall to the floor immediately and lifted the cloth of the closest tent.

"Clear," I announced after I inspected the interior. "Can you roll through here?"

"Of course," Victoria confirmed and within seconds, both of us were inside the tent. Watson took just a bit longer to enter in the same way, clumsily getting up from the ground.

Immediately, we were engulfed in a hot and sticky darkness. It was clear that the tent had been left undisturbed in the sun all day, as the air was stale and reeked distinctly of unwashed clothes. On the floor was a thin carpet, which felt sticky to my hands, so I made a point of touching it as little as possible. As my eyes adjusted to the darkness, I could make out the sparse furniture, consisting of at least three low beds and several small tables. The overall state of the space quickly told me that there would be nothing of worth to us here.

There was only one object that caught my attention. A headdress with long feathers rested on the pillow of one bed, and as I bent down to examine the details, a sliver of light fell across it. The feathers immediately took on a blood-red shimmer. Surprised, I turned around, only to find Victoria cautiously holding open the door flap of the tent to judge the situation outside. She beckoned us over after closing the tent again.

"I can't observe much from here, but it seems like they have all gathered in the centre. There aren't any guards," she explained. "Not as far as I can make out."

"Maybe their meeting place is so secret and removed, they never had need for any protection. Or their ritual is so sacred, no one would even dare interrupt them," Watson wagered a guess.

"Or outsiders simply aren't allowed," Victoria added. "No matter the reason, I assume these cultists are distracted. We should search the tents to find Sherlock before they take him out there. We should still have about an hour, but we should assume less."

"Then we'll have to split up. Victoria, you will go with Dr. Watson and circle the camp clockwise. I'll go counter-clockwise and we'll look into every tent to spot my brother. There is no way to reliably contact one another without raising suspicion, so we will just have to be quick and do whatever we can."

Victoria showed me one last, encouraging smile, then beckoned the doctor to follow her and slipped out of the tent. Just like that, they were gone. I took a few seconds and a deep breath, then followed them outside.

The tents all looked remarkably similar -- especially in the falling darkness. As I searched for stable footing among the stones, so as not to stumble and draw attention to my presence, the members of the cult in the middle of the circle started a synchronous humming noise. It permeated the air, a sound so clear, I could hear it even over the growing wind. Still, the strange people made no attempt to leave. They sat in a half-moon shape in front of the central structure. Their robes fluttered and their headdresses looked like beaten, battered cockerels in danger of being carried off by the wind.

But there was no time to observe them any further. In the light of the fire, flickering bravely in the storm, the only other things I could make out on the pedestal were some wooden poles. It was safe to say that whatever they had in mind for my brother would take place exactly there. So as long as there was no one bound to the pole, we'd still have time to find him.

Turning towards the next tent, I lifted the cloth carefully. It was dark and had a stench just like the first one we had entered, if not worse, which made me wonder just for how long the cultists had lived out here in preparation for the ceremony. I finally found a slightly bigger tent, took a deep breath of fresh air and crawled into the interior. It was immediately obvious that this one served a different purpose, as it was empty, except for the chair in the middle -- and a person tied to it. The stench wasn't as horrible here, but there was an odour in the air I would never mistake for anything else: It reeked of fresh blood.

My presence had gone unnoticed so far, but I kept to the side of the tent as I circled around. It was hard to make out who exactly was sitting there, all tied up. Their body size was too small for Sherlock, but then again I didn't know what they had done to him in the last weeks. I only knew the person was injured, because even from the back, and with only the light of a single oil lamp, I could see them bleeding from a number of wounds on their arms.

Then I could also see clearly that it wasn't my brother, after all.

I inched closer and pushed the hair out of the person's face to discern just who was being kept here. To my slight surprise, it was no other than Elizabeth Moran, bleeding from a large number of cuts all over her body, blood smeared across her skin and what remained of her clothes. The only thing keeping her upright were the ropes binding her to the chair, and from the blood on top of them, I could conclude that she had been tied down, wounded and then simply left here. She was breathing shallowly and her skin had taken on a sickly white pallor. There was no way to know how much blood she had already lost -- I could only tell that she was in fact, still alive.

The ropes were bound tightly, and while I could have cut them easily, I didn't have the mind to do so. Here she was. The woman who had attempted to thwart me at every turn of our journey, finally at my mercy, all alone. Some part of me was absolutely satisfied by seeing her this way, and while I wouldn't have done her any harm personally, I gathered that my inaction would lead possibly to the same end.

But it wasn't my decision to make alone, as just then I heard the woman groan and move her head slightly upwards. The last thing I needed at the moment was a loud noise to alert anyone to my presence, so I put my hand over her mouth preemptively. While this only brought her to consciousness faster, at least I was able to contain

her shouts, which emerged muffled through my fingers. Elizabeth'
eyes flew open, panicked and unfocused. She struggled in her
restraints, clearly wanting to flee, but was effectively kept in place.

"Elizabeth, look at me," I hissed. "I'm not one of them. Surely
you remember me."

She shook her head and strained against the ropes, continuing
to utter unintelligible noises so loud I could barely stifle them. With
my free hand I strongly grabbed her head of unruly hair and forced
her to look at me. We stared into each other's eyes for a while, until I
saw the panic retreat and some sort of recognition arrive. Still, her
muscles relaxed only by a fraction, as I wasn't a cultist, but
potentially just as frightening to her. She took a few big breaths, but
never interrupted our shared gaze, with her big eyes full of tears, even
as I let go of her.

"Mycroft Holmes," she whispered, voice hoarse, the words
barely rolling off her tongue. "Why?"

"You of all people should know why," I said flatly.

She coughed as a shaky laugh rippled through her body. Her
eyes were unfocused and her head swayed back and forth. I grabbed
the lamp and held it up to her face to confirm my suspicion: Elizabeth
was under the influence of some drug that dulled her senses... and her
pain.

"Dear Sherlock..." she finally continued. "Go home. He is
dead."

"What?" I exclaimed, in that moment paying no mind to the
loudness of my voice. I grabbed her arms and closed my finger around

the cuts, eliciting a painful wince. "He *cannot* be dead. Tell me you're lying!"

"What does it matter to me? He is dead. It's the truth," Elizabeth let her head slump back, looking to the ceiling of the tent. "Moriarty…"

A violent sobbing noise escaped her and even more tears rolled from her eyes. She started to breathe heavily, only to be constricted by the ropes, which ended in a coughing spell. I stepped over to the entrance of the tent, and quickly drew back the cloth to check our surroundings. But the few cultists I could see were still humming their strange chant and seemingly in a trance-like state, so I discarded them from my mind.

A dull thumping noise had me spin around, only to find that Elizabeth had managed to make her chair fall over in the few seconds I had my back turned. Now only a muffled sobbing was audible. I sighed. Maybe it was indeed time to take pity on her. In this state, she wouldn't be able to even walk out of here. But not before I asked her some more questions -- so I knelt down in front of her.

"Where is Sherlock?"

"Moriarty," Elizabeth whispered. "He cut me. Those men, they touched me all over, squeezed my wounds to paint their faces with my blood…"

"You know you would have been better off if you had let me put you in a cell in Milan," I answered, but if she heard my voice, she didn't pay it any mind.

"He hates him, you know? It's only the hate for Sherlock Holmes, which kept him going all these years. He has lost so much in the fall. He can't think anymore. Gets headaches, has problems concentrating," Elizabeth simply stared to the floor in front of her and made no more attempt at struggling. She talked slowly, as if the words had to filter through a haze. "He learned that Holmes was still alive -- that he had escaped the fall with heavy injuries, but his mental faculties completely intact. That is when the *Desert Wind* found him. In his desperation, they convinced him that a *proper* sacrifice of Sherlock Holmes to the deity Seth would bring back his mind. Not just to kill him. No, he had to do it *properly*."

"And he believed them."

"Believed? He has made it his crusade... "

The tent started shaking violently just then, and I knew that the sandstorm had finally hit the camp with its full force. A voice rose above the roaring wind and shouted something in a language I couldn't comprehend.

"Go home, Mycroft Holmes. Go home and leave me to die."

I grabbed a bloodied knife from a nearby table. Elizabeth grew wide-eyed, her eyes betraying the shock she felt, but she kept quiet.

Then I raised the blade.

The cloth, which covered the entrance of the tent, was flapping in the wind. I slipped out into the storm and left Elizabeth alone with her own thoughts, now free of the ropes that bound her.

With my body pressed closely to one tent after the other, I advanced into the direction of the centre. But visibility wasn't my only problem. Even under my cloak, I was battered by the small particles, which hurt like pricks of a needle every time they hit my skin. Out of fear for the safety of my eyes, I couldn't advance directly against the wind, but had to run from cover to cover, inching forward.

The central structure was barely visible now, as the sandstorm clouded everything and the night had well and truly arrived. Still, the cultists kept to their formation, eyes closed, serenely meditating. The unrelenting wind tore at their clothes and destroyed the feathers of the few headdresses that barely held on in the battering. Blood was running down their skin, and I couldn't tell if it was Elizabeth's or theirs.

As I got closer, I could finally make out more details. There were now several figures on the central pedestal, but from the distance I couldn't make out who the shadows were. So I decided to circle around the tents to approach it from behind. The storm overpowered any noises, so I didn't worry about my footsteps, and the cloak looked just like the tent fabrics, pushed around in the wind, so I felt adequately concealed. But it wasn't my own safety I was worried about. I refused to believe Elizabeth's claim about my brother's death until I saw him with my own eyes. My only hope was that Victoria and Watson had reached him by now.

So it was with a shock that hit me like a dagger through the heart when I saw him, recognised him, as I circled around another tent: My dear brother Sherlock, bound to a wooden pole at one end of the structure, right above me. He hung limp, head only held up by a rope across his forehead. His body was being battered by the sand, which hit him without any barrier to protect him, as he was clad only in a pair of dilapidated, dusty trousers and showed bare flesh everywhere else.

Next to him were only two people: Another one of these damn cultists and James Moriarty himself. So my companions hadn't found Sherlock in time. I took a deep breath and released the safety of my gun. I knew there must be stairs to reach the top, which lay more than two metres above my head. It was impossible to climb in the wind, which was still growing impossibly stronger and I couldn't get a clear shot from my vantage point either. As I continued my way around, I temporarily lost sight of the trio, but redoubled my efforts to prevail against the wind.

Then a gunshot rang loud and clear, even over the noise of the storm.

I lost my footing as it startled me and my gun dropped to the ground, immediately carried away by a gust of the storm. I tried to jump after it, but lost track after only few seconds, as it disappeared between various other objects being blown about. There was no use searching for it, and I cursed under my breath.

"Don't move, you fiend!" I heard Victoria's voice then, bright, clear and full of wrath floating above my head in the storm. "Make one wrong move and the next shot *will not miss!*"

Victoria! She was up there, with Moriarty! I clambered to my feet as quickly as I could and scrambled to get around the base of the stone monument, almost falling several times due to the loose sand and resistance of the wind. Finally, I laid eyes on the stairs and climbed them using both hands and feet until I was on top and stood fully in the wind, eyes shielded.

Like this I could barely make out what was happening in front of me. The flames had been blown out almost entirely, leaving only embers to shed any light on the scene. Being robbed both of vision and freedom of movement by the sandstorm felt claustrophobic in a strange way I had never experienced before.

I reached out to the figure of Watson, only a few steps in front of me and grabbed his jacket. He jolted, but recognised me quickly. His arm was outstretched, gun pointed unwavering at Moriarty, no matter how much the gales tried to tug at the limb. Only a few steps in front of us, Victoria stood in the same position, weapon aimed at our nemesis.

Then I heard a laugh, chuckling and bubbling underneath the roar of the sandstorm, and it didn't take me long to realise that it originated from the professor, holding a large knife to Sherlock's throat, who was still bound and unconscious.

"There we are. Finally," he shouted and grinned widely. Thank you for coming all this way to witness our little show. I am now going to kill your precious detective and you will all watch me do it."

"Put down the knife, or I will shoot you," Victoria exclaimed loudly, above the roar of the storm.

"Oh no, my dear. *You* put down your gun, or I will kill him," Moriarty responded.

"You will kill him anyway," I said.

"Someone paid attention."

"It appears we are at an impasse, Moriarty."

"So it seems, Mr. Holmes, the elder. Tell me. How does it feel to see your precious younger brother in such a life-threatening situation?" Moriarty purred, which should have been impossible to hear above the noise surrounding us. He dragged the fingers of his free hand across Sherlock's exposed skin. His digits collected the blood from countless small wounds, which stemmed from the onslaught of the sand in the air and drew little patterns on his stomach. "Are you mad? Angry? Desperate?"

"I refuse to give in to your taunts. Release him now!"

Moriarty laughed again, in his strange way. "Or what will you do? Shoot me? I am dead already!"

"Tell me something I don't know, professor," I said as a calculated response.

"Don't call me that!" he hissed, face distorted with anger where just a second ago only amusement had shown. "Never call me that again!"

"Why not?" Watson asked, surprise obvious in his voice at the madman's reaction. "Professor?"

"Stop it!" Moriarty screamed and pressed the knife to Sherlock's throat so hard it drew blood and coaxed a reaction out of him. He squirmed uncomfortably and finally let out a strangled noise, which only made the knife press in further. "Ah, back with us, Sherlock?"

"Holmes!" Watson exclaimed, but didn't dare move towards him yet. "Holmes, are you alright?"

"Dr. Watson, ever the faithful dog."

"Shut your mouth!" Victoria stepped closer, weapon still raised. "Get away from him!"

"Victoria, get back!"

"Yes, listen to the smarter Holmes. Step away from me, Victoria."

"Vic... toria?" the voice of my brother drifted shakily over on the wind, eyes still closed, but reacting to a familiar name. "Victoria? How...?"

"Now, now. I don't want to interrupt the touching reunion, but if you don't want to lose one of your family members, I would suggest you throw away the guns now," Moriarty inclined his head slightly.

"But..." Victoria hesitated.

"*Now!*"

"Just do it, Victoria," I said flatly. "We won't get anywhere otherwise."

"Very wise, Mycroft. Much wiser than your younger brother," Moriarty smiled. "Now, throw them over the edge."

Watson made the first move -- his gun flew towards the lower ground in what would have been an elegant curve, if not caught by the storm and carried out of sight in an instant. The look that Victoria exchanged with us was fearful and angry at the same time, but even after sending a silent plea to me, I just shook my head, and her gun took the same journey as the doctor's.

"Your turn, Holmes," Moriarty ordered me as I didn't move. "Your gun."

"I lost it."

"Nice try. You always carry a gun. Our friendly detective here told me. He told me everything. We had a very nice time, Sherlock and I, very nice, indeed…"

"I *most certainly* dropped it!" I shouted. "Down there. When I heard the shot earlier, I was surprised and stumbled. The wind… it carried it off."

"And I am supposed to believe that?"

Victoria exchanged a questioning look with me, but I could just shake my head and patted down my pockets to signal that I really didn't have any weapon on my person. I removed the cloak and my suit jacket, both of which were carried off by the wind immediately and turned around, so everyone could see my empty weapon belt.

"I'm telling the truth!"

There was a little pause in Moriarty's movements, and he lowered the knife from Sherlock's throat to his unprotected stomach. He could still hurt him fatally, but at least the blade wasn't pressing into his throat anymore. While my brother seemed to be slowly regaining consciousness, he was still far from lucid. His body was constantly assaulted by the storm and he blinked as if he couldn't see properly, which wasn't surprising considering his state.

When Moriarty waved for me to get closer, I hesitated.

"Come on. Just a bit closer, so I can check if you are *really* unarmed," he said with a voice coaxing and sweet, which then dropped to an authoritative tone within seconds. "*And do it now.*"

Watson looked at me with an unsure gaze and Victoria just shrugged. To get to Moriarty, I had to move against the wind, which made it hard to advance quickly. I was already tired from just standing in the storm, and now I raised my arms protectively in front of my head as I inched over to Moriarty's position. Just as I was only two steps away, he pointed at a position right in front of him and I obediently followed his instructions for now.

The madman started to pat me down methodically, but then I saw something move quickly from the corner of my eye. Moriarty screamed and cursed. Then there was the metallic noise of the knife falling to the floor. Sherlock had regained enough of his faculties to be able to kick the blade out of the professor's hands while taking advantage of the fact that Moriarty had no more vision in his right eye.

I jumped for the blade immediately, which was already being pushed away from us by the wind, but my antagonist was just as quick in his reaction. We fell to the floor and both struggled to reach the knife. Even though the man was kicked by Sherlock repeatedly, he managed to hit me squarely in the face and grab the knife before I could put my hands on it. I could barely hold onto his arms to prevent him from cutting me or anyone else.

"Mycroft!" I heard Victoria shout and run towards me, but then I saw a shadow jumping at her from the side, toppling her slender form to the ground in a heartbeat. The cultist, who had been up here before with Moriarty, had waited on the sidelines, hidden by the storm, for the right moment to strike. He was upon Victoria with a blade of his own.

Watson decided to fight off her attacker first, leaving me to deal with Moriarty alone. We scrambled for dominance over the knife, pushing it back and forth between us, rolling dangerously close to the edge of the stone structure in the process. Sherlock was out of our reach now, which was a blessing and a curse, as he was now fully awake and shouted his wrath over the storm with a voice hoarse from neglect, but powerful nevertheless. I was just glad we weren't close enough to hurt him with the blade by accident.

"You are a dead man, Mycroft Holmes," the professor hissed while he kicked me to loosen my grip on the weapon. "I will kill you and then I will slice up your precious Sherlock. Or I will make you watch."

I concentrated all my strength on getting out alive, instead of wasting my breath on senseless taunts. From the corner of my eye I could see the acolytes beneath us, still all in trance, continuing to sing. It was then I first considered that they were in a drug-induced stupor. But it had been the wrong thing to contemplate at the wrong time. Moriarty had seen the moment in which I was distracted by my own brain, which could never be turned off, and ripped the knife from my hands.

He jumped up, placed a heavy, dirty boot squarely on my throat and the other on my right hand, then pointed the blade directly at my face. I could barely breathe and clawed at his leg with my remaining hand, but the pressure on my trachea was too much. Moriarty grinned at me triumphantly and lifted his boot slightly before pressing down in earnest. I didn't lose consciousness completely, but blacked out long enough for Moriarty to think I was indeed incapacitated. I tried to grab him as he walked into Sherlock's direction, but the only thing I managed to hold onto was thin air.

"Sherlock Holmes!" he screamed, positioning himself directly in front of my brother. "Now you will pay for what you did to me! For the glory of Seth *I will end you!*"

I wanted to scream, but my battered throat didn't produce any sound. In that moment Victoria picked up the cultist, threw him from the pedestal in a feat of adrenaline fueled, inhuman strength and launched herself towards Moriarty, but it was too late. The blade was already moving down.

My world went black.

A single gunshot sounded loudly over the wind. I saw Sherlock's body splashed with blood and then the knife untainted at his feet. Moriarty lay on the ground, wounded by a shot to the shoulder. I wasn't taking any chances now, summoned all of my strength and launched myself at the body of the professor. With a fluid motion I grabbed the ceremonial knife and pushed it deep between his ribs, into his heart. Underneath me I felt him struggle and gurgle, but it was over within seconds.

Just like that, the storm faded, and the sand in the air fell to the ground like a rain shower, as if the wind had simply been switched off. It left everything in an eerie silence, now bathed in the silvery light of the moon. After the strange darkness, it felt as bright as daylight, in that magical, time-stopping way only the full moon can achieve.

In the deafening silence of the storm's aftermath, I recognised the sound of metal, hitting the stone floor. With great effort, I peeled my eyes from Sherlock and looked around to find the origin of the noise. On the top of the stairs, barely standing upright, clothes in rags and blood running down her body, stood Elizabeth Moran, panting heavily, the gun she had used to shoot Moriarty at her feet. She had her eyes trained unwaveringly on the figure of the professor on the floor. No one dared to move, as if the spell could somehow be broken, but then Elizabeth collapsed while exhaling a shaky breath and just like that, we were back in reality.

"Sherlock!" I shouted brokenly, as my throat was still hurt. I coughed heavily. "Sherlock, are you alright?"

Watson reached him before me and removed his friend's restraints. Victoria simply collapsed at his feet, all energy drained. I managed to stand up and walk over to them on shaky legs. Sherlock fell into the doctor's arms, completely limp and exhausted. I took the cloak from Watson's shoulders to spread it out on the floor and we carefully placed my brother on top of it. Even this simple action made him groan and grimace in pain.

"Congratulations, Mycroft," was the first thing I heard him say after opening his eyes again. "Victoria is a good match for you."

"Sherlock, I swear I'll kill you with my own two hands."

I leaned down and put both arms around my little brother, letting him wrap his bloodied limbs around myself in turn. We remained like that for a long while, while tears formed in my eyes from sheer relief and exhaustion. As we finally separated, Sherlock's eyes had already taken on their usual, mischievous spark.

I knew there and then that everything would be just fine.

EPILOGUE

A gentle breeze brushed my cheek and woke me from the light slumber I had drifted off to in the late afternoon. The sun was still in the sky and bathed the room in a golden glow. I watched the dust motes dance in the air over my head, while my brain slowly woke up. Everything felt sluggish, in a way only a nap in the middle of the day can leave you disoriented and tired... which is ironic, because you were trying to achieve the complete opposite. The wind brought the smell of dinner up to the third floor. I smelled spicy tomato sauce -- not surprising given my current location.

"*Hungry?*" Gregorio asked from the doorway.

"*You're only asking because* you're *hungry*," I chuckled.

"*True*," he shrugged and walked over to the bed, dropped into the sheets beside me.

I rolled over and pressed a kiss to the Italian man's lips.

"*There's a letter for you*," Gregorio held up a piece of paper.

"*Only one person knows where I am. Give me a minute, please?*"

"*Fine*," he answered. "*But only if you come back here afterwards.*"

I smiled at him and rose from the bed. My head was a bit woozy, but I made my way to the window and opened the letter under the warm rays of the early summer sun. It was one of Victoria's briefings, which she continued to send even though I never answered. Sherlock was fully recovered on his way back to London. I had expected the news to arrive weeks ago. Maybe he had decided to stick around for a while.

After the ordeal in Egypt, we had to remain in Alexandria during our trial. In the end, Victoria had been suspended from the Service for two months, and her status of branch leader had been stripped from her for the time being. I had been suspended for an entire year, but there was no rank they could take from me. We reached Rome soon after, where the trio had built themselves a nest in Victoria's home faster than you could say Greek Interpreter. It was endearing, in a way, but I didn't feel like being a part of it. No, I had a different respite in mind and he was lying on the bed behind me.

"*Anything... bad?*" Gregorio asked then, as I took my time to digest the information.

"*News about my brother*," I answered and sighed. "*And a request for me to return to work early. I am to report to Munich within a fortnight.*"

"*So, are you leaving?*"

"*Eventually. But for now, I have other things in mind...*"

Also from MX Publishing

MX Publishing is the world's largest specialist Sherlock Holmes publisher, with over a hundred titles and fifty authors creating the latest in Sherlock Holmes fiction and non-fiction.

From traditional short stories and novels to travel guides and quiz books, MX Publishing cater for all Holmes fans.

The collection includes leading titles such as *Benedict Cumberbatch In Transition* and *The Norwood Author* which won the 2011 Howlett Award (Sherlock Holmes Book of the Year).

MX Publishing also has one of the largest communities of Holmes fans on Facebook with regular contributions from dozens of authors.

www.mxpublishing.com

Also from MX Publishing

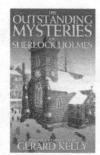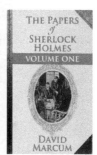

Our bestselling books are our short story collections;

'Lost Stories of Sherlock Holmes' , 'The Outstanding Mysteries of Sherlock Holmes', The Papers of Sherlock Holmes Volume 1 and 2, 'Untold Adventures of Sherlock Holmes' (and the sequel 'Studies in Legacy) and 'Sherlock Holmes in Pursuit', 'The Cotswold Werewolf and Other Stories of Sherlock Holmes' – and many more......

Also from MX Publishing

"Phil Growick's, 'The Secret Journal of Dr Watson', is an adventure which takes place in the latter part of Holmes and Watson's lives. They are entrusted by HM Government (although not officially) and the King no less to undertake a rescue mission to save the Romanovs, Russia's Royal family from a grisly end at the hand of the Bolsheviks. There is a wealth of detail in the story but not so much as would detract us from the enjoyment of the story. Espionage, counter-espionage, the ace of spies himself, double-agents, double-crossers...all these flit across the pages in a realistic and exciting way. All the characters are extremely well-drawn and Mr Growick, most importantly, does not falter with a very good ear for Holmesian dialogue indeed. Highly recommended. A five-star effort."
The Baker Street Society

www.mxpublishing.com

Also from MX Publishing

The Missing Authors Series

Sherlock Holmes and The Adventure of The Grinning Cat
Sherlock Holmes and The Nautilus Adventure
Sherlock Holmes and The Round Table Adventure

"Joseph Svec, III is brilliant in entwining two endearing and enduring classics of literature, blending the factual with the fantastical; the playful with the pensive; and the mischievous with the mysterious. We shall, all of us young and old, benefit with a cup of tea, a tranquil afternoon, and a copy of Sherlock Holmes, The Adventure of the Grinning Cat."
Amador County Holmes Hounds Sherlockian Society

www.mxpublishing.com

Also from MX Publishing

The American Literati Series

 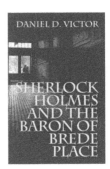 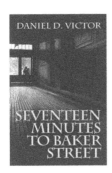

The Final Page of Baker Street
The Baron of Brede Place
Seventeen Minutes To Baker Street

"The really amazing thing about this book is the author's ability to call up the 'essence' of both the Baker Street 'digs' of Holmes and Watson as well as that of the 'mean streets' of Marlowe's Los Angeles. Although none of the action takes place in either place, Holmes and Watson share a sense of camaraderie and self-confidence in facing threats and problems that also pervades many of the later tales in the Canon. Following their conversations and banter is a return to Edwardian England and its certainties and hope for the future. This is definitely the world before The Great War."
Philip K Jones

www.mxpublishing.com

Also from MX Publishing

The Detective and The Woman Series

The Detective and The Woman
The Detective, The Woman and The Winking Tree
The Detective, The Woman and The Silent Hive

"The book is entertaining, puzzling and a lot of fun. I believe the author has hit on the only type of long-term relationship possible for Sherlock Holmes and Irene Adler. The details of the narrative only add force to the romantic defects we expect in both of them and their growth and development are truly marvelous to watch. This is not a love story. Instead, it is a coming-of-age tale starring two of our favorite characters."
Philip K Jones

www.mxpublishing.com

Also from MX Publishing

Sherlock Holmes novellas in verse

All four novellas
have been
released also in
audio format
with narration
by Steve White

Sherlock Holmes and The Menacing Moors
Sherlock Holmes and The Menacing Metropolis
Sherlock Holmes and The Menacing Melbournian
Sherlock Holmes and The Menacing Monk

"The story is really good and the Herculean effort it must have been to write it all in verse—well, my hat is off to you, Mr. Allan Mitchell! I wouldn't dream of seeing such work get less than five plus stars from me..." **The Raven**

Also from MX Publishing

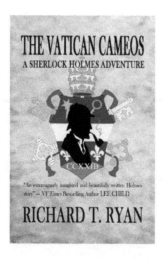

When the papal apartments are burgled in 1901, Sherlock Holmes is summoned to Rome by Pope Leo XII. After learning from the pontiff that several priceless cameos that could prove compromising to the church, and perhaps determine the future of the newly unified Italy, have been stolen, Holmes is asked to recover them. In a parallel story, Michelangelo, the toast of Rome in 1501 after the unveiling of his Pieta, is commissioned by Pope Alexander VI, the last of the Borgia pontiffs, with creating the cameos that will bedevil Holmes and the papacy four centuries later. For fans of Conan Doyle's immortal detective, the game is always afoot. However, the great detective has never encountered an adversary quite like the one with whom he crosses swords in "The Vatican Cameos.."

"An extravagantly imagined and beautifully written Holmes story"
(Lee Child, NY Times Bestselling author, Jack Reacher series)

Lightning Source UK Ltd.
Milton Keynes UK
UKHW02f2318241018
331145UK00014B/391/P

9 781787 05212